THE TURRET

STARCLAN FOUNDATION

Starclan Book I

By James Warren McAllister

Cover Design and Art Work
By
James W. McAllister

Titles and Lettering
By
Robyn Dickson

To my Angel, The Lovely Cindy, who always believes in me.

I have no idea why, but I'll take it anyway. Perfection is hard to resist.

Table Of Contents

Prologue

House Of Providence
Syracuse
Standard Earth Date June 21 3761

"Mother Mary, will you tell me a bedtime story?"

"You just go to sleep, lad. You'll dream better stories than I would ever tell you." The old nun bent and lightly kissed the young boy's forehead as she tucked him in. *The poor lad, so brave after losing his parents like that. Well off, but no family nearby at all. Well, no one young enough to raise a child. Father, after all these years, you still pull my heart so!*

She walked slowly out of the room, the walk of the very old. No one in the orphanage knew just how old she was, nor could any of them recall a time when she was not there. Rumor had it she had founded the orphanage almost three hundred years ago, but no one believed that. Once, a curious young priest had begun searching the archives to find out, but every time he left the records room the answer had faded from his mind.

Mother Mary headed straight to the chapel, mumbling as she moved, one foot methodically and painfully placed just a few inches ahead of the other.

"I don't know which is worse," Mother Mary paused her steps to glance up, then continued as she spoke softly, "the ones you send me that shouldn't be here, aren't ready, can't be, or the times you don't send me any."

"The ones you send, they do make me feel young again. For a time. So much like... Aahh. Triple A! Hah! They kept me smiling, those three! Alex, Allison, and Alistair." She sighed, nodding her head at the warmth brought by old memories.

"Each time I ask you, is it time? Now again, I ask you, is it time, at last? I will stay as long as you need me, but please...I am so weary!" Mother Mary winced at a twinge in her hip.

"As you wish, then," Mother Mary nodded again. "I have no complaints. I am your servant, your tool, to employ as you see fit, as always."

It took a good deal of time and effort for the old woman to reach the chapel. She stayed inside, praying most of the night.

Just an hour before dawn, she began her slow trek back to the young boy's room.

Chapter One

Near Stonefield Castle, Tarbert
Loch Fyne, Scotland
Standard Earth Date July 4 3425

Commodore Nial MacAlister walked up the steps to his Kintyre country home. The setting June sun cast a pinkish-purple glow over the heather behind the thatch-roofed home; how he loved this time of year!

As he reached the door of the simple cottage, he heard the sounds he had been longing to hear over the past two years.

"Daddy! Daddy!" Little Jock threw open the door and leapt into his father's arms.

"Jock! You'll conk your poor father out before I've a chance to welcome him properly!" Gwenifer MacAlister smiled as she looked from her five year old son to her tall, handsome husband. She swore he got more handsome each year he was away among the stars.

"Leave the lad alone, Gwen. You'll have your own private time to properly welcome your husband home." Nial's eyes twinkled as his words smiled at his blushing wife.

"Daddy, are you gonna stay this time?"

"Son, a man needs to answer his call to duty. Honor is important, as is truth and courage. Jock, we will be moving soon, near a spaceport in a place called New York. Do ya think you would like that?" Nial cast a quick glance at his wife as he told her and his son of the move. "The Space Force calls, and I must answer, son. It is my chosen duty."

"Does this mean we'll see you more than once a year, Daddy?" Little Jock looked at his father with wide, brown eyes, pleading for more time with the father he so idolized.

"It could be, my son. It could be." Nial looked his wife in her eyes as he said this, promising that which they both wanted so desperately.

Later that evening, after the youngster was asleep, as the husband and wife lay contentedly in each other's arms, they discussed the move.

"It will be better for him, Gwen. He's so smart, the schools here will bore him quickly. There he can learn enough to find his path."

"I know, but I'll miss this country. I'll miss the views over Tarbert. But you are right. Will you be able to be home more?"

"My assignment there is overseeing the research into my gravity control systems. I should be able to get home for several days at least

1

twice a month. I've bought a place overlooking a lake, I think you'll like it. Land is reasonable there, we can keep both this house and Glenbarr Abbey."

"I like that. Enough talking, Oh Mighty Clan Chief! Come, let your wife finish welcoming you properly!"

***

West Lake Road
Skaneateles, NY
Standard Earth Date May 12 3426

"Oh, Nial, 'tis a gorgeous view indeed!" Gwenifer MacAlister gasped.

"Daddy, is all of that lake ours?"

"No, Jock. The lake belongs to everyone. But we may use it for swimming, boating, and fishing, as long as we respect the laws about such things."

"Laws?"

"Laws are the rules that allow many people to enjoy the lake the right way, without spoiling it. Now, young man, let's take a look at your new room!"

***

West Lake Road
Skaneateles, NY
Standard Earth Date July 25 3430

"Mommy, what do dreams mean? Do they tell us things for real?" The ten-year-old boy breathlessly tried to interrupt his mother's needlepoint.

"That, Jock, is a question people have been asking forever! Maybe if you tell me your dream, my darling, I can help." Jock's mother kept her eye on her work.

"I saw a pretty woman standing with a baby, my baby. Her hair was made of gold, shiny and glowing, mommy, and when she smiled at the baby, her eyes got all soft, like you when you smile at me. And there were five other children there, all smiling and laughing."

2

"Did she say anything, Jock?" Gwenifer asked her son with a raised eyebrow.

"She said, 'He's a part of you, so I can't help but love him.' What does it mean, Mommy?"

Gwenifer MacAlister set down her needlepoint and smiled brightly at her son. "It means you will live a very happy life, my son!"

***

Skaneateles Junior High School
Skaneateles, NY
Standard Earth Date September 4 3430

"I dare you to go say hello to her." Don teased.

"Cut it out! Just because I said she was cute doesn't mean…"

"Jock, you don't have to ask her to marry you! Just go over and say 'Hi, I'm Jock' or something."

Jock looked at the pretty blonde again.

"I think I'm getting Bird flu. My chest feels funny. Like tingly and hollow at the same time."

"Bwahahahaha!" Don laughed loud enough that the two girls and everyone else in the lunchroom look at him.

"Hey!" Jock punched Don's arm.

"Go on, you know you want to. Ask them to come sit with us, why don't ya."

"Okay, okay. Geesh!"

Jock walked up to the girls' table and stood next to the blonde one.

"Hello. My name's Jock, what's yours?"

"Oh. Dream! You were in my dream!" *It's HIM. From my dream. And he thinks I'm cute!*

"Uh, okay… sure."

"Sorry. You just startled me as I was talking to Aggie here, about, em, a show."

"So, um, what show was it…"

"Sandy."

"You were watching a show called Sandy?"

"No, silly, my name is Sandy."

"I'm Aggie. Hi. What's your friend's name?"

"Huh? Oh, that's just Don."

Aggie leaned and waived past Jock, "Hello, Just Don!"

The girls giggled a bit, then Sandy batted her eyes, "Jock MacAlister, What do you want?"

"Don wants you two to come sit with us at lunch."

"And you don't?"

"I, ah, um, yeah, I do, too."

"Will you carry our trays?" Angie winced as Sandy elbowed her ribs.

"Um, both of them? Uh, well, okay!"

"We will not sit with you two. You two may come over and sit with us, Jock MacAlister and Just Don."

***

New York State Fairgrounds
Syracuse, NY
Standard Earth Date August 22 3431

The banner above the amphitheater read, "REMEMBRANCE." The crowds pressed in, nearly a quarter of a million people standing before the two hundred foot viscreen.

"Today as we open the Great New York State Fair, we remember Nili Patera." The announcer stepped back as the giant viscreen came to life.

"I am Martina Wells," the space-suited woman began. "My husband, Albert, said I should record this, in case someone ever finds it. He thinks they need to know what has happened. I don't think anyone will be left to find it.

"It all started yesterday. We had been a quiet mining and archeological colony. We exported some light metal ores and some artifacts. We have never been able to identify who or what left them. The artifacts are only artistic: statues, images, sounds, and the like, but never any technology. The best we can determine, they are hundreds of millions of years old." The woman turned her head, looking over her shoulder, her wide eyes shining with the camera's light.

"We were eating breakfast when the bombardment hit. Huge explosions from small asteroids accelerated to hyper-velocities slamming into our settlements. Nili Patera was a small settlement, well apart from the "big three." So, we got to watch the destruction of Gagarin Base, Glenn City, and Challenger Colony. Five minutes each.

Nothing left.

"Then the alien troops came. They used some beam weapon that melts or explodes everything. We had nothing; weapons were banned on Mars by treaty decades ago.

"We got out just in time. We are hiding now in an excavation, some kind of art gallery of something." Again the woman looked over her shoulder. "There is a vault here, and we've closed ourselves in. Albert, me, and...and little Martin. We think we can hide, but we have only a little air, just enough to last about twenty-four hours.

"Martin is only eighteen months old. Why must this happen to him? Why? I can't stop crying thinking about him. Albert is heartbroken too. He keeps sobbing that he is supposed to protect us. Darling, what could you do? What could...what was..."

As the woman turned her head, her image flickered into static snow.

The announcer stepped up to the podium.
"Today, we remember Bear Mountain Bridge."

"My name is Sergei Andropov. I'm from Brooklyn. Gonzo said I should record this. I've only got a minute." The sweaty, camouflaged face of a young brown haired soldier filled the amphitheater's screen.

"I sat hunkered down behind the barricade. Gonzales was on my right. I saw him shivering a little in the 90-degree heat. Hell, so did I. I looked back at the bridge and took a deep breath. This even smelled wrong. August on the Hudson River shouldn't smell like burnt flesh and feathers.

"We beat them back six hours ago. We made them turn and run away. That felt good. It had never happened before.

"The clouds were scarce, so we knew they'd hit us with the beams again. Energy beams are not visible. But they still burn through sand, wood, steel, and skin. Like going through so much soft-serve ice cream. We dropped the smoke grenades to scatter the beams. Then we just had to deal with their mag-guns.

"Our mission was to hold the Bear Mountain Bridge. If we managed to do that, then New York City could survive a little longer. If we didn't, well, then humanity's fate is up to the French. Downstate New York was all we've been able to hold in North or South America. They told us this morning Australia is gone now.

"The defense had not gone well at all. The three colonies on Mars and Moon Base Armstrong were hit with a bombardment from space, then over run in less than a day. The twenty thousand alien troops arrived on Earth right after a massive bombardment. We think they used asteroids. Now Brazil is just a cratered swampland. The San Andreas Fault even opened up.

"Most of their troops landed in the Great Plains of the United States. From there they pushed north and south to secure their flanks before fortifying the Rockies in the west. Then they began coming east.

"We call them 'Birds,' though we had no idea of their biology. They stand about four feet tall. Half of that is two backward-bent legs. They're covered by a light coat of grey/brown feathers. They wear armor that stopped a lot of our bullets, and use a variety of energy beams and projectiles against us. The worst are the beams. The only way we can counter them is with smoke. Sometimes it works. Of course, that makes our shooting less accurate. Their projectiles travel very fast. Soldiers sometimes kept fighting after holes appeared in them. If they miss, you heard a thunderclap as the air slaps together behind the bullet.

"We didn't have anything heavy, no tanks or artillery left. We did have a few ancient GAU-21 heavy machine guns. And we had the high ground, at least until the Bird aircraft showed up. A British fighter-bomber counter attack was supposed to tie them up over a staging area they had near Montreal. I guess that didn't go too well.

"To my left, I noticed the grim look on Southworth's face. I took another deep breath and let it out slowly. I scanned the other side of the river. The Birds had to cross the bridge to get the ports of New York and New Jersey. We've placed a line of nukes just south of our position, and they know it.

"When they came, I never saw them until the battle was well underway. Until we had lost a quarter of our men to their beams. Both Southie and Gonzo went silently with several holes through them. The rock ledge behind me had dozens of glowing half-inch wide holes from beam strikes. I crouched down a little lower and waited. My hands were shaking, I was so scared.

"Our smoke grenades went off just then, and the alien's hypervelocity mag-guns opened up. I heard dozens of the thunderclaps. The rocks around and behind me exploded from multiple impacts.

"The Birds were just coming into our range. I could see them gathering on the other side of the Hudson. I looked through my targeting scope, and saw half a dozen birds drop almost at once as their heads exploded. The Birds seemed confused, and another eight dropped. Our snipers were good.

"The Birds were just at the edge of my range, so I held my fire. Orders were to open up once they got halfway across the bridge. Just as the Birds started moving, my attention was drawn up; something blurred overhead, and I felt a searing heat from behind me. Our snipers were gone.

"I looked up as the first Birds hit my aiming point. I opened up. Every quarter second burst from my M-46HV carbine fired seven 3mm tungsten bullets at 4,800 feet per second. The high velocity rounds would penetrate most armor at this range. Birds started falling on the bridge, then the heavy machine guns opened up.

"I was concentrating on the bridge, so I never saw the tanks. They saw us. Heavy rounds hit us at 12,000 feet per second, impacting with the same energy as a heavy naval shell. Hundreds of these hit all along our positions. Somehow I survived. I don't think many others did.

"The Birds were pouring across the Bear Mountain Bridge when first French sub-orbital fighter-bombers hit. The Napalm was effective, but not effective enough.

"Twenty of the French ships attacked. All were shot down. The last dozen before they could release their payloads. We made the Birds pay heavily for the bridge. My guess is about two thousand of them died on the bridge. But another four thousand made it across.

"I'm out of ammo now. I still have my bayonet. And my knife. And one grenade. Yeah, I'm scared.

"It's funny, the things you remember. Near my face is a small patch of damp grass, a little patch of green in this grey, smoking hell. I smell the grass from high school; I'm back at football practice, doing push-ups. I smell the grass each time I let my body down. It smells green and sweet. Just like this grass. Sweet, just like her. What was her name? Linda. We lay down on the grassy hill the night after the last game, gazing at the stars. Holding hands. I wonder where she is. I miss those days. A lot.

"I can't withdraw, I can't even roll over; my legs are pinned under a pile of rocks that fell from the last mag-gun barrage. They stopped hurting a little while ago. I can't feel anything below my thighs now. My legs just feel wet. Where would I go anyway? Commands stopped coming over the comm channels when that flash behind me wiped out the snipers.

"If anyone finds this recording, remember what the 10th Mountain Division did here. We did all we could.

"I hear them near me. Now I…"

"Daddy, wh…" Jock started as the viscreen went blank.

"Shh, Jock. Listen. Watch. Not everyone gets to see this live," Nial whispered.

"Today, we remember Over Bear Mountain Bridge"

"Robert asked me to record this in Anglaise. I do not know why, except maybe he is recording his in Francaise, and wants a monopoly. Hah!" The grinning face was barely discernable through the helmet's visor.

"We got the scramble call an hour ago. Oh, we had been briefed some time before that. . A soldier's fortune, no? Wait, wait, wait, a lifetime for a heartbeat's moment of frantic battle.

"The *Americans* were losing. Inconceivable! They never lose. They may get bored and quit, but they never just *lose*. Impossible! Well, enough of our politicians waiting for the Americans to win; now *we must* win, or we all die.

"The world depends upon *us* now. Some of the American and Canadian resources have trickled in, but we are nowhere near as strong as they were. And they are being beaten. We must fight better!

"We have no choice. That is not really true. We can fight and win, or we can die. Every single one of us. That is our choice. The oiseaux do not talk, do not negotiate. They only kill.

"Our superiors have taken the gauntlets off, as you say in Anglaise. The first flight went in with napalm and explosives. I hear they inflicted severe casualties, but that they were all shot down. How do you shoot down a ship traveling at Mach 6? Incredible!

"The boost from Paris was hard. I always hate the boost! Magnetic rails shooting us to unbelievable speeds. Thank the Lord it only lasts a few seconds. I feel like a, what, sandwich? Panini! Pressed back into my seat under an oppressive force. Then nothing, no weight, no sound. Up and over the 'top' of the Earth. I see the glimmers in the distance. Alien ships, orbiting MY world! I carry one very special package for them. I arm it, and set it free. It will drift in a sub-orbital glide until it is very close to the oiseaux ships. I hope it will be too small, too close for them to shoot it down, like they have all the others.

"I roll the ship and get a terrific view! I have seen this dozens of times on training missions, the wondrous blue globe. This time I see South America, smoking, brown, smudged and broken, nothing but mud left. The scale of the thing hits me, and I nearly vomit. How many

8

billions dead? I have been to Rio. I know people, I knew a woman there. No more. *Sacrebleu!*

"The intense sadness turns into anger. Anger I can use, to keep me focused. I want nothing but to kill them all. If that damns me, then so be it! Mon Dieu, forgive me, but I do!

"Nose over; computer fixing targets thousands of kilometers away. Tiny green, red, and yellow dots on my HUD. Arming the big ones; I have the nukes now. This is to the death, *une lutte `a mort*. Die, you *salauds*!

"I've got something tracking me, my ship, she knows. Countermeasures on our ships are designed for very general work, the Americans designed theirs for the way the Chinese track you. Too specific. The oiseaux track differently than the Chinese. Whatever is tracking me loses its lock. Perhaps Robert will catch that missile! I hope not. As much as I kid him, I like Robert.

"My targets are approaching fast. Even my mission, though it lasts but a few seconds, is mostly waiting. An instant of combat, then more waiting. I release my atomics; they will free-fall for a time before they accelerate to their targets. They are now out of my hands. I hope the programmers were competent.

"Now I have a few moments to select targets I can hit with my rockets and plasma cannon. My computer targets a large, flat vehicle, roughly oval in shape. There was nothing in the briefing like this, so I target everything on it. The rockets are gone now, and I keep the trigger depressed on the plasmas until they shut down from overheating. Now I can pull up, hitting the final booster back to the edge of space. Damage assessment will be someone else's mission.

"A bright flash snaps my head to the window, but I see nothing. My ship rocks, tumbling as if God has hit it himself. I can't do anything, so what will be....que sera, sera.

"I roll over again, trying to see the alien ships once more. There! Fewer, amidst sparkling dust. HITS! We've hurt the bastards!

"I see also many streaks, and flashes. Then my arc takes me out of view.

"I have a few seconds of communications now. Robert is gone. Damn! The force at Bear Mountain Bridge has been badly mauled. The alien ships were also hurt badly, and an American supply ship is....*that* was what the streaks were! They accelerated to high velocity and exploded their ship, so the debris will ram the aliens! *Those* are the Americans my great-grandfather spoke of with such awe! The ones who came and save *his* great-grandfather! The ones the world has seen too little of since. Now I get the reports, of the Americans fighting with knives when the bullets ran out, with nails and teeth when the knives broke. And of the Chinese, and others, taking inspiration from them! Now, we French as well! *Vive la Americans! Vive la France!*

"Communications are out now, due to reentry heat. I have an alarm, but there is nothing I can do. A rip in my ship's skin, near my left leg, is letting the superheated air in. Flames surround my legs. Soon I will be burning. It hurts very much. Not much time left. I think of what my great-grandfather told me, and I hope I made a diff..."

The viscreen went dark once again.

"Today, we remember the SS Jeremiah Wadsworth."

Nail hugged his son a little closer. "Your great-uncle, Jock." Several people nearby turned and looked at Nial, some mouths agape in awe.

"Is this on, Johnson? It is? OK." The man on the screen looked exactly like Nail MacAlister.

"Eh-hem. Captain's log, SS Jeremiah Wadsworth. Joel MacAlister, Captain. We have received the reports of the invasion, and the dire situation. We have, the entire crew, decided on a course of action.

"We began accelerating at maximum thrust from Europa orbit. We figured that at that distance, the aliens wouldn't notice us until we hit them. At this point, we have exceeded the structural design limitations of this ship by at least one order of magnitude. Our engines remain at full thrust. Our engineer estimates our relative velocity at intercept to be nearly three-quarters light speed. We are sure the aliens will feel our impact. Heh, Davey Johnson came up with that one.

"From what we can tell, the aliens haven't seen us. Could be they're focused on the Earth. We've got a bit of a surprise for them.

"Our engineer, Philip Bazaar, has rigged our reactor to explode when we intercept the alien fleet. Even if we are not on a direct collision course with one of their ships, the core overload will turn us and our cargo, twenty thousand tons of uranium ore, into a shotgun blast they can't escape. At least, that is the plan.

"We haven't been able to contact anyone, so this log will be the only record. Philip says it's a relativity effect, or something. We'll eject a distress buoy with it soon. First, I want to say to my wife, I love you very much. To Jerry, Jen and Jack I love you all...very much.

"My crew is... this is the best... Cargo Master Davey Johnson. Engineer Philip Bazaar. Navigator Rico Veronesi. Cargomen Doug

Collins and Steve Witowski. Remember them. They are all special men.

"Davey, it's your turn. Keep it short, Phil, Rich, Doug, and Steve need to go, too. Yeah, I'm cryin'. See me about it when you're done."

"Today we remember United!"

"Are we on? Are we broadcasting?" A man in a dusty suit asked someone off camera.

"Good evening. This is Andrew Parker. I am broadcasting over the old antennas, radio, and television, they were called. I hope someone has the equipment to hear us.

"Tonight, we have good news.

"Our forces, the Tenth Mountain Division, have engaged the aliens north of New York City. Although they suffered severe losses, the alien advance was halted.

"Furthermore, French sub-orbital attack craft have hit the stalled alien army very hard, using conventional and atomic weapons. Preliminary reports indicate near total destruction of the alien forces. All French attack ships are reported as lost.

"French, Chinese, and Russian ships have also inflicted severe damage onto the orbiting alien fleet. And a commercial cargo hauler has run a... excuse me...they...a-hem. The SS Jeremiah Wadsworth has run at maximum acceleration into the alien fleet. Just before contact, the reactor core of the Jeremiah Wadsworth exploded, turning the ship, and its cargo of asteroid ore, into a spread of hypervelocity projectiles aimed at the alien fleet. All crew aboard... heroes, all.

"We should never forget the brave souls who have fought and won this...great victory.

"The alien fleet has been destroyed! Their ground forces have nowhere to retreat to now!

"We are hearing that Chinese and South African troops have landed along the West Coast and the Gulf of Mexico. Word is that they have liberated Oregon, California, Nevada, Mexico, Texas and Louisiana. Eurozone and Russian troops have landed on the East Coast, freeing Washington D.C., Philadelphia, and Boston. Troops from India, Indonesia, Pakistan, The Saudi Arabian Empire, and Israel have landed on Australia. Reports are still sketchy, but indicate that the Birds are in full retreat on every front!

"We will try to broadcast updates every two hours. I will see you then.

"Ladies and gentlemen, Godspeed, and goodnight."

The announcer stepped up to the podium.
"Today we remember VICTORY!"
Jock was surprised at the loud cheering from his father.

***

West Lake Road
Skaneateles, NY
Standard Earth Date June 2 3432

"Here, Jock, can you see this? See how the reach of the weapons from each one overlap the fields of fire for the others? See how every approach to the system is covered?" Nial MacAlister looked at his pride and joy sitting on his lap. *How he has grown! Ten years old already! I can barely keep him on my knee; this will end soon, he's growing up. So big! So strong! So smart! How happy, how sad!*

"Gee, dad, this vidagram makes it look like nothing could ever hit us like the Birds did! Those guys in the Turrets must be top-notch!" Jock's preadolescent enthusiasm was boundless. Power, strength, skill meant everything, not yet tempered by the choice of application nor by the finesse earned through experience. *But, they will be*, Jock thought. *My young boy is learning.*

***

Skaneateles Junior High School
Skaneateles, NY
Standard Earth Date September 9 3432

"Jock MacAlister, stop staring at me please." Sandy smiled. "What do you want this time?"

"Um, yeah. Well, I'm, uh. I thought we could do a project for the science fair together."

Sandy frowned and said quietly, "That's NOT why you're here! Don't ever lie to me again. Even a little."

"I, I'm sorry. Sandy? W-would you, um, do you want, maybe…" his voice cracked as the words stuttered out.

"Jock MacAlister, what is wrong with you? Spit it out!"

"Doyouwanngotothefallformalwithme?"

"Yes, I will go to the dance with you, Jock MacAlister."

***

Skaneateles High School Athletic Fields
Skaneateles, NY
Standard Earth Date May 24 3436

"Aren't they beautiful Jock?"

"Your eyes? Yes. Yes, they are."

"No, the stars, silly!" Sandy snuggled a little closer into Jock's side, resting her head in the crook of his arm.

"You'll be flying around them in a few years."

"Why would you say that?"

"Because you will. You'll go to the Academy, become an officer, and save the world."

Jock raised his eyebrows and looked at Sandy.

"I've never told anyone. I don't know if I'm good enough…"

"Oh, silly. You've got the second best grades in our class, you're going to be State Champion in wrestling the next three years, and you have a scientist father in the USF. Of course you're good enough."

Jock sat up and looked at Sandy, her blonde hair glowing in the starlight.

"What? State Champ? The next three years…what? How?"

Looking at her in this light took his words away.

"You hate to lose. You won't." Her smile faded quickly.

"What?"

"Jock, be…be careful. When you go to the Academy." She held onto him tightly.

"Sandy, how did you know I wanted to go to the USF Academy?"

"I just seem to know what's going to happen around you. I told you you'd make State finals this year. I told you you'd win the science fair. I know you're going to the Academy." Her arms tightened a little more. "Just be careful. Promise?"

"What has you so worried?"

"I don't know. I just know there's something dark hanging there, dangerous." She took a deep breath in, "but you will save the world!"

Jock smiled at her, "Well, what's this about me having the second best grades?"

"You don't think I'm letting you beat me, do you?"

Sandy set her hand on Jock' chest and pushed him back on the grass.

"What are you going to do? You've never told me, and I can't see the future like you can."

"It's not seeing the future, really. It's just a sort of buzz that is around you. I don't get that with anyone else."

"Good!"

They lay for a few minutes just watching the stars.

"Jock?"

"Hmm?"

"Do you love me?"

"I, um… I don't know… I…"

Sandy sat up and slapped Jock's chest.

"Jock MacAlister, you promised me when we first met that you'd never ever lie to me again!"

"Come with me to the stars."

"No way! I don't even like the rides at the Fair! I'm going into business law. Somebody has to run Starclan for your father."

"Sandy," Jock pulled her shoulders down to him. He bent her head down and kissed her forehead before looking into her eyes. "I just want to spend forever with you. Like this. I love you, Sandra Wilson."

"You will. But we both have things to do first. Now kiss me handsome. Then we have to get back to the dance."

***

Skaneateles Lake Hobie Cat Regatta
Skaneateles, NY
Standard Earth Date August 28 3440

The fourteen-foot long lime green catamaran sliced through blue-green Skaneateles Lake with one hull out of the water. The tall, well-muscled young sailor held tightly to the line in his hand as he stood on the side of the raised hull, leaning down towards the water's surface to balance the force of the wind. This last leg of the race had put him in the lead, and now the finish line was rapidly approaching as his back was skimming inches above the waves at just over twenty-six knots.

Jock glanced up at his sail, judging the feel of the wind through the line in his hand. He glanced through the spray hitting his face to the finish line, and then back to the other boats. The boat was sailing right at her limits, as usual. He loved that feeling of riding the edge! He loved the clear blue sky, the wind, the smell of the lake. Life was good.

The horn sounded as Jock crossed the finish line clearly ahead of everyone else, as usual. Jock was used to winning, plunging into every undertaking at full speed. Oh, how he hated to lose. Jock let up some tension on the sail, and bent up as the cat's second hull dropped into the water. The small boat slowed to a more leisurely pace. He looked around the lakefront, taking in the picturesque little town, and thinking this could be the last time he would see it from a boat. In ten days he left for the United Space Force Fleet Academy. And, a different kind of sailing.

Jock looked over to the marina, turning the boat smartly towards the dock. His three closest friends were there, waving and sporting big grins. There was the perpetual pair of Agnes and Don, and Sandy. His Sandy. Every drop-dead gorgeous blond inch of her, glowing in the sunlight, had been a part of him since they'd met in ninth grade. He almost lost his grip and fell overboard looking at her. *Tonight I'll ask her.*

"All hail the conquering hero!" Don cupped his hands around his mouth to help his shout carry.

Jock laughed to himself. *Don, the master of hyperbole!*

"Yeah, right! Here, grab this line, and help me tie her up!" Jock shouted back, as he threw the mooring line exactly one-half meter short of the dock. Don leaned out, realizing the joke just in time; he still made a great sight flailing his arms about to regain his balance.

"Funny!"

"Okay, here you go!" As Jock tossed the line to Don this time, he looked past his friend to see the USF Marine Corp staff car that rolled down to the dock. *What are they doing here?* The reason hit him like a sledgehammer to his gut when he saw his mother in the car, hands over her face. Jock froze, his cat hit the dock, nearly throwing him into the lake.

DAD!

***

Jock stopped in the middle of the Quad as the crowd flowed around him. Still numb from his father's death, he was having a hard time focusing on the task at hand. He didn't even remember how he got this far.

His mind wouldn't stop replaying that day at the lake. His mom's face, her tears. How Agnes, Don, and Sandy had tried to comfort him. And how he had pushed them all away.

Sandy. She had run to him, and she held his hand as they walked to him.

Every time he thought of Sandy, he saw the Marine colonel telling him, "Son, there's been an accident."

He saw the vid of his father's death.

It all looked so wrong.

It wasn't an accident.

No matter what they told him.

The world around Jock began shrinking into that private pinpoint of pain again.

"Well, helloooo, handsome!" The tiny voice squeaked out of a short, olive-skinned girl with shining black hair and bright, smiling eyes. "I'm Angela. Angela Soriano. And you are?" she said, extending her hand while flashing a grin.

Jock looked at the girl, then her hand, and robotically reached out and shook it. "Jock. MacAlister."

"Oh, you're the brilliant Clan Chieftain I've heard about! Wonderful! Here, follow me, and we'll get through this orientation thing." Angela snaked her arm around his and started to lead him through the crowd towards the auditorium.

Jock allowed her to lead him, her arm pulling him into reality as much as it pulled him into the auditorium. Still, he wasn't watching where he was going when the two in front of him stopped. He walked right into them before Angela could pull him back.

"Oh, um, sorry!" Jock stammered his apology to the two oblivious

16

people he bumped into. The collision knocked Jock a little further from that pinpoint.

"What exactly are you trying to say?" The shapely honey-blonde haired girl with her hands on her hips and an amused look on her face demanded.

"I said, um, that, um, your, eh…" The tall, thin young man stammered.

Jock looked from one to another. Something here pushed his pain aside, pushed everything connected to that pain into a dark box deep inside his mind. Was it the pretty girls? Or was it that these three didn't know about his father, and seemed to delight in each moment. Jock thought he could make new memories with them, memories never associated with that horrible pain.

The futile efforts of the tall thin young man amused Jock enough to snap him into action. "What he's trying to say is this; your eyes reflect my soul like shimmering pools, and your hair outshines the morning sun; when you smile wise men are but fools, all my senses your beauty stuns!" Jock grinned.

Both the tall young man and the blonde turned and stared at Jock.

"Yes, that's it, exactly!" The tall young man exclaimed, slapping a hand on Jock's shoulder.

The blonde turned to the tall one, and then looked back to Jock with glazed eyes. "Say that again!" she asked softly.

"Your eyes reflect my soul like shimmering pools, and your hair outshines the morning sun; at your smile wise men are but fools, all my senses your beauty stuns." Jock said in a quiet baritone voice as he smiled broadly at the blonde beauty.

Angela was staring, mouth wide open, her arm in a vice-like grip on Jock's arm as the blonde sighed heavily.

"Hello. My name is Sharon Malone. What's yours?" The blonde asked Jock. *Oh, my! I have GOT to stay near this one! I can't breathe!*

"I'm Patrick Campbell!" The tall young man chimed in.

"Jock MacAlister, at your service, Pat, Shar. Here is my new friend, Angie." Jock motioned to the girl clinging to his arm.

Sharon looked at Angie, then at Pat, and laughed. "OK, then, Musketeers, let's get ourselves orientated!" She grabbed Pat's arm, and Jock's free arm, and the four of them walked into the auditorium.

Jock realized he was smiling for the first time in ten days.

Zimm's Lagrangian Scrap and Ship Sales
L-5 Lagrangian Point
Standard Earth Date January 6 3441

The well-worn shuttle-pod slowly drifted past the huge reactor section of the tug. Dennis Trap eyed the massive heat sinks closely, for he had done his research. If the dense metal fins designed to dump excessive heat from the iron-fusion reactors into space were damaged or loose, the multimillion-credit tug could end up as an expensive chunk of fused scrap metal attached to a pilot's seat.

"So, Mr. Trap, Dennis, heh-heh, what do you think? A fine ship, isn't she!" Tally Zimmer was a dark, sweaty, fidgety little man, his hands rubbing each other or some part of his ruddy face or greasy brown hair at all times.

Dennis glanced to the left of the reactor. Just past the radiation shield that separated the crew module from the three reactor-plasma drive units, Dennis watched the lunar disk roll past in the background. He still found it hard to believe he was this close to his dream.

Twenty years he had spent in the Corps, turning young kids into Marines. At first he thought about driving a truck. A little research told him that they're all automated, and it's more like riding than driving. But space tugs, now that could fit the bill! No one to bug him, he could pick his own assignments, and do some real piloting. So, he shelled out the credits for the space tug piloting classes, did his apprenticeship, and got his license. Now, if he could swing a little financing at the age of forty-five, he had enough for a substantial down payment for a beat up old tug. With the price of this one, though, he could pay cash, if he negotiated well enough.

"She's a nice looking ship. Before I test-drive her, tell me something, Zimmer. I'm curious; why so cheap? You should be asking ten times your price for this tug." *Hell, it's even got a fresh coat of white and red paint!*

"Well, umm, Mr. Trap, you see..." Tally's hands rubbed over each other faster as he spoke, "there is a history with this tug. This was the tug that, eh, well, this tug was named, heh-heh, "Thistle", eh, hm."

"So?" *So, no one wants it because it has a pansy-assed plant's name?*

"Mr. Trap, Dennis, the S. T. Thistle was the tug captained by Allison Og." Zimmer's hands broke apart and began tugging at his earlobes and collar.

"So?"

"You don't know the story of Allie Og? She murdered over three hundred innocent people!"

"That cruise ship thing? But, this is a tug, isn't it?"

"That it is, sir. But sometimes tugs are, eh, were used by cruise lines for 'special' charter trips, far out from Earth. Instead of cargo barges, they haul pleasure barges out past the asteroids, past any, eh, um, jurisdictional issues. Cruise ships don't have that kind of range or speed. Heh, eh, Allie Og took one of these pleasure barges out past Saturn. Rumor has it she found out the barge was hosting a snuff-cruise; she claimed there was a docking gravity clamp malfunction. When she lit her engines to begin the trip back to Earth, the barge swung around into the engine exhaust cone. The backwash from the plasma drive thrusters crumpled the barge, killing three hundred guests and fifty-six staff. She was convicted of 320 counts of murder."

"What the hell is a "snuff-cruise"? Were they sniffing something?"

"I would rather not speak of such things, Mr. Trap." Tally's hands stopped moving as his eyes looked out of his pale face, focused on his shoes.

"Wait, if there were 356 people on the barge, how did she only get convicted of 320 murders?"

"Her defense was able to prove that thirty-six of the people on the barge were already dead; they were there to be, um, killed for the…" Zimmer paused, closed his eyes and swallowed hard,"…eh…*entertainment* of the guests. They were twelve sets of children and their parents." Zimmer was trembling now.

"How can…people…who…. wow. Assholes." Dennis took a big breath as he studied the floor of the pod, looking for a place to spit the bad taste of this story out of his mouth. After a moment's thought, he looked Zimmer in the eyes; "I can understand why the people shy away. I'll take her.

"Wha, what? You're going to buy her, sir? Even after that story?" Zimmer's face brightened as his eyes lit up.

"Zimmer, the way I look at it, that tug removed 320 bags of evil shit from the universe. Now, if you can take a couple thousand off as a cash discount, I'll sign, and you'll get paid, today. In cash. Where's the paperwork?"

"Let me dock the pod, Mr. Trap, and then just follow me, sir!"

Dennis couldn't figure out how Zimmer could pilot the pod with his hands rubbing over each other like that.

***

Syracuse University
Hendricks Chapel
Syracuse, New York
Standard Earth Date June 1 3444

Father Joseph Champlin noticed the pretty blonde girl was back again. She was in her usual position, kneeling at the rail with head down. The Father knew from experience the tears were hidden that way.

He had offered solace and counseling countless times over the previous four years. She had politely refused each time. He prayed for guidance as he walked over to her one more time.

"Child, it pains me to see you troubled so. You've not found the answers you look for. If you won't let me help you with your troubles, at least let me guide the direction of your search. How are you seeking your peace?"

Sandy kept her head down. She knew the kind face that voice belonged to.

"I've been asking why…"

"Sometimes we are not meant to know why. I sense this may be your last time here. Will you tell me what your troubles are?"

A slight shake of her head was her answer.

"Then try this, my child. Ask God to take your pain and anger for you."

Sandy lifted her reddened face to look at the priest.

"Father?"

"You have only to ask, Sandra. When you are ready, I will be here, God will be here. You always have only to ask."

United Space Force Academy
Commandant's Office Complex
Cape Canaveral, Florida
Standard Earth Date June 18 3444

"Hey, c'mon! Don't shove!"

"Outta my way, pipsqueak!" The dark haired, lanky 6′ 4″ Ensign tried to pull the slightly shorter but stockier officer in the crowd in front of him to one side, but found the man's shoulder unmovable. When the shorter man's heel dropped down on top of his foot, he let go of the shoulder.

"OW! Hey! Damn it, Jock! That hurt!"

Lieutenant Junior Grade Jock MacAlister turned and grinned at his friend, "Now, Ensign Campbell, is that any way to treat a superior officer?"

"Jesus, Jock, you almost broke my foot! Have you seen our assignments yet?

"No, I can't get up there yet. Something, or SOMEONE," Jock cupped his hands around his mouth, "IS HOLDING EVERYONE UP!"

"Oh, Jock, HUSH!" came a voice like ringing bells from the front of the crowd. "Got 'em!" A shapely arm waved three envelopes above the crowd.

The crowd in front of Jock parted like the red sea, and every eye on every male present focused on the Lieutenant JG holding three envelopes high in her hand.

"Well, hurry up, Shar!" Pat called.

Sharon Malone walked slowly to her friends, exaggerating her normally entrancing walk for the benefit of the men in the crowd. Sharon was the complete dream package: what a mother dreams of for a daughter-in-law, as well as what her son dreams of during the night. She had a strikingly pretty face; lovely glacier-blue eyes, full lips, a turned-up button nose, a splendid figure, and constantly blushing high cheeks. Sharon was a great friend, kind, gentle but tough, strong, loyal, and had an astronomical IQ. And Sharon Malone always seemed to get what she wanted, almost. While she qualified for advanced placement to graduate as a Lt. JG instead of an Ensign, she came in second at the Academy to Jock MacAlister. And even though he was her nearly constant companion, escorting her to various functions as well as to the last two formals, she had not been able to entice him into more than a kiss on her cheek. Once Sharon reached Jock and Pat, her show-walk ended. The crowd went back to the task of shoving to get at their assignments.

"Mr. Campbell, your assignment, Sir! Open it, please!" *Please be something good for him!* Sharon thought.

Pat fumbled for a moment. It wasn't the thought of what could be in the envelope, but the realization that once he opened it he had less than 24 hours to spend with his girl and his two best friends. The four had been nearly inseparable since their first week at the Academy, when Pat had stammered while trying to chat up Sharon, and Jock had intervened on his behalf by 'translating' Pat's puppy love gibberish into Shakespearian sonnets for Sharon.

"Oh. Well, Okay! I guess." *The four of us will end in 24 hours, whether I open this or not. Even IF Angie says 'yes'…so…*

"Well, what is it?" Jock prodded his friend. While Pat's jokes with Jock were almost always physical, Jock was the more athletic of the two. At six feet, one inch and two hundred five pounds, he combined speed and power well enough to win two national collegiate wrestling titles. Jock though always played mental jokes on Pat, but nothing ever cruel. Pat was a good friend, and smart enough to easily qualify for advanced placement himself. IF he had ever studied, which he almost never did. Jock kept telling Pat that he'd be the smartest one of the group, if he only tried a little harder.

"I've been assigned to the staff of Admiral Alimonte." *Those words mean our friendship has 24 hours to live. But I like it anyway!* Pat grinned.

Sharon squealed with pride and joy as she hugged her friend, and Jock slapped him on the back.

"Great news! That's a prime assignment, Pat! Now, Jock, Mr. First-in-my-class, it's your turn!" Sharon handed Jock the envelope. *Is it too much to ask that we have the same assignment? Please? Of course it is! But, please?*

Jock looked at it for a moment, took it from Sharon's lovely hand, and promptly stuffed it in his shirt pocket. "I already know where I'm going. Shar, you go next." *They'll not like it. I have to be ready for that. I want this last day to be a happy one for all of us. I don't want to lose their friendship. I don't want any of us to remember this day with sadness.*

"Always the gentleman, hey Jockie?" Shar leaned over and kissed Jock's cheek lightly, then lightly blew in his ear before she pulled back. "OK, here goes! In twenty-four hours I report to…here! I'm assigned to be an associate professor in naval history and battle tactics while I study for my PhD. Jock, that's a policy/command career line!" Sharon just stared at nothing for a full minute before Jock spoke up. *NO, no, no, no! Jock won't be anywhere near here, he'll be on Mars station or a patrol cutter or something far away, I know it! Don't cry, it's THE assignment I've been working for these last four years, how can it disappoint me so?*

"Pat, this is a record for her to be silent. I've got it at 75 seconds and counting...." *Is she going to cry? What's wrong?*

"You!" Sharon lightly slapped Jock's cheek. "This is an honor, but it means at least three more years before I get into space! Still, it IS an honor!" *But it's too much time away from...away from YOU!* Sharon felt her eyes filling, but could not take them off of Jock.

"Shar, are you telling me you did NOT try for that assignment?" Pat knew the answer before he asked.

"Well, of course I did!" *It means I get to stay here and never see these two and Angie for at least three years!* "Now, Jock, spill it! Where are you going?" *They NEVER give two of these. Still, he has the highest grades ever here; he would get whatever he asked for. Please?*

"You didn't do what I think you did, did you?" Pat was concerned about his friend. *He asked for a Turret! The damn blockhead asked for a Turret!*

Jock pulled out the envelope and opened it. He pulled out the paper and glanced at it.

"Whoo-hoo! I've been assigned to command a Turret! Asteroid Defense Station 1437, to be specific. Just what I've wanted since I was a kid!"

"God, Jock, how could you!" *Don't cry. At least he won't meet anyone better for two years. Unless...no! Please, not that! What was the number? 1437? OH, NO! Maybe that's not the number. I'll recheck it later.*

"Geeze, buddy, that's a one-way ticket to nowhere for your career!" *Damn it, Jock, they'll forget all about you out there! Three years and they'll decommission them all, and you with them!*

"It's also a prime automated weapons development research station, so I get to experiment on what I think is cool! Anyway, for right now, who cares? I got what I wanted, for once! Now," Jock draped an arm around each of his friend's shoulders, "How are we going to celebrate?" *I've got to keep them focused, and then make them take the oath. Before I get too drunk to remember it!*

"We could go back to my place!" Shar grinned at the two men. *Sure, it's a long shot, but....*

"You learned how to cook? Great! I have to find Angie, first." Pat quipped. *There's the softball, Jock.*

"What are you cooking, Shar?" Jock added. *A long fly ball to deep center field…* Usually when the guys ribbed Sharon, they double-teamed her. It made it much less personal. And, it helped each guy keep things light.

"Well…Angela's at Mama Rooney's." *Damn! Shut out again. Maybe later, after a few beers!*

"Lead on, my Queen!" Jock chuckled.

"After you, Princess!" Pat echoed.

"My two knights in shining armor!" Sharon laughed as she put an arm over the shoulders of each man and the three walked out of the hall. *I'm gonna miss this!*

***

Skytop Apartment Complex
Syracuse, New York
Standard Earth Date June 18 3444

"Sandy, are you sure you don't want to come home for the summer? It's not much of a drive in. Your friends, your mother and I would love to have you for a little while longer."

Sandy closed her eyes and took a deep breath.

"Dad, my clerking job is too important to spend two hours a day commuting. Besides, you and mom can come out to see me, just call first. I think I'll be working long hours, from what they tell me." She plopped onto her unmade bed, fighting the urge to pull the phone from her ear.

"Sandy, Don and Aggie will be home soon. And, uh, sometimes, you know dear, sometimes, I hear the Academy gives leave after gradu…"

"STOP! DAD, JUST STOP."

"I'm sorry hon. I just… I want you to be happy is all."

"I know, Dad." Sandy swallowed hard. "I will be." *Someday.* "I have to go now Dad. I love you."

"I love you too, sweetheart. You call if you need anything, okay?"

"I will, Dad. Bye."

"Why does he always do that!" Sandra screamed at the walls around her. She slid down the bed and pulled the covers up over her head.

"Why do I keep waiting for Jock?" Her sobs were building again, that all too familiar pattern of starting small and rising until they caused her physical pain.

"Dear God, please take my pain for me. I can't anymore..."

Her sobs quieted when sleep came.

***

Mama Rooney's Bar And Grill
Cape Canaveral, Florida
Standard Earth Date June 18 3444

Mama Rooney's Bar and Grill sat as close to the Academy campus as the law and the Navy allowed. A modest establishment, it was cleaner and served better food than most bars near military bases. Still, it saw its share of 'altercations' each month.

"Patrick! Jock! C'mon over!" Ensign Angela Soriano somehow made her tiny voice heard over the din of the bar. "I've saved you a table!" *Damn, she's with them!*

My mousey little floozy of a roommate is trying to horn in on me again! Damn it! "Hi, Angela! I'm so glad we ran into you here! We'll be happy to join you for dinner! Are you buying?"

"Angie! Hi!" Jock exclaimed.

"Hey, Angie!" *She does look good today!* "Where are you posted?" Pat asked as gave her a quick kiss while he held her chair as the three sat down around the table.

"R & D command, Mars City. Isn't that super?"

"Isn't that super?" Gag me, please, Angie! Jock hates that candy talk. But, maybe it's not aimed at him? "That's great, Angie!" Sharon beamed.

"Where are *you* going, Jocko?" Angie Soriano batted her eyes at the new Lieutenant, JG. Angie was known for two things among the other cadets; her continuous and ineffective flirtation at Jock MacAlister, and her complete and unrivaled mastery of physics.

"Jock pulled the ADS duty he requested. He'll be out among the 'roids for two years!" Pat droned.

"Jocko! You won't have any time to come see me? Maybe I can work it out to come see you then!" *Yeah, big boy, you and me alone on a deserted asteroid...my perfect dream! Almost...* Angie cast a quick glance at Pat.

"Angie, they don't allow visitors to ADS sites. They have to be kept secret." *Is she for real? She acts like an airhead, she looks like an airheaded Island Girl, and she has a genius level IQ!*

"Hey, Angie," Pat injected, "what would you like to eat? My treat!"

"Oh, Pattsie, you'd buy lil ole me dinner? Why, I'll have the usual, handsome!" *He's so sweet, and kinda cute. What happens to us after tonight? Why have we never talked about it? Why does the thought of never seeing him again make me want to cry?...*

"Jock, let me buy you dinner!" Sharon pleaded. *Let me...pleeeease!*

"OK. But before we order, we all need a drink, and THAT is on me. Hey! Wanda!" *OK, this could work. I just hope Angie keeps her eye on Pat. They're good for each other.*

"Hey, it's the Four Musketeers! The last time you'll be in here, kids! What'll it be, Lieutenant?" Wanda liked these kids; they were fun, good-natured, and tipped well.

"Four Glenfiddich, neat, with ice in separate glasses. 15-year old stuff, Wanda!"

"You've got it, sugar!" *Hope the kid can afford it, he tips well!*

"Jock, have you thought about, well, that this is the last time we'll see each other for a long time, maybe, well..." *I need to know you want to see me after tonight! Please! Please! Please!*

"Yeah, Shar, I have." *Every time I wanted you, but couldn't get Sandy out of my mind.* "And that brings me to this. I have a proposition. The four of us have been together constantly pretty much since we arrived on campus. Pat and I banged heads for a few days, and then became best friends. Angie and Shar butt heads, but you two have been roommates for three years, and you spend holidays at each other's homes. Each of your fathers has offered Pat and I careers with their companies after our service ends. The four of us were practically all each other's dates at every formal. And we now face a time when we only have a few hours left. How do we make sure we never forget each other?"

"Geeze, Jock, I'm gonna cry here." Angie pouted, as a tear formed in her eye.

"Yeah, handsome, me too" Shar echoed.

"What do you have in mind, Sport?" Pat's quiet voice cracked a little.

"Well, now, follow me..."

***

"Jeepers, Jocko, you didn't tell me it would HURT!" Angela smiled as she rubbed the circular tattoo on her right shoulder; a ring with 'FORTITER' inside it, and a fist thrusting a dagger up through the center.

"What does this say, anyway?" Pat quizzed. Six drams of Glenfiddich later, his close up vision was *just a little* blurred.

"Jock, does this mean we're engaged?" Shar kidded. She and Jock had gone much lighter on the Scotch than had Angie and Pat.

"No, Shar, that would take a ring. This does mean you're all part of my Clan, Clan MacAlister." Jock reached into his pocket, but did not take the ring out. *Damn it! I can't! Why not? I've got it here, why can't I? Sandy!*

"Well, it's sort of a 'ring'!" *Oh, what I'd give for a REAL ring! PLEEEEEASE!* "Clan MacAlister, eh?" Sharon looked up at the shop's sign, a big neon star with "The Limit" inside it, and a small s after the star. "Starclan MacAlister! And anyway, what does 'FORTITER' mean, again?"

"It means, 'To Go Boldly Forward'. Just like we are. Going boldly forward into the rest of our lives. Starclan! Shar, I like it!" *And I love you, even though I'm too much of a coward to tell you!*

"We all have these tattoos. Now what?" Sharon looked at Jock. *Say something. Do something. You're down to three friggin' hours!*

Angie leaned into Pat and whispered into his ear. Pat's eyes got wide, and a slight grin spread onto his face.

"Ah, guys, Angie is a little worn out, and I'm gonna, um, escort her home, for safety's sake, ya know."

"Angie!" Shar stood up and hugged her roommate.

Angela whispered something to Shar as she hugged her, and then Angie stepped to Jock, tenderly planting a kiss on his cheek.

"Jocko, you be careful way out there!"

"I will, Angie. You be good, ya hear?" The two friends hugged for a moment, Angie placing another kiss on his cheek as she stepped back. Pat came over to Sharon and she started crying as she wrapped her arms around his neck. Sharon whispered something to Pat, and he

27

kissed her cheek gently.

"Jock", Pat said as he moved to his best friend. "I, um…I don't know."

"Yeah. I know. Look, just stay sharp, and study once in a while, will you?"

The two friends extended a hand and ended up in a quick hug. Then Pat was off, Angela's head on Pat's shoulder as she hugged his arm.

"That just leaves us then, Jock."

"Yeah, um, I, uh, guess it does. Do you want me to walk you back to your room?"

"No, Jock. I can't go to my room tonight. It's…occupied." Sharon said as she turned to look at Pat and Angela walking away.

"Oh? OH! Um, eh, well!"

"Jock, it's not that. They're going to talk about their future. They may or may not end up in bed."

"Um, Sharon?"

"Yes Jock?"

"Would you, do you wanna come back to my room? I think it'll be sort of empty tonight if you don't." *Like it has been for four years.*

Girl, you've asked for this for four years, and here it is! What is stopping you? He's all alone with you now, go for it!

"Jock," Sharon looked at Jock with big doe eyes, "I'll go, if that, if that is how you want to remember me." Sharon hung her head. *I've tried to get him to ask THAT question for four years, and I'm turning him down? Yeah, he IS worth more than that!* She looked up at Jock again, "Why haven't we talked about us, Jock, about what happens to US after tonight?"

"Sharon, that's not what I meant, not what I wanted to ask you." Jock swallowed hard. *Tell her now, you won't get another chance.* "This is." Jock's hand shook as he held out the open ring box. The modest diamond inside shining brightly in the streetlights, it's twinkle reflected in Sharon's eyes.

"Oh! Jock!" *Oh my! Oh my! Oh my! Oh my GOD!* Her mind raced as her body froze. "Jock, can we do this, being apart for two years? PLEASE tell me *you* can!" *Pleeeease! Pleasepleasepleaseplease! Say we can!* Sharon's eyes pleaded with Jock.

"I can, Sharon, what about you? Can you wait two years to be my wife?"

"Yes, Jock, I've already waited four!" She exclaimed as she wrapped her arms around his neck, and her legs around his hips as she pulled him closer and pressed her lips to his. *As long as SHE doesn't screw me over again! He'll be stuck with her until her deployment ends in three months.*

They didn't go right away to Jock's room. They held each other close and kissed like they never had before under the clear, star speckled skies of the cool, early summer night. After a time, they walked off holding hands.

They soon found themselves in front of the Academy chapel. Jock went to lead Sharon inside, but she pulled back.

"It's been such a long time, Jock, since I was ten. I, I haven't been…I'm afraid." *Jock, what does this mean, if we go in there? If we place our love before God, and everything? We can't back out then….I'll go! For him! With him! Anywhere!*

"Then now is a good time, Shar. C'mon. You're with me. You're always safe when you're here, and when you're with me."

"This is where you spent all that time alone, after your mom died. We couldn't find you, and you wouldn't ever tell us." *You should have let us in, let me in! It hurt us when you didn't.*

"Yeah." *That was a hard time. I should have let you in. I was too much in shock. I almost…*

"Shar, I've tried to tell you so many times, but every time I started to, I saw the day they told me about dad."

"Jock…"

"Sharon, when my dad died, I shut out all of my friends. Sandy was my girlfriend. I just shut her out. I was afraid that if I had another girl, something bad would happen again. I was going to ask you to be my girl the day I got the call that my mom died. It started all over again. But this time I couldn't leave, I couldn't run away. I couldn't shut you out."

"Jock, I'm so sorry."

"Sorry?"

"That I couldn't help you. Promise me, you'll never keep me out. That's what this means, Jock," Sharon held up their engagement ring. "We two as one. In everything."

"I promise."

The pain Jock had hidden deep in that dark box began to fade a little as they held each other.

Sharon looked over Jock's shoulder at the words over the imposing chapel entrance: MacAlister Chapel.

"Jock, is that…?"

"My Great-Great Grandfather was Chaplin here for 45 years. The graduates from those years chipped in and built this to remember him."

The two never did make it back to Jock's room. Instead, they walked around the campus for three hours in the cool night, under the stars, holding hands, holding each other, talking in silence as they gazed into each other's souls to confirm what they already knew. Until the waking birds told them it was time for each of them to pack their things and move away, out to a new life.

***

Skytop Apartment Complex
Syracuse, New York
Standard Earth Date June 18 3444

"This is very good wine."

"Shut up and kiss me again."

Sandy's eyes snapped open as she bolted upright in her bed. It took a moment for the dream to register.

"That was Jock. And me. We were old."

She started at her words.

"I said his name without breaking down. Jock. Jock! JOCK!"

She looked around the apartment, and then focused on the clock. She picked up her phone.

"Eleven fifty. Well, he said anytime." She ran her netsearch and hit the call link.

"I really have to clean this place up," she mumbled as she listened to the rings.

"Yes, Sandra?"

"Father Champlin, I, can, can I talk with you. Now? Please?"

***

Canaveral Earth/Space Transit Hub
Cape Canaveral, Florida
Standard Earth Date June 19 3444

The last good-byes having been said, the four friends stopped at the Spaceport. Jock was the first scheduled to leave, his shuttle to lunar orbit, and six months of training before blasting out to his Turret.

Jock grabbed a window seat on the tram to the launch gate. He looked out at the three waving friends, wondering when he would see them again. Angie and Pat would be married soon, and Jock would miss it. Jock and Sharon had to wait for his assignment to finish; there was no leave from an Asteroid Defense Station. Both guys knew why they planned it so poorly; they had never been happier, and planning like that meant this happiness would end.

Jock smiled and leaned out the window to wave, as the tram started moving. His three best friends stood arm-in-arm on the side of the road, a perfect picture waving at him.

They never saw the bus that killed them.

Jock did.

Deep in that dark little box buried in Jock's mind, the pain began to grow again.

CHAPTER TWO

Lunar Launch Station
Tsiolkovskiy Crater
Standard Earth Date July 16 3444

"Lieutenant, your ride is in here." Lieutenant Commander Jericho Bucktooth motioned for Jock to follow him through the doors behind the large and intimidating Marine guards. Jock followed him up to the doors, and stopped. Six months of concentrating on his training had kept him busy. Too busy to think about...

"Go ahead, Mr. MacAlister, open the doors."

Jock pushed the doors open and walked into the brightly lit room. A catwalk ran around three of the four walls of the sixty by thirty foot room, bordering the sunken center where the probe was supposed to be.

Jock did a double take as he looked at the center of the room, for there was nothing there! He walked up the catwalk, and as he came closer, his stomach started flipping. The dizziness grew, the nausea grew; just as Jock was about to double over, the Lieutenant Commander flipped a switch on the wall and the vertigo disappeared. A forty-eight foot long charcoal black needle shape floating in the center of the room replaced it.

"Wow!" was all Jock could say.

The center of the probe was about six feet wide and ten feet long. From there, it tapered smoothly into a needle-sharp point on each end. The exterior of the craft was a mirror finish, glass-smooth, without visible variation or seams.

"OK, Jock, keep your eyes on the probe." LC Bucktooth flicked the switch to activate the gravity screen again. The charcoal needle shimmered into invisibility as the gravitic field bent the light waves around the pod. Jock felt the dizziness begin until the LC said, "Keep telling yourself it's still there, Jock. Reach out, touch it."

Jock reached a tentative hand out and touched the cold, glass-like surface his eyes told him was not there. As he ran his hand over the smooth surface, the vertigo faded. His hand seemed to leave ripples in the air as he moved it along the probe's surface. Jock picked his hand up and looked at the space where the probe was, and noticed a slight shimmering effect. If he concentrated very hard, he could see the needle shape in the shimmer. He thought, *if this ship was moving at zero-point-three times light speed, it would be undetectable.*

"Lieutenant, may I speak with you a moment?" Jericho Bucktooth brought Jock over to a door off the catwalk, motioning the young officer inside. Jock walked into a small room of bare gray walls, which was nearly filled by one grey metal table and two sparsely padded grey metal chairs. Lieutenant Commander Bucktooth followed Jock, closing the door behind him.

"Jock, how are you?"

"Excuse me, LC?"

"Jock, the recordings are off. This is an "off-the-record" conversation. How are you doing?"

"Sir, I've done pretty well learning the mission profile, flight controls, ADS controls and capabilities…"

"Stow it, MacAlister! I want to know how you *feel*! And call me Jeri in this room."

"Sir, eh, Jeri, I don't…"

"Stop bullshitting around the bush!" Jeri slammed his hand down on the table as he stood up and leaned over Jock. "You watched your fiancé and your two best friends get run over by a bus, and there was nothing you could do about it! How are you dealing with that?"

Jock took in a deep breath. So many things boiled deep inside him, things he had kept buried under textbooks and equipment manuals for six months; tears, sobs, uncontrolled bawling. He had kept it all neatly boxed up inside. Now his CO was prying the lid off of that box. Mom. Agnes. Don. Sandy. He could shut them all out. He couldn't shut out his CO.

Jock felt the world around him shrinking into that suffocating pinpoint again. Crushing him tighter and tighter, all of it building up pressure…

"Son, what happened to you would sidetrack anyone. It wasn't like a battle, no one expected casualties. And you watched your love and your friends splattered as they waved good-bye to you. Tell me how that makes you feel!"

Jeri's graphic words opened the lid to that box a little more. The images in Jock's mind added to the pressure there.

"It, um, it, makes me feel angry! Sad! Cheated! It…I…They…" Jock's head fell on the table as his pain exploded, his body to his soul shaking. Jeri placed a strong hand on Jock's shoulder, and waited as Jock's pain boiled over. *This is the strongest kid I've seen come through here, and the brightest. He didn't deserve this.*

"They got a bum deal they didn't deserve, Jock. And so did you. It's Okay to be angry about that, about the happiness that day ripped out of your life. But it can't take the memories of what you four had shared. Nothing can take those from you, son. Tell me about the first time you met them, each one. Start by telling me about the dark haired girl…"

***

Stealth Probe 1138
Lunar Launch Station
Tsiolkovskiy Crater
Standard Earth Date December 28 3444

"Comfortable, Pilot?" The half-bald, mustached face asked.

"Like a bug in a rug, Chief." Jock replied.

"OK, son, Godspeed to you, Sir." Crew Chief Vito Kowalski slapped a big hand on top of Jock's helmet. "Glad to see you perked up and smiling, Son."

"Thanks, Vito." Jock looked up at the Chief's face, the ever-present unlit stub of a stogie trying to fall from his lips. The entrance hatch closed, sealing Jock into the stealth probe for the next twelve days. Bucktooth was a smart guy. Even though Jock had passed all his training requirements with flying colors, he realized that twelve days sealed in the needle-tipped probe no one could see would have driven him insane if he hadn't released his feelings about Angie, Pat, and Sharon. Plus there was the long buried anguish over the deaths of his mother and father that he had never dealt with. Now, thanks to LC Bucktooth, Jock would be thinking of the good times he had had with the three friends and with his parents. *That is one good officer. I hope I can be as effective if I ever make it that far.*

"You got your hat on straight, Lieutenant?" Jeri's voice came over his comm.

"Aye-aye, Sir! Thanks to you, Sir! I mean that."

"Stow it, son. Consider it part of your training. You'll have plenty of chances to use it."

"Copy that, Sir. I still am grateful, Sir."

"MacAlister, get the hell out of here!" Jericho Bucktooth grinned.

"On the schedule, Sir!" Jock looked at the readouts in front of him. The stealth probe was sitting on a launch cradle just outside the main propulsive rails. The basic process was that of a high velocity railgun, lengthened out over the lunar surface to keep the acceleration tolerable for the human bullet. Once every six months the railgun pointed close enough to ADS 1437 to launch a replacement. There was a reason for the stealth launches and undetectable probes. Jock thought of that Remembrance Day with his father at the fairgrounds 13 years ago.

Eighty-eight years ago, the Earth had been invaded, and Humanity had come close to extinction. Due in large part to the actions of an otherwise inconsequential freighter captain named Joel MacAlister and his crew, who managed to turn their creaky old ore carrier into a shotgun blast that destroyed most of the alien fleet, Humanity survived. The result was the construction of the ADS systems at certain favorable gravitational points around the solar system. This put overlapping early warning and point-defense systems into the most likely paths of any future invaders. The ADS sites were almost undetectable by design, and any ships traveling to them needed to be as well, or an invading force would simply bypass the "Turrets".

And now Jock, great-nephew of Joel, was about to be launched like a dart at one of them.

Twelve days. What would I think about? What would I do? I have no input into the flight until the last few kilometers.

Jock went through the checklist yet again, for the twentieth time he figured. *Busy work!* Oh, well, he was getting the assignment he had dreamt of since he was ten. Command of a Turret!

"T minus ten minutes, and counting!" the computerized voice informed him. Jock thought about the launch; 1,100 kilometers of magnetic accelerated hell as he was boosted to the speed that would take him to the Turret in a dozen days. 100 million kilometers in twelve days! One third of light-speed!

Now he had a few minutes to think…if he hadn't chosen a Turret assignment, would his friends still be alive? If he had asked Sharon last year, at the formal when he first realized it was the right thing to do, would they all be alive and happy?

Jock rubbed his right shoulder and screamed, "FORTITER"!

"…in three. Two. One. Launch." The computer stated calmly. But Jock never heard that "launch" part, as the acceleration slammed him into the gravchair.

Twelve days in isolation is a longer time when you have to live it than when you just talk about it. Jock had little to do now, as the entire process was automated up until the last few hours.

I've been over the last few hours at the Academy at least twelve times.

There is nothing I could have done. The bus driver had a heart attack; he was dead before he could have seen my friends. How long has it been? Twenty minutes, great! Mom, she died of a broken heart. Dad was her life, dad and I. Nothing I could have done there, either. Dad, I wish…dad, I wanted to spend every second I could with you. The trips to the lab you took me on sparked my interest in gravity research: the accident in the lab. I'll find out what killed you, dad. I promise.

"Computer, run simm Mac-A-1."

"Simm initiated."

Jock watched the vid of the research lab his father oversaw. He watched as his father moved into the staging area near the gravitronic field. The other technicians looked at their readouts, one screamed in panic, and the entire lab imploded, collapsing in upon itself. His father and three technicians included, sucked into the microscopic singularity at the center of the field. As the field collapsed, all that was left of the people, the lab and a quarter of the building was a baseball-sized sphere of super dense matter.

Again and again Jock watched. At first it distracted him from thinking of Angela, of Patrick, of Mom, but most of all, it kept him from thinking of Sharon. And Sandy. He felt so guilty about shutting Sandy out of his life after his father died, that he didn't contact her for the four years he was at the Academy. Yet his feelings for Sandy were what kept him from embracing Sharon for four years. Now the guilt of those precious few embraces, of planning to marry another woman, made thinking of Sandy even more painful. So he buried her memories very deep.

Studying his father's death almost kept all of that guilt out of his mind. It kept him from remembering Sharon's golden hair, how soft and shiny it was, how it's smell always made him smile, how soft her skin was, the taste of her lips the last night together…

I need to get off of that. I'm not ready yet.

"Computer, replay at one-half speed."

"Replaying at one-half speed."

Something's not right there!

Hilton D. C. Resort
Room 513
Arlington
Standard Earth Date December 28 3444

"How could you have screwed this up so badly? Do you know what he's going to do to us? You were supposed to whack that MacAlister kid, instead you whacked *his* kid!" Harry Ashton growled at his partner.

"It's not my fault. The guy really croaked! We had it set up so he could claim a heart attack, and he really had one!" Ralph Mitchell begged.

"Even so, the only way one of us will survive this is..."

"NO, no, wait! Harry, Harry, don't!"

***

Stealth Probe 1138
Lunar-Oort Transit
Standard Earth Date December 29 3444

Jock lay staring at the neutral grey panel above him. Finding the strength to look into certain memories was not an easy task.

One at a time he lifted the mental images out of his mind's keep. Angie, that first day, in awe of some story she had heard about him. And how embarrassed she was when Jock found out later that she had researched the three smartest cadets in her class before hand.

Patrick, his unconditional friendship, his aversion to studying. And his infatuation with Sharon's beauty...

Sharon. Sharon. All thoughts of her go to that last night: *The wind was cool, and smelled faintly of cherry blossoms. My hand shook as I slid the ring onto her finger. She was afraid of going into the chapel, oh, but how wonderful it was inside! When we kissed, that exhilarating feel of her skin, the smell of her soft hair, the electricity of her lips, the magic of her fingers...*

"Sharon, I'll never forget you. I'll never waste time that way again. I miss you. I love you. Always."

Jock fell asleep. He dreamt of the things that should have been.

***

Chrysler Building
55th Floor
New York City
Standard Earth Date December 31 3444

The 55th floor of The Chrysler Building had only one occupant. The private elevator stopped only there, and opened up into a large reception area, where a pretty, yet efficient looking receptionist guarded the two massive, dark stained wooden doors. Behind the doors was a meeting room, designed to hold a dozen VIPs comfortably.

A well-dressed yet brutish looking man dragged the swollen, half conscious Harry Ashton through the doors, past the polished mahogany table and into the private office beyond.

"Here he is sir, just as you requested."

"Thank you, Mr. Hale. You may leave him now."

"Yes sir."

"Mr. Ashton, the results of the assignment you were given were disastrous. I send you to remove a thorn, and instead you kill my daughter. And, I hear you have taken some steps to try and protect yourself from the consequences of your failure." An evil sneer crept onto the bald man's darkened face. "In so doing, you presumed to take action for me, from me. You assumed my place." The words were spat out as if sour milk. "I have some friends that I think will enjoy meeting you."

The half-bald man walked over to the large mahogany desk and pressed a button.

"Mr. Stack, I have someone here I wish you to introduce to your hounds."

Harry began screaming then. He stopped screaming soon after he was introduced to the hounds.

***

"How is the kid doing, Bucktooth? Will he be able to handle what he will find there?"

"Better than I would have been able to at that age, Admiral. He's pretty damn strong. It's a shame to send him out there, though. And damn bad luck on the assignment."

"We've tried to talk him out of it for two years. He's not only the highest scoring in physics, history, tactics, and strategy but in diplomacy, as well. Everyone wanted that kid! And, this is the ONLY ADS site available before we shut them all down."

"I still don't think that's a good idea, Sir."

"Neither do I, or any of the Joint Chiefs. But, the decision's been made. The new plasma drives are supposed to enable a fleet of ships to take the place of the Turrets, and we just don't have the budget for both."

"Well, Sir, I still don't like it. Or sending MacAlister out with...*her* there."

"They are simply the two best minds we have on Gravitic Drive Theory. I'm betting they'll start working together on it pretty quick."

"If they don't kill each other first. You're setting them both under a huge emotional Sword of Damocles, Sir."

"Take care of this kid, Bucktooth. And take care of the girl when she gets back. She'll likely be a wreck. Or, more of a wreck than when she went out."

"I'll keep an eye on him, sir. And I'll do what I can for her as well."

"I know you will, Jeri."

***

Jock woke up after eight hours of sleep. He felt much more at peace with himself than he had in a long time. Now a refreshed Jock was back at his self appointed task of investigating his father's death. Why did the gravitic field expand, what collapsed the controls?

Jock watched the vids over and over again. He looked at the data readouts over and over again. And he looked at the data feeds superimposed upon the vids over and over again. Jock came to the uneasy conclusion that the gravitic field was normal right up until his father came into the control room, and then, as if a switch had been thrown...

Something's just not right there!

Jock called up the vids of each technician and observer. He thought he may have seen something, but he needed more information, a better data feed with more detail.

Later. Jock had come to realize that after reviewing the same vid five times, he stopped seeing details. So he alternated.

He went back to his theory of gravitic beam control. Running simm after simm of his theory, tweaking each little detail just a little here, a little there. After a few hours of working on that, he just needed to stop thinking, stop trying to solve puzzles.

So, he remembered.

He remembered watching Pat play basketball. He was deceptively powerful with that thin frame, and very quick. He smiled at the memory of Angela's vicious logic on the debating team; so much joyful ferocity in such a small package. Sharon. Every time he brought up a memory of her, his mind went back to the softness of her hair, her scent, like flowers on a spring morning, her touch, like an angel's breath. To the first words he ever said to her, that said what he thought the best:

"Your eyes reflect my soul like shimmering pools,
And your hair outshines the morning sun,
When you smile, wise men are but fools,
All my senses, your beauty stuns!"

And then his mind wandered out of that comfortable room of memories, into places his guilt darkened; Don, his best friend, the kindest person he'd ever met, never saying a bad word about anyone. Aggie, always smiling, the most perceptive person he could imagine.

And Sandy. The dances. The Proms. The Friday nights on the lake. The way her head fit perfectly on his shoulder. They way he felt… whole when he was with her. The shimmer of her eyes whenever she looked at him. Her joy when he won a wrestling match. Laying next to her on the summer's grass, holding her hand as they looked up at the stars…

He fought through the darkness of his guilt. How he had cut them all off after his father died, and how he had closed the door on them completely after his mom passed. How his mom's death, or his reaction to it, had almost cost him Pat, Angie, and Sharon as well.

How they all could have helped him deal with the deaths, as Lieutenant Commander Bucktooth had. How they all would have become friends. How he would have had to choose between Sandy and Sharon. How he couldn't have made that choice.

Was that why I kept them out of my life after I got to the Academy? I knew I'd have to choose? But, wasn't that choosing of a sort?

No, it wasn't choosing; it was the memories of Dad teaching Don and me how to sail. Of Mom teaching Sandy and Aggie how to make haggis. Of the talks with Dad about being a Man, about right and wrong, about honor, duty, and kindness. About girls, how a real man treated women. And how that topic had always came back to Sandy.

It took Jock three days to fight through that darkness he had draped over those memories. He couldn't bring them fully into daylight yet, not until he asked her forgiveness.

And that had to wait another eighteen months.

After seven more days, he thought he had his gravity answer. He also thought he'd had his fill of the subject of gravitics.

And, he still hadn't figured out why his father was dead.

***

Stealth Probe 1138
Lunar-Oort Transit
Standard Earth Date January 7 3445

"Deceleration program commencing in ninety minutes." The cold computerized voice announced. Jock wondered why the USF never gave a bit of personality to a computer's voice.

Battery power had run the stealth probe Jock was riding in until now. The small gravitic generator was scheduled to start now. Jock watched the readouts that told him the hydrogen atoms were being slammed into each other, releasing great amounts of energy. .

Jock monitored the startup of the reactor. This was a critical moment in his trip. If the reactor did not fire, Jock would become an interstellar traveler, drifting endlessly through the universe. Thankfully, that had never happened. Yet.

The reactor started, and Jock saw the power available increase. He initiated the IFF transmission so the ADS would not vaporize him, then the gravity beams as he reviewed the deceleration profiles calculated before his launch. He was dependent upon those calculations, since his stealth probe had no way of verifying his position, course, or velocity.

At the predetermined point, Jock's probe energized the gravity beams and began slowing into the orbit that should place him into the docking port of ADS 1437.

Two thousand, four hundred Asteroid Defense Stations were commissioned in the three decades after the Bird invasions. Originally armed with railguns, missile batteries and laser emplacements, the ADSs were continuously upgraded throughout the years. Huge numbers of missiles were maintained, but upgraded with newer, faster, more maneuverable missiles. Lasers were upgraded with better ranges, faster recharge times, and more power. Railguns fired larger, denser projectiles at higher velocities. And sensors were improved to the point that anything coming within a half light-year of the station was identified.

The stations were comprised of groups of asteroids clustered in gravity wells about the system's perimeter. The habitation module was in a large asteroid near the center of the cluster, with various sensors and weapons systems spread out among the smaller rocks. ADS 1437 was more like a series of powerful forts, each with supporting fire from its neighbors, rather than one turret.

The most recent upgrades had included experimental gravity beams, still not perfected. Studying gravitics gave Jock ideas for other weapons, such as gravity well 'moats' and projectile gravity imploders. These later devices would act as explosive projectiles, except that instead of releasing energy through explosions, they turned their energy into a concentrated gravity field, which would act as a mini-black hole.

Jock monitored the startup and initiation of the systems, but everything was automatic, so there was little for Jock to do. As he came closer to ADS 1437, his probe slowed, and the sensor collectors deployed. Jock soon had a vid feed of the surrounding space, including the many rocks, pebbles, boulders, and planetoids he was gliding through.

Jock looked at a large planetoid dead ahead, seeing the docking bay doors open, transforming the rocky surface into a gaping landing field. His probe seemed to float into the opening, settling down without any effort on his part. *Gee, I'm sure glad I spent all those hours in the simms learning how to fly this crate!*

The probe settled onto the landing bay floor, as the darkness signaled the closing of the exterior bay doors. Jock was anxious at the prospects of meeting his station partner. He felt remiss that he had not studied her files on the trip out; it was his only official assignment.

Quickly Jock brought up the files, scanning the background, the last two evaluations, and the most recent perf-proj, or performance projection. This computer-generated report was an electronic guess of the sailor's performance over the coming two years. Jock read it, and started to worry.

His partner's IQ was nearly off the charts, ten points higher than Jock's. But her perf-proj was a disaster, just awaiting fulfillment; total mental breakdown within six months. Great.

The probe's hatch opened, jarring Jock back into the present. Her name, he hadn't memorized her name! He glanced at the image on the darkening screen, the name under it, and felt a chill go up his spine: Shannon. Shannon Malone. Malone… Jock's shoulders shook as his eyes rapidly scanned the bio file. Sibling, twin sister, Sharon Malone!

She never told me about a twin sister!

The image of his three friends waving flashed to the front of his mind. That image zoomed in on Sharon, closer, closer, the bus…

"Aaaagh!"

Jock tried to sit up as he screamed, slamming his head into hard, cold, unyielding metal. The jolt snapped his head back down and his mind spun back to the present.

The dark prison he had so recently escaped threatened to lock him away again.

Calm down. Remember the good times, like Bucktooth taught you. Deep breaths.

It took a moment for Jock to feel presentable. Still, one thing worried him.

Twins. She'll probably look exactly like Sharon, so man-up and deal with it!

Jock hit the release switch to open the probe. Bright light hit him, forcing his trembling hand up to his forehead.

He felt a lump growing there.

Oh, just great!

***

Asteroid Defense Station 1437
Landing Bay Alpha
Standard Earth Date January 9 3445

"Welcome aboard, Lieutenant." The cold computer voice spat at Jock.

I would have expected the Ensign Malone to show up and say, 'hi', at least! Jock thought. He looked around the small landing bay; barely big enough for him to stand next to the transport stealth probe he'd ridden out from the Moon.

"Hey, El-Tee Jay-Gee! Nice ta-meet-cha!" a familiar yet strange voice greeted Jock.

"Hello?" Jock looked around, trying to find her.

"Over here, lover boy!"

Oh, God, no! Please let me handle this.... Jock spun around and saw her. Sharon, but not Sharon.

"Ensign Malone?" He weakly inquired.

"Yeah. So, is this the stud my lil sis has gone so gaga over?"

"Shannon, when was the last news from home delivered here?" Jock walked towards the voice.

"Well, if you're as smart as sis says, you'd know. Six months ago." An unkempt blonde stepped out of the shadows, and stood with arms crossed, staring defiantly at Jock.

Oh, God! I can't relive that! Jock stopped, and stood in silence for a long time.

"Well, what happened? You marry her, she get run over by a bus, what?"

"Ensign, follow me." Jock swallowed hard, his suddenly dry throat leaving his voice barely a whisper. *It's just no fair! I shouldn't have to do this! I shouldn't have to relive that again.*

She shouldn't have to find out like this. No one should. Damn total stealth isolation!

A few more deep breaths and the stretching of his muscles calmed Jock a little.

This is a function of the assignment I had asked for. Suck it up.

The two walked in silence towards where Jock remembered his quarters were supposed to be.

Think of her as a subordinate!

Finally arriving at the door to his quarters, Jock went inside and sat at the desk there. "Ensign, sit down."

"Yes, Sir!" she said with mock seriousness.

Jock stood up as Shannon sat down. Even though the room was small, Jock paced head down. Every few steps he shook his head.

There's no easy way to do this. No magic words. No special phrases. Damn it! I shouldn't have asked to come here!

"Hey, LTJG, what's going on? You clench that jaw any tighter you're gonna need dentures."

Jock stopped walking and looked through Shannon.

"Shannon, Sharon is dead."

The gorgeous blonde looked at Jock, her expressionless face cutting his soul into little pieces.

"That...that's not funny."

"Sharon and I were engaged. I asked her the night after graduation. When I boarded the tram to the spaceport, Sharon and my two best friends were hit by a bus. The driver had a heart attack, and the bus ran them over as I watched them waving..." Jock swallowed hard again, swallowed those tears he couldn't let escape just yet, "waving goodbye. To me." *Stay upright. God, I just want to lie down and cry!*

Shannon stared at Jock for a long time. She wavered side to side for a moment. "You were engaged to her?" her voice came quietly to his ears.

Jock told her the story of that last night. Everything. Even the parts he would never tell another. He had to tell it all, to get through telling it at all.

"You were engaged to my twin sister, and then you watched her die. Now you have to tell me about it. How are you so…damned composed? Because I'm about to lose everything right now." Shannon did not wipe the tears flowing down her cheeks.

"Shannon, I…It's not easy. I loved her with all my soul."

"If you told her the things you said you did, I believe you. I… I." Shannon took three big, deep breaths. "Oh, Shar is gone! Oh, God!" The ensign fell to the floor, unconscious.

She looks just like…STOP THAT! SHE IS NOT SHARON! "Ensign, Ensign Malone, are you alright?" Jock knelt next to her, holding her head. *God, she looks just like Sharon! How am I…why this test?*

"Wha-what's going on? Sharon? Sharon's dead?" Shannon sat up, and squinted at Jock. "She loved you more than anything. She must have been very happy when you asked her. Tell me that part again. I know it must hurt, but…please tell me again." Shannon stared up at Jock through her tears.

Jock nearly melted, looking Sharon's twin with that much emotion flooding her eyes. So, Jock told her, through the tears and sobs. It helped that she wore her hair tied up in a way Sharon never did. He hoped she smelled different too. Jock focused on that while he told her his feelings, his regrets for not owning up to his feelings earlier, and his guilt for her death. Jock held nothing back. At the end, Jock placed a hand on her shoulder while he told her his heart, his tears hitting her face while he spoke.

"She told me about you in the last letter I got from her, about a year ago. It wasn't long, but twins can say a lot with a few words. You've had some time to deal with this. Give me my time for that." Shannon stood up, composing herself as best she could. She looked right through Jock standing next to her. Suddenly she leaned over and lightly kissed Jock's cheek. Before he could react, she was gone.

She does smell like Sharon. Am I screwed, or what! I'll either come out of this the strongest person ever, or I'll go nuts.

Jock sat on his bunk for several minutes, just letting the last few minutes fade on their own. When the numbness wore off, he moved to his duffle and began unpacking. *Yeah, this would be challenging. In many, many ways.*

***

Shannon Malone drummed her fingers on the monitoring panel. "Where the hell is he?" she glanced at her watch again. "He's half an hour late, and I'm hungry and tired."

Shannon reached out and tapped several inputs until she brought up the video of Jock's quarters. *I shouldn't be doing this, he could have my ass....ha-ha! Poor choice of words. He's sleeping! The SOB is sleeping!*

Shannon set the system on auto-track as she stood up. Her feet hit the floor with just a bit more force than the ADS gravity generators would have accounted for as she marched to Jock's quarters.

She hit the codes on Jock's door and froze as she focused on the back of her hand; her watch. She grabbed her datatab from her belt and checked the time...DAMN! *How could I have misread the time like that? It's 05:30, not 08:30!*

"NO! NO! NO!"

The scream shocked and frightened Shannon. She gingerly stepped into the dark room, and stuck her head into the Lieutenant's bedroom.

"SHARON! STOP! STOP THE TRAIN! I'VE GOT TO GET TO HER!" Jock thrashed in his bed, the light from the corridor shining off of his sweat-drenched hair and face. His blankets were flung across the room, and he clutched his pillow tightly in the grip of his nightmare.

Shannon watched Jock as he quieted down. She turned and walked back to the passageway, not bothering to wipe the tears streaming down her cheeks. She held her sobs until she heard his alarm go off. She closed the door to Jock's quarters and ran sobbing to her own.

***

Jock stared at the large video screen, watching his father implode in slow motion once again. *Something's not right. What IS IT!*

Shifts on the ADS were ten hours on, fourteen hours off. The automated systems ran the ADS for the six hours that both of the crew were off. The shifts were supposed to overlap for two hours for the crew to work together. But some how Shannon was always somewhere else for those two hours, fixing a system or running a diagnostic. The first day he got here, he'd shown up ten minutes before his watch began, only to find Shannon had just left. Each day after that he had come in ten minutes earlier than the day before, with the same result. He hadn't seen her since that meeting in the landing bay. Today, he would show up exactly on time, just to see what happened.

Jock had spent every waking off-duty minute studying the vid, pouring over each frame, following the movements of each person over and over again, and burying his mind in it, using it to shut out everything else.

He couldn't figure out what it was, but there was something wrong in the vid.

"Ding-ding-ding" his datatab alarm told him his watch began in five minutes. Jock stopped the vid, and began getting ready.

A final adjustment to his uniform, and Jock turned and walked to the door. He reached for the handle and pulled it open. As he began to walk through, he pulled back with a start.

Shannon!

"It's the lab assistant next to your father. Run it again." She said, brushing past Jock to the small meeting area of the commander's quarters. "Here, look." She was adjusting the controls before Jock could think of a thing to say.

"Uh, Shannon! Um, my, a, my watch is starting, I should be in CIC…"

"You know that the station computer will contact us if anything shows up. There! See it?" Shannon pointed her finger at the right hand pocket of the assistant's lab coat.

Jock stared up at the scene he'd looked at a thousand times. Now, as

48

Shannon played the three tenths of a second forward and back in a continuous loop, Jock saw it; the pocket moved! Someone had altered the recordings!

"What…" Jock looked at Shannon, who was already watching him.

"I watched the vids of Sharon's…that bus was heading straight for them before the driver had the heart attack. They were part of a hit, Jock, a hit meant for you." Her eyes were aflame with her anger. "We need to find out who did this. Now, tell me everything your father ever told you about his work."

"Well, he was working on using gravity control to stretch and compress space. As a means of driving a ship at FTL speeds, and on using gravitic thrust, where the gravity force is applied like tires to a road, driving a ship without fuel, and a power plant design that used gravity to hold a proton and an electron in close proximity without allowing the electron to orbit the proton, which could end up producing a lot of energy."

"All that, before lunch, hey?"

"Excuse me?"

"Look, do you have any notes of his, or anything like that?"

"Yeah, I brought them all. I was hoping it would lead me to the reason for the implosion. Something there just isn't right, like you said."

"Right. Now, I'm starved. C'mon, follow me to the mess." Shannon grabbed his hand and pulled him out of his quarters.

Jock followed Shannon, though he wasn't exactly sure why. His sense of duty, his training screamed that he should be in the Combat Information Center, or CIC, scanning the computer's reports. Yet, somehow, this impetuous reflection of Sharon was leading him around as if he were a puppy.

"Jock, you're too close to the problem. Give me what you have, and I'll look at it overnight." Shannon said as she punched in the menu choices. "I've got yours, too. Save us a table."

Jock looked around the small room, then walked over to the only table in the mess and sat down. He waited patiently until Shannon brought the two steaks, baked potatoes, and corn on the cob over.

"Here, Jocko. Now, about your father's research." Shannon said as she stood next to Jock.

"Look, Shannon, my father's research, it's pretty intense…"

"Can it. My IQ is forty points higher than Sharon's. " A hint of anger touched her voice. "And I know hers was ten points higher than yours. How you ever outscored her on all those tests…"

"I worked harder. Well, I worked better. Okay, I'm not sure how that happened."

"You really are just as dense as she told me, aren't you? You beat her because, for the first time in her life, she was distracted. Distracted by you!" Shannon nearly yelled her response as she grabbed Jock's shoulders.

Jock stood up, glaring at her. Shannon saw the pain burning in his eyes, and immediately regretted the tone she had used.

"I'm sorry, Jock. That was selfish of me. We both loved Sharon. I just wish…"

"What? You wish what?" Jock put his hands on Shannon's shoulders and stared intensely into her eyes.

"I wish I had been distracted by someone like you instead of… Jock, haven't you wondered why I'm here, and Sharon went to the Academy?"

Shannon looked straight back into Jock's eyes. He thought for a moment, he saw Sharon's eyes looking back.

"Why" was all his suddenly quiet voice could reply.

"I was in love. She was a girl from high school. She enlisted, and I followed. Then she got pregnant, got herself discharged. And here I am, on a career path to nowhere, jealous of my dead twin sister, talking to her… fiancé. Thinking what I could have been. I…"

"Shannon, please, you just beat me up, don't beat-up yourself now!"

Shannon sobbed as she buried her head in his shoulder. Jock put his arms around her, trying to tell himself he was comforting a friend. Much to his own disappointment, a large part of him tried to pretend that he was holding Sharon again.

They stood there awkwardly for several minutes as Shannon's emotions finally found relief. She composed herself, and stepped back from Jock.

"Thank you. I needed a bit of 'family' support. Now, back to work."

***

Asteroid Defense Station 1437
Research Simulations Center
Standard Earth Date December 29 3445

"No, that won't work; the magnetic flux field has to be synchronized to focus the gravity wave. See, like this." Jock was deep into the physics, confident in his education and understanding playing off of the raw intuitive brainpower of Shannon's intellect.

"That won't let you go where you need to. See, in order to compress the spatial fabric, you need to apply the gravity wave over a larger, unfocused area, and then bring it into focus as you shrink the wave's footprint. In order to do that, you need to be unfocused initially."

"Wait, that makes sense, but we need to apply it this way; start focused on the initial wave application, then change the focus this way," Jock hit several controls, changing the graphics on the screen to illustrate his point, "Then move it out. The problem becomes releasing the wave and applying it again to the next point in space. We can't do it fast enough. They say that is why my father died. Hmm…"

"What are you thinking, Little Brother?"

"We don't need to move the wave! What is the theoretical limit on the length of the gravity wave?"

"Theoretically, there is none."

"Right. So, using your "unfocused" approach…"

"Cute."

"…we set the wave to grab the space in front of the ship, ALL the space in front of the ship, and focus it all at once, like this." Jock confidently hit a control, and the simulation ran perfectly.

"Jock, that is what your father was doing! Look at these readouts!" Shannon shouldered Jock away from the screen controls and quickly entered in her inputs. The video of the lab Jock's father died in came up, frozen at the point in time of the gravitic wave activation.

"See, those figures on the screen. Here," Shannon magnified the display, "see it?"

"Yes! YES! THAT'S IT!" Jock threw his arms in the air, and then jumped up. When he came down, he turned towards Shannon, "You found it!" Jock grabbed Shannon's head and planted a big kiss hard on her lips, then immediately froze. "I, God, Shannon, I, I'm sorry, so sorry!"

"Hey, um, eh, it, it's Okay, Little Brother! We're family, remember?"

Jock sat down quickly, heart suddenly beating wildly. *Clear your head, Lieutenant.* "Shannon, am I wrong, or is this a relatively simple software adjustment?" Jock felt as if he'd just finished a wrestling match.

"Well, that and about a hundredfold increase in power output." She glanced down at Jock. "Jock, did Sharon ever tell you who our father was?"

"Mr. Malone, I assumed. She never spoke of her family, she always changed the subject. She did mention once, our sophomore year, that he wanted me to come work for him after my first term."

"And, she knew who your father was, and how he died?" Shannon took a small object out of her pocket, flicked a switch on it, and set it on the table.

"Yes, she was there when Pat dragged it out of me one night in our freshmen year. Why the jammer?" Jock pointed to the object on the table.

"Jock, look at the screen, the logos on the lab coats, on the stationary, the computer screens. Jock, what company was your father leading in the gravitic research?"

"General Aerospace Developments. I knew that."

"Who is the CEO, Chairman Of The Board, and majority stockholder in General Aerospace?"

"That's easy, he's in the newscasts all the time, heavy into politics; Howard Ma...Malone? He's...you're..." *Oh, shit!*

"Yeah, Howard Malone was almost your daddy-in-law." Shannon sat down. "He is pure evil, Jock. Stay away from him. Drop the investigation into your father's death, and never mention it again."

"But, Shannon, I..."

"Drop it, Jock." Shannon's voice had become hard and dark, determined and fearful together. Her brow furrowed as she continued, "I'll prove what happened to Sharon and your friends. I have some, eh, contacts, resources. But you should know that he's had people killed. And worse. Many times. I've heard the orders he's given, just like he was trading stock or buying a bottle of wine. We argued about it, and now I'm here. Yes, there was a girl, I did love her, but she didn't get pregnant. She just..." Shannon gulped hard trying to swallow that lump in her throat, "...died. Training accident they said," Shannon tried to swallow the lump again, "Sharon argued too, but she handled him a lot better than I did."

"Shannon, do you mean, your father tried to have me killed? Had my father killed?"

"Yes, Jock, that is exactly what I mean. If you drop this, he'll forget about it. Please, please!" Shannon took each of Jock's hands in one of hers, and looked into his eyes. "Please?"

"I wish you would stop looking at me that way. It makes it hard, em, er, a, to concentrate…"

Shannon kissed Jock hard on the lips. She held the kiss for a long time. When she let Jock back off, she sensed that something had changed in him. *This should make it even harder!*

"Well, Ensign, thank you."

"Sir!"

"Thank you for making me realize you are not Sharon."

"Hmm. Mission accomplished then, Sir."

"You know I can't drop it."

"I also know I'm leaving here tomorrow, and I've got eighteen months to handle it so you won't have to." Shannon's eyes still held Jock's. "Sir."

"Shannon, don't do anything foolish."

"I promise you, Little Brother, Sir, that every move I make will be carefully and very thoroughly planned and thought out."

"I don't doubt it for a minute. Shannon, you aren't Sharon, but you are my friend. Please, be careful." Jock placed his hand on Shannon's arm.

"Come with me, and bring the jammer." Shannon grabbed Jock's arm and led him down the hall to her quarters. "Did you really make that up about her eyes, and all? Tell me again!"

"Your eyes reflect my soul like shimmering pools, and your hair outshines the morning sun, at your smile wise men are but fools, all my senses, your beauty stuns!"

"That's what I thought. C'mon, hurry up!"

A few hours later, smiling, damp, and sweaty, as she traced the tattoo on his shoulder with her finger, she asked him what "FORTITER" meant.

***

Asteroid Defense Station 1437
Combat Information Center
Standard Earth Date May 2 3446

"PERIMETER ALERT!"
"PERIMETER ALERT!"
"PERIMETER ALERT!"

The station's computer used a voice expressly designed to be annoying for this alarm. In this case it was effective, as Jock MacAlister burst into the room fresh from his shower. Ensign Emerson Bird was leaning back in his chair at the sensors station, hands behind his head and feet up on the control console. Jock slid into the weapons station, carefully adjusting his towel.

"He-ha! We've gotta boogie, JG!"

I think this guy is cracked. Something's wrong with him. "What is it, Emerson?"

"Some kind of mass moving in a nonconventional orbit, SIR!"

Jock's screens activated as he sat down, and he checked to see that no external lights or emitters were active. There was the boogie; two hundred meters long, white and red paint, crew compartment, heavy reactor shield, and three-iron fusion/plasma drive units.

"It's a Randall Class Space Tug. Looks like…number…Thistle. Huh. Damn computer cut my shower short for a faulty IFF transponder? Emerson?" *Where the hell did he go? Nutcase!*

"Ha-ha-ha!" came over the comm.

Great, he's in the showers!

"Computer, get me tight beam transmission to that tug."

"Um, hello!"

"Thistle, this is Lieutenant MacAlister, commanding officer ADS 1437. Are you aware your IFF transponder is not transmitting?"

"What? Oh, hell, dammit! Hold on a second…" Jock heard what sounded like someone kicking a metal box, followed by several industrial strength curses.

"There, it should be on now, JG."

"Affirmative, Captain…what is your name, sir?"

"Captain Trap, Dennis Trap. Hell, I'll answer ta Gunny."

"OK, Gunny. How did you know about the JG?"

"Your voice ain't dense enough to hold that second bar yet, Sir."

"Well, your IFF works now, Gunny. Just make sure you keep it on. We're always looking for targets to practice on."

"Understood, Lieutenant. You take care out here, Sir."

"You too, Gunny. Keep warm." Jock closed the connection, and hit the files for Gunnery Sergeant Dennis Trap. *Hmm. Long record, good service. Thistle, eh? Pretty but prickly. Hmm.*

***

ADS Debriefing Center
Tsiolkovskiy Crater
Standard Earth Date May 2 3446

"So, Lieutenant Commander, what do your five months' worth of testing say? Is my marbles bag full, or am I a nutcase?" Ensign Shannon Malone sat in the small gray room nearly filled with one grey metal table and two sparsely padded grey metal chairs, looking intensely at Lieutenant Commander Bucktooth.

"Your tests tell us two things. First, you are perfectly sane, notwithstanding your request to be discharged with a new identity. Second, you are, eh-hem," the LC pointed to Shannon's swollen belly, "very pregnant."

"I already knew that, Jeri." Shannon glanced down at the evidence. "I told you, I seduced him. What about the reassignment, the new identity?"

"You can stow that nonsense with me, Malone. The psych tests all ADS crew candidates go through would have revealed that, and neither one of you were even close to the cutoff. But, you both did have a unique trauma shared in a unique way. Shannon, are you trying to hide from Lieutenant MacAlister? What happened out there?"

'Look, LC, we've been over this a million times. You've put me through all the truth tests and psych evals in your book, and everyone else's book. You know nothing happened on that station that I did not want to happen. Everything we did was within the regs. Don't tell me I'm the first girl to come back with an extra passenger on board."

"Not the first, not by a long shot. But you are the first to come back and ask for a new identity. Shannon, there is no recording in this room. What is going on?"

"If I leave the debriefing quarantine without a new identity, I will be dead within a week, and, the same thing will happen to Jock when he has to come back." Shannon leaned over the cold metal table, as close to Jericho as she could get without leaving her chair. "Give me the identity, so Jock can survive."

Jeri held his place, leaning slightly over the table. He stared into Shannon's eyes for several seconds, mentally reviewing her evals and psych tests.

"Tell me what you know about Jock's father."

"He was murdered. The records of the test he died in have been altered. He…"

"Enough." Jeri barked the command with such an unquestionable authority that Shannon's irreverence was shattered and she fell back hard into her chair. Jeri pulled a pen and a single form from his pocket and slid them to Shannon without taking his eyes off of hers.

"Ensign Shannon Malone, if you sign this paper, you will get your new identity. You will also pursue the issue that is eating at your soul. But you will do it following the orders of your superior, and within the regulations of USF Marine Corps Intelligence Service. Is that cle…"

Shannon signed and pushed the paper back to the Lieutenant Commander.

"I am now an official 'McIce' Captain. There is one thing I need before I leave here. Where can a girl get a decent tattoo around here?" Shannon smiled as she clasped her hands behind her head. Somehow, the chair didn't feel so cold now.

***

Asteroid Defense Station 1437
CIC
Standard Earth Date December 4 3446

"Ensign Bird, you're early! You have the comm." Jock stated wearily. Between Bird's oddball antics, missing Shannon's intellectual companionship, and the stress of dealing with that frenzied last night before she left, Jock was exhausted.

"Early Bird! Heh-he, good one, Louie-tenant! Ha-ha! Early Bird! Hey, where's my worm? Heh-he!"

Jock walked out of the CIC and walked down the short corridor to his quarters shaking his head. He passed through the door and through the small office/foyer, diving on the bed. As tired as he was, Jock couldn't fall asleep; his mind kept replaying those haunting thoughts, like a computer stuck in a feedback loop. Shannon. His father's death. Sharon. The last night with Shannon, he never dreamed it could be like *that*! Sandy. The gravity drive, FTL applications, power plant solutions, weapons. Shannon. Sharon. Pat. Angie. He even thought back to older friends, Don and Agnes, married now, and Sandy. Sandy. *How could I, why did I lock Sandy out?* Thinking of Sandy calmed him some, but he still couldn't sleep. He tossed and turned for a while, then reached under his pillow and looked at it again. The note.

"Dear Jock. I'm not Sharon. And no, I'm not in love with you. I was always the mischievous one; Sharon was always the good girl. No matter how much trouble I got into, no matter how many awards Sharon won, I never wished I was Sharon. Until last night. I hate to, but I have to say goodbye this way:

The silence of a falling star
lights up a purple sky.
And as I wonder where you are,
I'm so lonesome, I could die.'"

There was a password and a file. Jock had not had the guts to open the file before. But he needed to stop his mind rehashing....what? That he didn't wait, and miss out this time, a second chance? He knew that it would have been different with Sharon. Or Sandy. That at least he had an amazing memory of a woman he would probably never see again? That, never once that night did he think about Sharon; he only thought of Shannon; *her touch, her lips, her smell, her skin like velvet caressing him... Was that bad? Was he perversely unfaithful to Sharon? What happens when he gets back next month, between Shannon and him? Should he try to find her? Will she try to find him? GET OUT OF THIS LOOP!*

Jock sat up in his bed, grabbed his datatab, opened the file and entered the password.

Jock gave a start when an ancient song began playing; a mournfully sorrow-soaked nasal whine. Yet, Jock just had to listen to the simple waltz as the sad voice of the heartbroken man cried out the song:

D'ya hear that lonesome whip-poor-will
he sounds too blue to fly.
The midnight train is whining low.
I'm so lonesome I could cry.

I've never seen a night so long

when time goes crawlin' by.
The moon just went behind the clouds
to hide his face and cry.

Did you ever see a robin weep
when leaves begin to die?
That means he's lost the will to live,
I'm so lonesome, I could cry.

The silence of a falling star
lights up a purple sky.
And as I wonder where you are,
I'm so lonesome, I could cry.

Somehow, Jock's quiet sobs melted from the sadness of never seeing Shannon again, to the joys of that night with her, then to an unexpected place, the joys of Sharon; meeting her that first day, how the beauty of her formed the poetic words as he spoke, how her easy smile muted the pain of his father's death, how she spent every holiday break with him after his mother died, just seeming to show up, and the closeness of that last night they had together, closer than the last night with Shannon. Jock's sobs warmed into memories of Sharon and his friends, the things they shared with him, blanketing him in a soft, quiet comfortable sleep, a good sleep that had eluded Jock for a long time now. Sleep that kept Jock from seeing the other file. A file named "FORTITER".

And then the station alarms woke him up.

***

S.T. Thistle
Far Oort Cloud
Standard Earth Date December 4 3446

"I understand you have a schedule! I'll help you keep it, but I'm too far away, I can't get to you until…but…I…wait a minute! I can't tow you in unless I can dock and secure your load. I…Sure. Okay. I understand. Next time. Right."

Dennis Trap slammed his fist into the comm panel as the connection closed.

"OW! DAMN IT!" His fist bent more than the metal of the comm did.

Rubbing his hand, Dennis sat back and closed his eyes. Another job lost. *I'm just a crappy salesman, I guess.* He shut down almost all his systems to conserve power. In space, energy was life, but energy was also money. Even the iron required to power his ships cost money. And Dennis Trap did not have much left.

It had been a tough three years. Dennis had started out all right, undercutting his competition and securing some plum contracts. Then something went wrong, and a barge was lost. The penalties nearly bankrupt Dennis; he had to borrow against the Thistle to keep going. If he didn't get a contract soon...

The retired gunnery sergeant opened his eyes at the instant just before the alarm began, as if anticipating it. Passives showing an object moving fast, over one half light speed. Nothing he knew of could match that, unless it was on a suicide run. Some instinct told him to keep his head down, and think about lines of fire; twenty years in the Corps had taught him to trust *that* instinct. Where was that ADS?

Dennis activated the Thistle's 'enhancements', and then he sat, waited, and watched...

CHAPTER THREE

Asteroid Defense Station 1437
Commander's Quarters
Standard Earth Date December 5 3446

"PERIMETER ALERT!"
"PERIMETER ALERT!"
"PERIMETER ALERT!"
The computer blasted the alarm into Jock's dream, erasing his wedding reception kiss with the faceless blonde bride.

Training had been intense at the Lunar Station, and Jock's muscles knew exactly what to do, awake brain or not. He was out of bed and into his pants and tee shirt before the third 'perimeter alert' sounded. Exactly 6 seconds later he slid into his station in the CIC.

"Report, Ensign Bird! What have we got?"

"HA! Looks like a real, honest to Jupiter UFO, Sir! Ha-ha-ha!"

Damn, he's irritating! How did he ever pass the psych tests for this assignment?

Jock looked at the vid screen Emerson indicated. It was big, fast, and unlike any ship he had ever heard of. Jock thought, *if I had a power plant fifty times more powerful than what we have now, that is the ship I would build around it!*

"Velocity reads as one third light and decelerating. It looks to be about two hundred meters long, about thirty five meters at its widest point. A lot of protrusions on it, many looking like lenses. Sensors, comm arrays, weapons? Several small ports; the right size for large missiles. Exterior color flat black. No lights. I'm getting scanning EM waves, likely sensors. Mr. Bird, what do you think?"

"Um, Sir, this isn't one of ours. Heh. Heh."

"Let's see what he does for a while. Confirm all our emission are cold?"

"C-con-confirmed, Sir!" Bird was shaking slightly as he realized just what was happening.

"Relax, Emerson. They could look right at us and only see another group of rocks in space."

The two men sat and watched as the strange ship stopped right at the System Lagrangian point their station was assigned to guard. The ship sat quietly for several minutes, then a cluster of projections on its

60

hull began glowing bright orange. Both Jock and Emerson grasped the arms of their chairs a little more tightly.

"Is that a weapon charging?" Emerson's voice quivered.

"It's not aimed at us, if it is. It is pointed out of the System." Jock answered in hushed tones.

A bright orange flash filled the screen. As the men's eyes readjusted, the strange ship seemed dark once more.

"Communication. This must be a scout ship! Ensign, get the Taclink ready." Jock's cool voice calmed the jittery ensign as much as having a concrete task to perform did. Jock energized the gravity beam projectors, and focused them on the space occupied by the strange ship.

"Taclink online, Lieutenant."

Jock opened the Taclink comm. "CODE RED. ADS 1437 has contact with unknown object. CODE RED. Appears to be alien vessel. CODE RED. Believe communicating out-system. CODE RED." Jock closed the record comm link.

"Message encoded." The station's computer announced a moment later. Jock activated the control, which sent a small tightly focused laser burst directly at the Nili Patera System Defense Complex. They would have the information in seconds, and the transmission would be undetectable unless you were right in its path with an active optic sensor.

Jock relaxed a little now. Even if they were vaporized, the defenses would be active. *Now, that's a pretty thought!* And, unless these ships were FTL, Jock figured they had years to prepare for the main "arrival", IF they were hostile.

"Ensign, are all reactors on line?"

"Yes, Lieutenant. All reactors at 100%."

"Projectile weapon status?"

"Railguns and missile batteries all show green, Sir. Including your 'specials'."

"Thank you, Mr. Bird." Jock acknowledged the ensign as he entered a few more settings into the gravity beam controllers. "Hang on tight, I'm going to lock them up here."

Jock activated the gravity beams, modified and enhanced with his software 'adjustments' as suggested by his work with Shannon. The ship on the video screen shook slightly, but held fast as Jock and Emerson watched thrusters and then main drives pour out huge amounts of energy.

"Looks like you caught a big one, Lieutenant!"

"Yeah, let's hope he doesn't break the line!"

The thrusters and drive units on the alien ship suddenly went silent. Numerous protrusions on the ship's hull began moving, as if searching for…them.

Ports opened. The flames of missile thrusts burst from the openings and peeled back towards the ship's hull. But the missiles stopped as soon as their nosecones cleared the port. Jock's gravity beams held them all in place.

The alien ship became quiet again, a dozen missiles floating half in, half out of their launch tubes, having exhausted their fuel. Two of the lenses rotated, and beams of energy touched a nearby chunk of rock, instantly vaporizing it into an expanding globe of plasma.

"We need to silence that quickly, before they get lucky and hit the gravity beam emitters. Ensign, see if you can take out those sensor arrays with the lasers. Maybe we can blind their aim."

"Aye-aye, Sir" Bird fired several laser bursts at the alien ship, but every shot seemed to stop about a hundred meters from its hull.

"Okay, time for plan 'B'." Jock entered more commands, and a thin, focused gravity beam reached out and disrupted the molecules holding one of the sensor arrays to the alien's hull. Again and again, Jock targeted a protrusion on the alien's hull, effectively chopping them off by ripping the molecules in their supports apart. It took several minutes before Jock had disabled every antenna, sensor, and beam emitter. The alien beams had destroyed three ADS laser emitters and one ADS missile platform, but nothing vital had been hit.

"Emerson, see if you can locate their power source." Jock had an idea.

"It seems to be here, Sir." Ensign Bird indicated a point near the main drive units, about one third of the way along the ship, forward from the drives.

"Good. Let me see here. Perhaps I can put them in the dark…" Jock's hands flew over the controls as he retargeted his 'gravity scalpel'. The tightly focused gravity beam neatly cut the ship into two pieces, separating the power and drive section from the forward two thirds of the hull. The two parts hung only a few molecules apart, still held fast by the main gravity beams, the atmosphere venting out of the gap. *Crap! I didn't think of that. I hope they have automated bulkheads!*

"I'm reading zero power output now, Sir. Temp readings throughout the alien ship almost match ambient space."

"Damn. Bird, you have the comm. I'm taking a trip over to look around."

62

S.T. Thistle
Far Oort Cloud
Standard Earth Date December 5 3446

"So, the young JG has captured that ship. Interesting. He must be a bright one." *I wonder what his next move is? They'll need someone to tow the ship in...*

Dennis Trap hit his thrusters, positioning the Thistle for a fast trip to the ADS. Then he sat back, and opened his datatab.

"I need to get better 'people skills'." Dennis said as he scrolled through the titles. "There, that's the one!" He declared, as he hit the computer comm. "Sally, open the book, "How To Win Friends And Influence People."

"Of course, lover boy!"

"Ye-up, that sounds like just what I need."

***

Asteroid Defense Station 1437
Airlock 7
Standard Earth Date December 5 3446

"Keep this comm channel open, Ensign." Jock was nervous about taking an EVA to the Alien ship. He was, in effect, an under armed one-man boarding party.

"Aye-aye, Lieutenant. Ha-ha-ha."

Jock rolled his eyes, then activated his powered armor, thrusting across the 80,000 kilometers to the alien ship. The armor was essentially a powered spacesuit with thick armor covering vital areas, and providing a power assist to his movements. It had a limited spaceflight capability, effective for inter-ship travel at less than 200,000 kilometers.

"Okay, Mr. Bird, remember, if I fail to report in every twenty minutes, reengage the gravity beams, contact Nili Patera, and just sit tight until they get here."

"Ha-ha-ha-ha! Aye-aye, SIR! Ha-hah!"

Jock scowled, then began breaking to avoid becoming a 'bug on the windshield', whatever that ancient phrase meant. The last few molecules of atmosphere escaping had pushed the two parts of the alien ship away from each other. The gap was now about ten feet, affording Jock an easy access point.

"I'm at the alien ship. Just moving inside." Jock looked into the larger section first, flipping his armored lights on. He gasped when his eyes registered what he was looking at.

The inside of the ship was essentially one large room. All the mechanicals of the ship were contained within the twelve-meter thick outer hull. Throughout the interior, parts of the outer "skin" protruded in, well beyond the average level. Jock figured it was due to large machinery. What appeared to be control stations were arraigned around the inside of the outer hull. Floating throughout the interior space were…Bugs.

Dull brown, oval bodies floated about. Most were tethered to duty stations, but some floated freely. Jock couldn't help but think that the floaters had been desperately trying to escape the depressurization of their ship.

"Bird, I'm in the ship." Jock transmitted as a way of recording his observations. "There are numerous alien bodies in here. Each of the bodies has eight legs, short in comparison to the body length." Jock moved closer to get a better look. "The legs aren't exactly jointed, more like meter-long tentacles with a hard covering in three sections. I think the gaps provide flexibility while the hard covering provides support. Some type of finger/claw arrangement is at the end of each of the four legs nearest the head."

"The bodies look like mostly soft muscular tissue, with a thick, hard support on the backside, like a boat's keel. There are two separate coverings on the underside. They look more… flexible. The legs slant towards the head. The head seems more mouth than anything else. The mouth has four pieces of the covering material, the two side plates overlapping the top and bottom plates. Each of the four plates had serrated edges that look sharp.

"Every one of these, I'll call them Bugs for now, every one has an olive-green sack floating near the heads, surrounded by numerous globs of pea-green liquid and attached to the Bugs mouth. It looks like if they were been trying to swallow these sacks when they died."

Jock gulped, realizing those sacks were the 'guts' of the Bugs, pulled out of their bodies by the sudden decompression of the ship.

"I'm glad I can't smell anything in here."

Scanning the interior so his suit recorders could document

everything he was reporting, Jock panned slowly as he checked for any signs of life. Convinced that none of the aliens were alive, Jock turned to check out the other section of the ship. The drives and power plant interested Jock the most.

"Beep!" his timer went off.

"Ensign, anything new on your end?"

"Anything new? New York, New Jersey, New Italian Ba…"

"Cut it, Bird!" Jock had had enough of this psycho.

Jock moved into the drive section, seeing only two Bugs stationed there. There was a bulkhead, with what looked like a massive door.

"I'm at a door, guessing this leads to the engineering section. All I have to do is figure out how to open it."

Jock's hand went to his gun, a two-pound "L" shaped device that fired a rod of compressed protons at two thousand meters per second. As he moved closer to the door, he noticed a U shaped handle-like protuberance on the door began moving, rotating around one end. Jock froze, and then backed up as the door opened.

***

Philadelphia Spaceport
Terminal D
Standard Earth Date December 17 3446

The tall redhead strode wearily down the spacebridge and into the crowded terminal. Her stylish but well-worn brown business suit downplayed but did not hide her nearly perfect figure. She carried a too-large briefcase on a shoulder strap. Her pretty face projected mild displeasure as she spoke loudly into her comm link.

"Hello, Robert? This is Susan Eastman. I've just touched down in Philly. Yeah, I can. Where? Okay, see you then." She closed the comm link and walked briskly, following the Baggage Claim signs.

One quick train-ride to Manhattan, and this can be over. Shannon thought. *Lost on the trip back, stealth probe navigation error. Will anyone buy that? By tomorrow, it won't matter. I never told them, Lord forgive me, I never told him. He'll know when he meets Jack. I knew. God help me, I knew and I did nothing! I knew Daddy had Nial MacAlister killed. Jock, Jack, Sharon, please, oh please, forgive me!*

The redhead picked up her bag, and then followed the signs to the

Maglev Train. She stopped at the counter, and purchased a one-way ticket to Grand Central Terminal, Manhattan.

***

S.T. Thistle
Far Oort Cloud
Standard Earth Date December 18 3446

Dennis Trap awoke with a start. Reading this damn book had taught him nothing about selling his services. It just kept putting him to sleep.

He took a quick look at his scanners. The ADS had brought what Dennis figured to be an alien ship close alongside the main asteroid. Dennis could zoom in and see the umbilicals stretching out to the two parts of the ship, and the glow of the lights inside. Soon, in about 3 days, Dennis figured, the Navy ships would show up. Then he'd be locked out. Again.

"Not this damn time! I've got nothing to lose, so what the hell!"

Dennis hit his drive units, and the S.T. Thistle began a moderate, nonthreatening acceleration towards ADS 1437.

***

Chrysler Building
55th Floor
New York City
Standard Earth Date December 18 3446

"Your man is in place, Mr. Hale? He understands what he is to do?"

"Yes, he does. The Lieutenant will never arrive at Lunar Station. His probe will have a launch "malfunction"."

"It better. I want MacAlister out of the picture. He has caused the deaths of both of my daughters. First Sharon, and then…her." The last word slithered out as if coated with putrid slime. "And, I want that alien ship!"

"I understand, sir. I have everything in place. Nothing can go wrong."

"I know it won't, because you will attend to the oversight personally."

"Yes, sir. I will leave immediately."

***

Asteroid Defense Station 1437
CIC
Standard Earth Date December 18 3446

When Jock's pounding heart slowed a bit, he peered past the open door into the dark interior beyond. There was nothing moving.

"The doors seem to be automatic and have their own power supply. I think… that's a computer interface port. I'll try to connect to it before I have to come back."

"I've got the panel off. Here's the access port. I think. Patching in… Bird, can you get me a direct connection with our system?"

"Bird? ENSIGN?"

"Where the hell is he?" Jock asked the air around him. "At least I'll be spared the laughing…"

Jock turned back to console. "I'm connected to the Bug system. It is a binary computer. I should have a usable interface…"

Jock saw his suits interface light up. "Good, ADS computer connection confirmed. Software interface with Bug system…"

Jock scanned the area around him again as he waited for the software to hack into the alien computer.

"Damned spooky."

"There it is. I'm in."

His life support running down, Jock returned to the ADS.

Seated at his command console, Jock searched through the information on the Bug computer, recording his preliminary report as he went for a tight laser burst directly to the Nili Patera System Defense Complex.

"I've found images of several classes of Bug ships. They are all warships. The Bug ship we captured here is a scout, looking for technologically active systems to target. The bright orange flash it sent out was a signal to attack *us*. They are from system known as Achird 12.

"I'm looking at the power plant specs. The alien power source is five times as efficient as anything we have. They also have a shield system and projected energy weapons. Their weapons are far beyond anything we have. If I'm reading this right, twenty of these scout ships could wipe out humanity today. Their SOP says that there are much bigger ships coming. Much bigger ships.

"The good news is that the Bugs do not have a FTL drive. They can make zero-point-nine light speed though. So, I figure we have about forty-two years to get ready.

"Lieutenant JG Jock MacAlister. End report"

This was Jock's last watch. He would go from here to join his already packed bags in the stealth probe for the trip back to Lunar Launch Station.

And Ensign Emerson Bird was late.

Screw this, I'm leaving! Jock had finally found the files Shannon had left him; everything they had discussed, written down in scientific text. He decided to absorb it all, along with what he had learned from the alien ship, on the two-week trip back.

Jock left CIC, and jogged to his quarters where he barely slowed down to pick up his small bag. He got to the launch bay just in time to see Emerson Bird leaving it.

***

S.T. Thistle
Far Oort Cloud
Standard Earth Date December 18 3446

"Collision alert, darling. Collision alert, darling!" The computer's sultry voice overpowered Dennis like cheap perfume. *I have to stop trying to customize these things! I'm just no damn good at it.*

Dennis sat up and started playing on his control console. In a moment, the video screen showed a graphic of the Thistle's course and speed and the course and speed of the unknown ship from in-system.

"Damn, they must have left a lot sooner than I figured. Well, let's pour the coal to her, then." Dennis reached for the drive controls and slammed them past the safety stops. The Thistle's acceleration at maximum thrust slammed him into the chair. Hard.

"Oooohhhh, Shiiiiiiit!!!"

Stealth Probe 4649
Oort-Lunar Transit
Standard Earth Date December 19 3446

Jock sat in the cramped confines of the probe, thinking he would never have to do this again. *Just over an hour out, and well on my way home. Then what?*

For some reason, likely because his training was highly detailed, Jock hit the computer input and checked his initial course and velocity. Not that he could do anything about it, but...

"This is NOT good! Computer, recalculate!" The numbers didn't change. The course and speed Jock was on would get him to Earth in exactly four years, three months, and two days.

The probe had fourteen days of life support.

"Aw, shit!"

***

S.T. Thistle
Far Oort Cloud
Standard Earth Date December 19 3446

"What was that?" Dennis said out loud. He had just caught a flash of light, almost like a railgun muzzle flash, on the surface of the ADS. *Did some one leave?*

"Insufficient information for little ole me to give poochie-kims a good answer!" Sally responded.

"Sally, take a nap!"

"Oh, Okay, then. Goodnight!!"

Can a computer pout?

The former marine adjusted some settings on his sensors, and had the computer predict course and speed...*Damn peculiar. Way too slow to get anyone home, or any info packet. Could it have been a misfire?*

Dennis adjusted the course of the Thistle. If it was a misfire, he was the only hope the occupant had of not ending up a Popsicle.

***

Stealth Probe 4649
Oort-Lunar Transit
Standard Earth Date December 20 3446

Jock went through every tape and file that Shannon had left him, and every video and note he had taken on the alien ship. He had the answers: power generation an order of magnitude higher, the drives and weapons to use it, how to beat the Bug invasion, and the Faster-Than-Light drives.

But, what good would it do him? He'd been able to hack into his guidance computer system, and had turned on his reactor early. All he needed now was something massive to push off of. That was the problem; nothing would be close enough for two years.

"ALERT! ALERT! ALERT! Collision course!" The computer screamed. He saw it on the limited sensors carried by the probe; it could only be that tug, the Thistle! Jock hit his hacked computer, and flashed a quick IFF, the only transmitter he had. On and off, on and off. Jock hoped the old marine would see and understand the ancient code...

***

S.T. Thistle
Far Oort Cloud
Standard Earth Date December 20 3446

"There it is! A code...S...O...S! Well, I'll be damned!" The gunnery sergeant slapped his thigh. "Lock onto that IFF broadcast and give me a course alteration for intercept."

"Sure thing, handsome!"

"Now, all I have to do is figure out what to do once I get there!"

"Heh-he, just slide it right up inside, sugar!" The deep, husky female voice caused the old Sarge to blush. Just a little.

Dennis rolled his eyes and tried to think. *Adapt. Improvise. Overcome...*

The big Space Tug had a huge amount of thrust, which made it nimble when not towing barges, which had been its status way too often lately. Trap let the computer plot the intercept and control the thrusters while he tried to figure out how to get the occupant aboard.

"Let's see…it's fifteen, no, sixteen meters long and two meters wide. My shuttle bay is fourteen-point-five meters by eight-point-three meters. Damn I can't…wait a minute. Computer, give me the diagonal measurement of the shuttle bay."

"Diagonal measurement of the shuttle bay is sixteen-point-six meters along the floor, stud."

And a touch more from top inside corner to bottom outside corner! I can do it.

***

Stealth Probe 4649
Oort-Lunar Transit
Standard Earth Date December 20 3446

"All scanners, on-line now!" Jock's hacked computer interface filled the tiny vid screen with the image of the Space Tug's three huge drive pods. *What is he going to do? I don't have a space suit!*

Just a moment later Jock felt the docking gravity beam lock onto his probe. Okay, so if this guy could make it to a base in less than two weeks, he'd buy the old marine a beer. No, he'd buy the guy his dad's favorite single malt Scotch. He could see the green labeled bottle now, fifteen year-old Glenfiddich. *Stay focused.*

Jock half expected to feel the acceleration begin, for the burn towards Europa, or even Mars. But, as minute after minute went by, he began to wonder. Suddenly he felt the probe move.

***

S.T. Thistle
Docking Position
Standard Earth Date December 20 3446

Dennis Trap hated zero-gee operations. He had extensive training, and more than a little actual experience in zero-gee environments, but he still disliked it intensely. But that didn't matter when someone's life was on the line. Someone depended on him pulling this off, and he was going to do it.

The retired Gunny moved out of the airlock. One of the 'perks' of having twenty plus years in The Corps was the access to military surplus equipment. Gunny had managed to acquire a low-hour Mark III cargo-handling suit, complete with high-thrust propulsion units and extra-strength tethers. He moved the massive rig out to the stealth probe, or at least out to where the gravity beams said the stealth probe was. He had a tough time finding the probe, until the landing lights lit up.

"Just stay put." Suddenly, the entire probe shimmered into visibility, a flat black, double-ended needle shape. *Good, that will help.*

Trap clanged onto the probe, but fortunately the gravity beams kept the momentum from pushing the probe out into space. He managed to clamp a GravTeth onto one end of the probe, near the needlepoint. He considered tethering both ends, but decided against it. It would be too hard for him to control and attach both lines.

The line secure, Dennis hit the control and cut the gravity beams to the probe. If that probe had any momentum away from the Thistle, Dennis could be dragged out into space along with it. Dennis held his breath, braced for the pull that did not come.

After a few seconds he exhaled, turned and hit the thrusters, pulling the probe straight to the left-hand edge of the shuttle bay.

"Sally, give me a clearance reading countdown, quarter meter intervals."

"Sure thang, Shuggar!"

"Oh, brother."

"Two meters, Darlin'."

The retired sergeant moved straight along the sidewall of the bay, building the direction of the momentum of the probe into the bay.

"One an' three quarters in, Handsome. One an' a half. Oh!"

At the halfway point on the wall, he stopped, placing both feet on the wall as he watched the tapered probe slide past him.

"Oh, baby, you're almost all the way in! One meter. Uh, three quarters! Ye-ass!"

When the first quarter of the probe passed, Trap pushed with both feet, both hands impacting the probe. Trap timed it so the hand closest to the front of the probe hit first, just to help begin the rotation.

"Half a meter, OH!"

The plan was working so far. Dennis had transferred his momentum to the nose of the probe, causing it to start rotating in towards the center of the shuttle bay. All he could do now is watch, sweating despite his suit's cooling system. The probe weighed nothing in the zero-G of open space, it still had several tons of mass. And several tons of momentum.

"Oh, Sweety, you're almost there! A quarter meter! Oh, Baby! You're IN!"

As it happened, the old gunnery sergeant with a disdain for math without practical application had figured it out perfectly, and executed that plan nearly so. The probe rotated as it glided into the bay, until the nose hit the high far corner just as the tail hit the floor in the near corner. As soon as that looked likely, Dennis hit the controls for the bay doors, closing the probe into the bay.

Dennis rolled his eyes at the computer's theatrics, and it nearly killed him as several tons of probe pinned his suit securely to the shuttle bay wall. He would have to wait until the doors closed and the bay pressurized so he could squeeze out of his Mark III suit.

***

West Lake Road
Skaneateles, NY
Standard Earth Date December 20 3446

"I think he looks just like Jock." Agnes said as she held the infant in her arms. "I just can't put him in that car seat!"

"I know better than to argue with you, Hon. He *is* a good-looking boy. I like the name, too."

"When will we get to Sandy's place?" Angie slowly rocked the little boy in her arms, smiling at his face.

"About six, I think. Why did she have to move into Syracuse?"

"Duh, she's getting her law degree from Syracuse University! Hey, slow down! Baby-on-board!"

"She doesn't know, does she?" Don reached down and stroked the infant's hair.

"Eyes on the road, and both hands on the wheel, mister! No, she doesn't. She's waited this long for Jock, how will she react to this?"

"You know her, Aggie. Not a selfish bone in her body, and she's devoted to Jock. She will be thrilled with Jack, and hopeful that Jock will come home. To her."

"I hope it works out this time. They were so good together. They deserve each other."

"Aggie, when he found out about his dad, he forgot about everything else. He didn't even tie up the cat, and he used to treat that sailboat like gold.

"Sandy gave him the space he asked for, but he had to leave before she could give him the support he needed."

"And she never complained. She went off alone, but always seemed happy. I don't understand her at all."

"Sandy always said Jock would come back when the time was right. Something about a dream. In a lot of ways, Sandy reminded me of Jacks mother. Six years she's waited.

"And Jack's mother. Shannon. I hope she'll be okay."

"Donald Wade, if there was a chance she'd be okay," Agnes looked up and gazed at her husband through moist eyes, "she wouldn't have left Jack with us. Those papers she left us about him, have you looked at them at all? She left him with people that love Jock. She's not coming back from where ever she's going. Don, I don't think she existed."

"Don't be silly, Aggie. I saw here...oh, I see what you mean. Undercover. What do we tell Sandy? What do we tell Jock?"

"When we get to Sandy's, we'll bring the papers in with us, darling. We'll all read them together. Just listen to her, a lot. It's got to be... Donnie, why is that truck...DON, LOOK OUT!!"

***

Grand Central Terminal
Manhattan
Standard Earth Date December 20 3446

A frumpy looking dark haired woman bumped into the porter as she exited the train. "Hey, c'mon awready!" her Bronx accent sounded over the buzz of the crowd. She hurried out of the terminal, a small bag slung over her shoulder. She walked a few blocks south and disappeared into the 42nd Street subway.

An elegant, gorgeous blonde wearing a sleeveless black dress exited the subway at Park and 33rd Street. People noticed the conspicuous clan crest tattoo on her right arm near her shoulder as she strode aloofly into Pompodious' Steakhouse. She walked up to the maître d', and asked him a question. When he answered, she brushed past him, walking straight into the exclusive private room he had indicated.

Three seconds after she entered the private room, the restaurant exploded. The entire city block was vaporized.

***

S.T. Thistle
Mess
Standard Earth Date December 20 3446

"Welcome to my humble abode!" You have your choice for dinner, peanut butter or ham on whole wheat. Optional processed cheese on either. No mayo, mustard."

"Anything is better than eating vacuum, Gunny." Jock was happy to be alive. Food would come later.

"JG, what do you know about a ship coming out here?"

"Not a thing. If there was one coming out, I would have known about it, even if it was due to arrive after I left. Why?"

"Take a look at this." Trap handed him his datatab, displaying the readout from his sensors.

"Have you received any IFF on this ship?"

"That's the funny part, Lieutenant. They're running silent and dark."

"Gunny, I don't like that. Not one bit."

***

Crouse Irving Memorial Hospital
Syracuse
Standard Earth Date December 21 3446

"Here he is, miss. He was thrown clear of the crash, and somehow he survived, barely a scratch. Both of the parents are deceased. I know they were your friends, Miss. I am sorry for your loss."

The doctor sounded tired, Sandy thought. He'd been up all night, trying to save Aggie. Don died instantly, they told her. Aggie hung on until she saw Sandy. *A baby! What do I do now? All my friends, gone! And Jock...does he even think about me anymore?*

"Thank you doctor. They told me something about papers?"

"Yes, the guardianship papers were held on the datatab found near the boy. His name is Jack, and the Wades had named you as his guardian if something...if you agree, of course."

"Yes, of course. He has no other family. Both their parents passed away within the last three years. Poor Jack Wade, I'll make sure you know how special your parents were! Do I take him now, Doctor? Is there some legal red tape or something?" Sandy Marx looked up at the doctor, her face calm and composed, but her eyes looking like a dam about to burst.

"Well, his name isn't..."

"Miss Marx?" The doctor's explanation was cut short by a strong baritone voice from the hallway.

"Yes?" Sandy turned to see a middle-aged Marine Captain in Dress Blue uniform standing in the doorway. *Oh, God! Jock!* Her mind screamed as her hand came up to cover her mouth. Her face went pale as her eyes widened in fear of what would come next.

The first dream began playing in front of her again. She saw herself holding a baby, and Jock standing next to her, smiling. Then the dream faded as her mind flashed back to the Marines telling Jock, ripping him from her. The empty look on his face, and how he shut her, and everyone else, out of his life after that. Throwing her into four years of hell. How her faith in that dream faded a bit more each of those years. Until she asked. Then she thought she understood, until now. If Jock was dead, the dreams, were they lies? The room started to get darker...

"Hello. My name's Jock, what's yours?"

"Oh. Dream! You were in my dream!" *He thinks I'm cute!*

"Uh, okay… sure."

"Sorry. You just startled me as I was talking to Aggie here, about, em, a show."

"So, um, what show was it…"

"Miss Marx, everything is fine, Ma'am. I am Captain Anthony DiBello." The Captain's voice and his hand gripping her elbow yanked Sandy back to the present. "I've come here to discuss some things with you. Doctor, if there is a room where we may be alone?"

Sandy's knees wobbled as the two men led her out into the hallway.

***

Lunar Launch Station
Tsiolkovskiy Crater
Standard Earth Date December 21 3446

Jericho Bucktooth looked at the message as the encryption decoded it. It took him three seconds to read it and slam his fist onto the table. The clear text stayed visible for twelve seconds, then all traces of the message vanished from his datatab.

The Lieutenant Commander sat and dropped his head into his hands.

***

SS Python
Mars-Oort transit
Standard Earth Date December 21 3446

"ADS 1437, this is SS Python, over." Captain Hans Richter called.

"Python, this is ADS 1437, Ensign Bird commanding. You are cleared for docking at Alpha port. Just follow the lights, gentlemen."

"Will do, Turret." Richter motioned to cut the comm link. *I wonder if he knows he will not survive this?*

"Mr. Bilingsley, can you target the docking port without damaging the alien ship?"

"Not a problem, sir. A two-kiloton missile should do the trick nicely. Just say when."

"Let's make sure we get all the data from the ADS computer first. Is it still transmitting Lee?"

"Looks like about another ninety minutes, sir."

"Very well then, stand by, Mr. Billingsley."

"Do not wait too long, Captain. There is a Navy ship on its way here. You have a lead of about two days on them."

"Yes, yes, I am aware of the time and dates, Mr. Hale."

"You are sure there are no more of the alien ships lurking about?"

"Mr. Hale, the only thing within twenty cubic AUs is an old ore-barge tug that went off in some wild direction yesterday. We are quite alone, I assure you."

***

S.T. Thistle
Bridge
Standard Earth Date December 21 3446

"You're sure of the mass of the two ship sections?" Dennis Trap was actually intuitively good at math when he saw a practical use for it, but he still didn't like doing it.

"Yes, I did the gravimetric measurements myself. Are you sure we can pull this off?"

"As long as you pilot the Thistle, I think I can grab the two ship pieces without slowing us too much. That other ship is likely to be armed." Trap kept entering data into his datatab. After a few minutes, he sat back and waited.

"Well?" Jock was a little nervous. He'd had a lot of training, but no real combat experience. This could be the first time something fired at *him*.

"Let the computer do her work. We'll know in a moment. Sally is a little old, but she is a solid computer. As far as I know, anyway."

"Computations displayed and ready for your inspection, Sugar!" Jock looked at Dennis with a raised eyebrow.

"It's not what I thought it was going to be when I installed it. I'm not good at customizing software, I guess, and I never thought I'd be using the computer this much." Dennis shrugged his shoulders. "Here, it's possible. This is the flight path that will take us past the ADS, and picking up the alien ship pieces will leave us with this trajectory. At full burn for two days, we can be on a high velocity lunar intercept they'd have a tough time matching. I'll leave the details to the real sailor."

"This old tug can outrun that freighter?"

"JG, you know that space isn't like sailing on a lake. Everything out here is thrust and mass. Those alien ship parts are big, but mass about ten percent of an average ore barge. Thistle has a lot of thrust, so we can out accelerate and out decelerate almost anything when we're that light."

"You said that freighter would be armed. How do you know that?"

"Well, if I was sending a ship out to steal an artifact from the Navy, I'd be armed. And, they won't leave your squirrely friend around to talk about them, either. My guess would be a couple of nuke-armed missiles; easy to install, cheap, untraceable, and easy to dump."

"Then, we've got to take out that ship. Any ideas?"

"Whoa, JG! Thistle is a tough tug, but it ain't no battleship! My plan is to fly by, snatch the prizes, and skedaddle out of Dodge. I didn't plan on combat."

"We need to take out that ship for two reasons; one, it's the last operating turret, and it sits right on the Bugs preferred path. And two, we need Bird alive, so he can talk about who they are. Do you have any weapons?"

"Well, just this, and two complete Mark IV armored recon suits." Trap hit some controls, and a panel next to the helm console opened up. A handle pushed up through the opening. Jock stared at the red trigger with the clear plastic flip-up guard.

"Impressive trigger. What exactly is that hooked to?"

"A two hundred meter railgun, triple-barreled, 12-inch bore on each. It telescopes out in front of the tug when you activate the trigger. Pre-loaded, I compressed the bullets myself."

"You what?"

"I just took the Thistle's three gravity beams and pointed them at a hunk of space rock, high iron content. Then, I hit the beams on it in reverse. Each of those bullets masses out at forty tons. The three reactors can feed juice directly to the gun, so the bullets go *real* fast. So fast Sally can't track 'em. I figure they're moving at about a quarter light-speed at the muzzle."

Jock just stared, open-mouthed, at the retired gunnery sergeant. "Gunny, do you know you outgun half the fleet?"

"You can never have too much firepower, JG."

"You have to show me how you did all that. But not now. How do you aim it?"

"Point and shoot. Sally aims." A circle and cross-hairs appeared on the video screen. "The bullets will go right straight through those cross-hairs. Every time."

"Gunny, you're right, Thistle isn't a battleship. But she is a monitor. I'm appropriating her for the duration. She'll be known as "Gunny One". You're drafted. Rank of Ensign. Now, Ensign Trap, what *else* can this ship do?"

"Aw, shit."

***

SS Python
Mars-Oort transit
Standard Earth Date December 21 3446

"Twenty minutes until download is complete, Captain."

"Are we in position to fire, Mr. Billingsley?"

"We will be soon, Captain."

"Captain, there is another ship heading this way, right at the docking port, at very high velocity! It's that tug, Captain."

"Target a missile on it, Billingsley. Fire when ready."

"Its speed is too high for a lock, sir, but it is decelerating. Estimate target lock in fifteen minutes."

"Fire when locked. Hold fire on the ADS; we may need our second missile for the tug."

"Will do sir."

***

Crouse Irving Memorial Hospital
Syracuse
Standard Earth Date December 21 3446

"Calm down, Miss Marx. I'm not here to tell you of anyone's death. Take some deep breaths, try to relax. I'm just here to, well, explain a few things."

Sandy took a deep breath, then another. It was hard to keep everything in, even after six years. Especially after six years.

"Captain," Sandy became more composed as she began to speak, "My last two friends on Earth have just been ran off the road by a truck that no one knows a thing about. A baby is dropped in my lap; a baby that was theirs, that I knew nothing about! And, the last time I saw a Marine in his dress blues, they drove my boyfriend away from me. So, yeah, I am just a LITTLE upset!"

"About the boy, Ma'am. His last name is not Wade. He wasn't the child of your friends. Not the two in the accident, anyway."

"Not their child...what are you talking about Captain?"

"The boy's name is Jack Nial MacAlister."

The room started spinning around Sandy again. A fuzzy light grew to envelope her.

"Sandy? W-would you, um, do you want, maybe..." The voice cracked as the words stuttered out.

"Jock MacAlister, what is wrong with you? Spit it out!"

"Doyouwanngotothefalldancewithme?"

"Ma'am? Stay with me, Ma'am."

The captain's baritone voice brought Sandy back to reality in time to see the world spun into total darkness.

***

Gunny One
Bridge
Standard Earth Date December 21 3446

Jock lay on the floor, hooking up the cable that stretched out of the bridge, through the shuttle bay, and into the stealth probe. He soldered the last connection and said, "There! We should have access to the probe's computer now. That will increase our computing capacity at least ten times."

"Sally, you still there?"

"Only for you, shugga!" came the sultry reply.

"Just checkin', darlin'"

"I feel sooo much better! You sure do know how to give a girl just what she needs, *stud*!"

"Okay. At ease!"

"Whatever you want, I'll give ya, baby!"

"Gunny, couldn't you have changed her…personality?"

"Other than sounding like a floozy, I sort of like her."

"Deceleration will finish in two minutes. Handsome."

"Thanks, Sally. JG, are you ready?"

"All set, Gunny. My bet is that ship will think we're going to stop to pick up the alien ship. If they're trying to target missiles, they'll have a tough time with us moving this fast. You pick up the pieces, Gunny, and I'll fly us past, while Sally targets the other ship. I'm firing all three bullets, just in case her aim is off."

"With that nav computer from your probe, you ought to be able skip a rock on that lake near your home from here. Let's do this."

"Deceleration terminated, Stud! Ship rotation commencing."

***

SS Python
Mars-Oort transit
Standard Earth Date December 21 3446

"Captain, the tug's stopped decelerating! It's still coming too fast for a good lock."

"He may be trying to snatch one of the alien ship sections. Fire missile one!"

"Missile one away, sir!"

***

Gunny One
Bridge
Standard Earth Date December 21 3446

"Missile warning, dear. Missile warning, dear. Missile warning, dear."

"They've fired at us, Ensign. One missile. Ensign?"

"Captain?"

"If this ship gets blown up, you're going down with it, Gunny!"

82

"Hah-ha, roger that, JG."

***

Chrysler Building
55th Floor
New York City
Standard Earth Date December 21 3446

"Gentlemen, Ladies! Order, please!" The tall balding man tried to shout with dignity over the confused din. A dozen board members in ten different conversations tended to raise the volume until everyone was shouting. Finally dispensing with all pretense of elegance, he slammed his fist loudly onto the table.

Every mouth closed, every eye turned to the tall man.

"Welcome. As you know, the unfortunate events of a few days ago have left us with a leadership, um, void. Again. I want to personally thank you all for coming here to confirm a new Principal. Please be seated."

***

Base Commander's Office
Lunar Station
Tsiolkovskiy Crater
Standard Earth Date December 21 3446

Jericho Bucktooth stood rigidly at attention, his arm in a perfect salute as Admiral Alimonte entered the room.

"At ease, Jeri." The Admiral said as he offered his hand to the Lieutenant Commander.

"Good to see you Sir."

"Good to see you as well." The Admiral closed the door, walked back to Jeri's desk and sat in a guest chair. "Computer, suspend recording, classification command, alpha-four-nine."

"All recording suspended."

"Admiral, none of her tests indicated…"

83

"I know that, Jeri. Relax, I'm not here to rip you a new garbage port. She was far too bright for our tests to show anything she didn't want us to see. We have other issues.

"Two weeks ago, ADS 1437 made contact with an extra-solar vessel. MacAlister managed to capture it, but it's cut in half and none of the crew survived. Preliminary analysis indicates this was a preinvasion scout vessel of advanced technology. MacAlister managed to capture it using some innovative technology of his own, developed with Ensign Malone's help.

"I've dispatched four ships to ADS 1437, three cutters and a fleet tug. There is a private ship that will be already there by now. We don't know who sent it. The only other ship in the area is an old independent tug operated by a retired gunnery sergeant.

"To make things worse, MacAlister's return probe suffered a launch 'malfunction'; he's adrift. Somewhere. I've held the decommissioning team here. Bird doesn't respond."

"Wow. I don't know what to say."

***

Gunny One
Bridge
Standard Earth Date December 21 3446

Jock MacAlister and Dennis Trap had squeezed into the tug's bridge wearing the Mark IV armored recon suits. Each had his helmet off to conserve power and air.

The Space Tug turned Monitor had swung around, the railgun telescoped out like an insect's stinger, just a little off the line of the ship's course. Jock had used the stealth probe's nav computer to confirm his calculations of just the right course and angle to pump a railgun bullet into the unknown ship. Now, it just came down to hitting the target.

"What's the status of that missile?" Jock asked.

"It's on a closer track than I thought it would be. It makes me nervous."

"It doesn't have to hit us to screw us up, Gunny. Unless you've armor-plated this thing..."

"Well, not quite enough for a nuke. A near detonation would pop us off course and screw up our electronics. So…" Gunny Trap hit six buttons in sequence on the panel in front of him, "…There, that should take care of it." Gunny calmly sat back in satisfaction.

"What did you do?"

"I threw sand in their face. I've got about two dozen "ash cans" positioned around the ship. Each is about two hundred kilos of asteroid dust, high metallic content, sitting on magnetically compressed springs. All I do is release them, and the sand flies out at high speed, messing up the guidance and then scouring the missile into harmless dust. At least, I think that's what'll happen."

"Damn, Gunny. They need you in weapons R & D!"

"Won't work. Too big a budget, I can't innovate. When it's my ass and my cash on the line, I seem to get ideas. Now it's time to button up."

"Helmets on!" Jock confirmed.

'Sally, link into our recon suits." Dennis fastened his helmet.

"Anything you say, *big* boy!"

Jock rolled his eyes.

"Missile destroyed, sweetie!" Sally announced.

Jock grinned and gave a thumbs-up sign to Gunny.

"Darling, twenty seconds to primary weapons fire. Another missile is inbound, stud!"

"It's going to fly right through the bullet's path, JG!"

"Well, Gunny, did you want to live forever?"

"Yeah, well, that was the plan. Or die tryin'. Check your suit one more time. Then concentrate on keeping us on course. I'll get the cargo."

"Main weapon fired." Sally announced.

Both men looked up at the video screen, staring at the freighter as they counted down in their heads.

"Impact in three. Two. One. Now, Sugar!"

Jock gasped at the sight on the screen. The freighter simply vanished behind a star-bright flash of light. When the light faded, there was nothing there.

"Missile status, Sally?"

"Missile is tracking an iron rich asteroid well off our course, love. Its fuel is exhausted. It is not a threat, killer."

"Got the big section," Dennis declared, "got the engines! Okay, Skipper, take us home!"

"Return trip insertion burn in three. Two. One. Burning." The two men were slammed back into their seats from the acceleration. After a few minutes, the engines shut down, and the men could move again.

"Shall we open up?"

"Aye-aye, Sir!" Dennis took his helmet off and looked at Jock. When Jock had his headgear off, Dennis said, "Good job, JG. Nice bit of strategy there."

"Gunny, I don't like to lose."

"It's been an honor working with you, JG. But, just remember, once we get back, I'm retired again."

Jock grinned. "Yeah, um, we'll talk about that."

***

Admiral's Quarters
Lunar Station
Tsiolkovskiy Crater
Standard Earth Date December 24 3446

BANG! BANG! BANG! The knocking on his door startled the Admiral.

"Come!"

"I have something you need to see, Admiral!" Jericho Bucktooth gasped as he stuck his head into the doorway of the Admiral's quarters. The Lieutenant Commander had run from the Comm center, about a quarter mile away.

"Well, come in then and show me, man!"

"Here, Sir!" Jeri tossed his datatab to the Admiral, "Lieutenant MacAlister! He's ten days out! He's commandeered that tug, drafted the retired marine, snagged the alien ship, and vaporized the privateer. And, Bird is still alive on the ADS, awaiting pick up!"

Admiral Alimonte stared at the Lieutenant Commander for several seconds before breaking into a huge grin. "Merry Christmas to you, too, Jeri. Sorry I didn't get *you* anything!"

***

West Lake Road
Skaneateles, NY
Standard Earth Date January 29 3447

Jock was still trying to figure out what to say as he walked up the steps of his home. He almost turned around four times. The smell of the crisp winter breeze from behind the house brought back a lot of memories, pushing any chance of eloquence out of his head. Just as he reached the door, he stopped and looked around. *Has it been that long? Since mom died, four, no, five years ago? Why haven't I been home?*

Jock turned back to reach for the door handle, but the door was already open. His eyes locked on the spot the door handle should have been, his hand, frozen, inches from touching a hand...the high school ring, his ring, on the finger there.

"Sandy!" The word rolled off his lips like a tear rolling down his cheek.

His eyes shot up to her face. Her stern look still surprised him, even though he had expected worse. They looked at each other for several long, long seconds.

Sandy opened her mouth, but no words came out. She closed it. Then Jock felt her hand in his. Then she smiled, and there was light in his universe again.

***

Chrysler Building
55th Floor
New York City
Standard Earth Date January 29, 3447

The young man sat quietly behind a massive desk, alone in a room that screamed power from every piece of furniture, every inch of flooring, every light fixture, window, comm system, monitor-every cubic inch of air. And it was his now. So much power...

He thought briefly how he had come to sit here; it was no straight line of ascension, though many would see it that way. He had to struggle to even be considered. But, he did have information on every board member. *And information was power, as father had liked to tell me. Before my bitch of a sister blew him up.*

First order of business was old business. Finish what his father had begun. Finish MacAlister, the bastard who killed his sisters. Next, get that alien ship, patent whatever technology he can, and expand his power.

Yes. Plan it out, let the experts fill in the details. Sheldon Malone clasped his hands behind his head and leaned back in his massive chair. He liked his new position very much.

***

West Lake Road
Skaneateles, NY
Standard Earth Date January 29 3447

"Tell me what Sharon was like," Sandy's quiet voice asked.

"Pretty. Striking. Funny, smart, patient..." Jock's words faded off as he looked at Sandy. *I don't want to hurt you.*

"Jock, it's okay. I've hurt as much as I'm going to over this. Really, I 'm okay. I want to know about her because she was part of your life. She's a part of you now." Sandy smiled, trying to ease both of them through the discomfort.

"Sandy, it's hard, describing her to you. I..."

"You still feel the loss." Sandy took in a deep breath. "I understand."

"It's not that at all, although, I'll always feel the loss. I can handle that now." *God knows I've had enough practice!*

"Sandy, I can't describe her because I'm...you won't believe me."

"Jock MacAlister, you've never lied to me before. You can't lie to me. I would know it."

"I'm thinking of you, Sandy. I'm thinking of all the time we lost, of how cruel I was to shut you out when all you wanted to do was help me. I'm thinking of Don and Aggie, and how I shut them out, too. How wrong that was. How I'll never get the chance to ask them what I have to ask you now; Sandy, I'm sorry. Please, Sandy, will you forgive me?" Tears built up behind the dam of Jock's eyes as he waited for the refusal he knew must come.

"I forgave you a long time ago, Jock MacAlister. After I did, the wait for you was a lot nicer. You wouldn't let me help before, will you let me help you now?"

"Sandy, I..." Jock buried his head in her shoulder as he let the dam burst. He stayed there a long time.

As he regained composure, Jock told her. About Pat's infatuation with Sharon, about Angie's too-obvious attempts at seducing him, about Sharon and Angie's sham antagonism. About how he had pushed Don, Aggie, and her into a closed corner of his mind because he couldn't handle the thoughts of his parents being gone. Of how pushing them away embarrassed him into staying away.

And then he told her of Shannon. And about the last night on the turret. About arriving at Lunar Station and seeing Jeri Bucktooth there, in Dress Whites. About being told of Shannon's death.

Through it all, Sandy held him, her embrace siphoning off his pain, and listened. She listened to the man she loved open up to her, as he had never done before. *Can I dare hope he still loves me? He does, I can feel it. But, tell me, Jock. Please!*

Jock felt his pain, the pain that Jeri Bucktooth and Shannon Malone had helped him deal with, evaporating with each word he told Sandy. After some time, just as he had finished, he sat up and looked at her.

"Thank you," he whispered. "I'm so, so sorry. How can you be here, waiting?"

"Your mom gave me the keys ages ago."

"I mean, how, why did you wait for me?"

"I had to. You and I are meant to be together. I love you, Jock."

"I don't deserve you. Not after..."

"I was tortured by it for a long time. I knew you'd come back, but I didn't know when. Or how. I didn't know why you shut us out, shut me out. It started to... I..." Sandy pushed him back and looked into his eyes. "Jock, tell me. Do you love me?"

"Yes. I love you Sandy. I always will."

"Did you love..." Sandra took a deep breath before whispering, "Sharon?"

"She made the pain less. I loved her, but, differently from they way I love you. I can't explain it. You are..." Jock ran his fingers over Sandra's cheeks. "You make me whole. You are part of me."

"Let me show you something amazing. Come on." Sandy smiled as she stood up, her face glowing in Jock's eyes, and extended her hand to him. "Jeri didn't tell you everything about Shannon."

Jock took her hand and let her lead him into his old room. His mind raced with thoughts; was she leading him as Shannon had, for the same reason? He had to stop her if she was, stop her from shattering every dream about her he's ever had…

They reached the door, and as Jock was about to draw back, he thought he heard something in his room.

"Go ahead, open the door." Sandy gently urged him, as if it was Christmas morning and his presents waited there.

His hand trembled, though he had no clue why it should. Jock opened the door.

Everything had changed. The walls were a different color, yet familiar. There were things hanging from wires, his trophies were gone, his bed, was now… a crib?

Jock stood in the doorway, dazed for a moment, then walked over and looked into the crib.

"He's so beautiful, Jock. He looks just like you." Sandy's smile lit up her voice as she spoke into his ear. She reached down and picked up the little boy.

"She named him Jack Nial MacAlister. I like it." Sandy began rocking the infant as she smiled at him, the baby cooing and giggling in response.

"Sandy. I. Wow! I, I never…I didn't know. I, I…" The lump in his throat took a fantastic effort to swallow.

"Shannon left him with Don and Aggie when I was at law school. They were bringing him to me when they were killed in the crash. He survived. She had made me his guardian, Jock."

"Sandy, you don't, I mean…" *JUST BLURT IT OUT THERE!* "He's my child with another woman. That doesn't upset you?"

"Jock, he's part of *you*, so I can't help but love him."

At that moment a ray of sunlight burst through the window, setting Sandy's hair aflame with a golden glow…

The dream!

"Oh, my God! Sandy, seeing you standing in the sunlight, holding my child, Sandy, I've dreamt this since I was ten!"

"Jock…"

"Sandy, there's something missing that was in my dream."

Sandy laid Jack down, and turned on shaking knees towards Jock. She raised her hand to gently stroke his cheek.

"Jock…"

Jock moved a little closer to Sandy, and reached up to gently cup her tear-streaked face with his hands.

"Well, in my dreams, there were six children. Our children, Sandy."

90

"Jock... I had the same dream..."

***

United Space Force Academy
MacAlister Chapel
Cape Canaveral, Florida
Standard Earth Date June 20 3447

"Hey, Griddles, who's that officer headed this way?" The pretty, dark-skinned Ensign asked about the tall officer, aglow in his dress whites, walking towards them as midnight neared.

"He looks familiar. Hey, is that MacAlister? LC already! I'll be damned!" Junior Cadet Charles Gridley told the girl clutching his arm. The two had been an item for the last year, but with Rhonda's graduation yesterday, they had spent the evening walking around the campus, talking about their future. They were still in their dress whites from graduation, Strolling around the campus in the late evening hours of the day after graduation, unwilling to release the excitement of the moment for mere reality.

"He graduated in '44, when you were a freshmen. Remember? He only has like the highest grades ever. In everything!" The two were visibly excited to see an honest to God Hero walking nearby on the day after their graduation.

"Oh, my God, Charlie, I'm assigned to his command, R&D!"

"What is he doing with those flowers?"

"Well, perhaps *HE* appreciates a gorgeous, brilliant *woman* when he hears about one!" Rhonda stepped to the side, hands on hips, posing with her head held high. "He's obviously read my transcripts, and..."

"Um, not so fast, sweet lips. He's laying them down outside the Chapel door. Now he's gone inside."

"Oh, my God, Charlie, don't you remember?" Rhonda Rhodes felt the hairs on her neck rise as her throat tightened.

"Oh God, you mean that story you told me about the three who died two days after graduation?"

The two spotted a few of their friends and called them over. The group talked quietly for a few minutes. Then they all moved towards the Chapel doors. Rhonda picked up the card with the flowers. It was simple, and said only, "Sharon, my love. Forever." One image was upon the card; an armored fist thrusting a dirk up through a circle with the word "FORTITER" inscribed upon the circle.

Rhonda gently replaced the card into the exact same spot she had removed it from, then looked at the others and nodded.

After a few minutes, Lieutenant Commander Jock MacAlister walked out of the chapel, his surprise at the sight greeting him hidden by his crisp salute to the half dozen newly graduated Ensigns and one Junior Cadet standing at sharp attention, saluting him on each side of the steps from the chapel steps and walkway. He recognized the Ensigns, freshmen his senior year, but he did not stop, holding his salute as he walked between them. As he passed each pair, their saluting arms dropped. While he appreciated their show of respect, this trip was not about him. He thought about another walk through saluting sailors outside the doors of this chapel. The walk he dreamed of, but never got to take. With her. Jock looked straight ahead and kept walking.

Rhonda stared after the head of Naval R&D as he walked away.

Charlie entered something onto his datatab, and then he put his arm around Rhonda's shoulder, drawing her closer. Her arm draped around Charlie's waist, resting on his far hip as her head nestled into that comfortable spot on his shoulder. She suddenly stood up, and looked at Charlie.

"I have to go take care of something. I'll be back soon. Don't move."

Charlie watched her walk down the hill.

A crowd of graduates and cadets gathered in the first light of morning to see what was going on.

Charlie explained it to them.

***

L-2 Shipyards Orbital Dock
Administrative Offices
Standard Earth Date August 20 3448

150 million miles above the Tsiolkovskiy Crater, the largest man-made object yet completed orbited the gravity shadow known as "L-2". The Armstrong Shipyards looked a lot like a kid's "Tinker-Toy" creation, girders creating a latticework of habitats and construction jigs around six "dry-docks". Building ships at L-2 on open jigs means that

nearly any design could be built without major renovations to the shipyards.

Floating in the gravity clamps of Dry-Dock 3 were the two sections of the alien scout vessel. Extra scaffolding was growing around the outside hull, allowing access and providing structure for the reverse engineering of this amazing ship. The airtight shell that would enclose the craft and allow a 'shirt-sleeve' environment for the study of it was nearly complete.

In an adjacent dry-dock, a frame was starting to take shape. One long keel, curving at the end, with a few frames curving up perpendicular to it, was anchored in the jig. The jig itself, already twice the size of the others, was being expanded outward. A long straight girder supported three tubes, each with huge copper coils winding around them.

Lieutenant Commander Jock MacAlister looked out the viewport at the new construction, and then scanned the other three jigs undergoing expansion. There would be three powerful new Heavy Cruisers completed by this time next year, and three more the year after that. Within five years, there would be enough infrastructures in place to build twelve ships per year. Within ten years, well over one hundred ships would be commissioned. By the time the Bug invasion fleet came, a fleet of nearly five hundred ships would be ready to meet them.

"Lost in thought, JG? By the time we get back, your reactor will be installed." A scruffy voice from behind pulled Jock's attention back to the present.

"Gunny! Glad to see you! Corporate let you out of your office, eh? I figured you'd be Earthside by now" Jock grabbed Dennis' hand.

"I had to kick some brass ass to get out. Figured you'd be here, so, here I am. When do we leave?

"About an hour. Thanks for doing this."

"No problem. I hear weddings are a great place to get laid, especially if you're the Groom. Or the Best Man."

"Gunny, you'd make Sally blush, I swear!"

"The little guy will have a blast, too. We'll see to that. Anyway, we'd better get a move on. Unless…you've gotten cold feet?"

"No, not at all. Not this time!"

"Good, because I'd hate to have to beat some sense into you. I may have to work up a sweat to do it. But I would, ya know!"

"Yeah, well, there's no time for that. Let's get moving, Pops."

Dennis Trap rolled his eyes, then grinned a little as he and the Lieutenant Commander headed for the shuttle hanger.

***

Saint James Episcopal Church
Skaneateles NY
Standard Earth Date August 24 3448

Jock held the ring up against the sunlit window.

"Good. That's the last one for now. I'll see you after the service." The photographer vanished.

"You ready, JG?"

"I sure hope so, Gunny. Here, you'd better hold this. I'll drop it down the drain or something."

"You'll be fine, Jock. You're just nervous. When the curtain goes up, you'll be fine."

"Thanks, Dennis." Jock took a huge breath and let it out immediately. "How long?"

"Just about now, I would say." The organ music began as if on Gunny's cue.

"Do I look okay? I my tux straight? My hair?"

"You're fine! Jock, GO!" Dennis gave Jock a slightly more than playful shove. The two walked onto the altar.

"Did we invite this many people?"

"Be quiet. When I kick you, say 'I do.' If I don't kick you, it's the wrong girl. Run."

Jock almost lost breakfast trying not to laugh. The organ changed tunes, the familiar song pulling Jock's attention to more serious matters.

He looked down the aisle.

There she was. An angel glowing in the sunlight. A few steps and he saw her face.

Jock remembered nothing but that face until Dennis kicked him some time later.

94

Belhurst Resort
Geneva NY
Standard Earth Date August 24 3448

Jock closed the door and let out a big breath. For an instant he was afraid to turn around. A smile grew on his face and he looked over his shoulder.

"We can unpack later. Mrs. MacAlister."

Sandy blushed, unpacking the suitcase. She turned to put Jock's underwear in the drawer and he was there, as close as…

"Jock."

"Sandy."

She dropped the briefs when her hands moved to his chest, her eyes never leaving his. Two small circles, then up her hands went to his face…

Jock pulled her to him, his kisses light and tender. Sandy's hands wrapped around Jock's neck…

Breathless, she pulled back, "What about dinner?"

Jock gazed into her eyes and smiled.

"You're all I need."

CHAPTER FOUR

L-2 Shipyards Orbital Dock
Construction Jig Alpha
Heavy Cruiser CA-1
Standard Earth Date May 4, 3449

"Dennis, are you sure?" Jock MacAlister frowned in the Captain's Station of CA-1, in the center of the deserted bridge. Around him floated the trappings of an ongoing ship's construction; pieces of wire, empty electronics boxes, used lunch wrappers, and other assorted flotsam.

"The lawyers are here now. They say we have to sign, or they'll hit us with two dozen patent infringement suits."

"Listen, Gunny, stall them. Tell them I'm on my way, and I'll make a decision soon." Jock cut the connection with Dennis' nod of affirmation, set his elbow on his knee, and began stroking his chin.

Dennis Trap was listed as the Owner and Directing Manager of Gravitas Propulsion. The company was founded as a subsidiary of his father's engineering firm, StarClan Engineering Company. Jock had deeded fifty two percent of it to Dennis, although it operated as a partnership between USF Research & Development and StarClan. The express purpose of the partnership was the rapid development of power, propulsion, and weapons systems to defeat the coming Bug invasion.

Now General Aerospace was threatening him with trillions in lawsuits if he didn't sign over his patent rights to the power plants, weapons systems, and gravitic drives that he had developed. They were threatening to delay the entire shipbuilding program!

Jock opened his comm link and hit a speed dial symbol. *Time for the big guns and the really big guns.*

"Yes, how may I help you?" The young and bored nasal voice grated on his eardrum.

"Sandra MacAlister, please. Tell her it's Jock."

"I'm sorry, sir, but The Hungyda, Hungyda, Hungyda and McCormick Law Firm does not handle athletes."

"Then tell her it is her husband, Solar Star Medal recipient Lieutenant Commander Jock MacAlister. I understand she handles *him* pretty well!" *Will this bimbo receptionist even have a clue?*

"Just pretty well, sir? Don't you mean, 'she handles him exquisitely'?

"Sandy, this is serious!" *She got me again! Will I ever learn?*

"Okay, Admiral, what's up? I'm NOT making a Burns Dinner tonight!"

"Sandy, I'm not an admiral! And yes, a Burns Dinner would be great, thanks for offering. But I need your help."

"Cooking haggis? Um, no."

"No, in legal matters. Now, I'm getting Admiral Alimonte on a conference call. I need your best corporate lawyer with patent experience to join us."

"Okay, that'd be Sims. I'll get him to join you. In the meantime, try not to fall apart!"

"Hold, pu-leeze!" The nasal voice came back.

"MacAlister, what can I do for you?" Admiral Alimonte's voice rang in Jock's ears.

"Admiral, there is a situation that threatens the entire ship production plan. I'm getting my company's lawyers on a conference call."

"Computer, suspend all recording, command authorization Peter Timothy One Zero Nine."

"Recording suspended."

"Okay, Jock, what gives?"

"Jock, I've got Ronald Sims on the line. What's going on?" Sandy was concerned now.

"Mr. Sims, Sandy, I've got Admiral Alimonte on the line as well. Here is what Dennis has told me so far:

"General Aerospace Developments is threatening to hit us with patent suits unless we pay them huge royalties on the power plants, weapons, and drive systems in the new ships. Their claim is that *my* designs are based upon my father's work, and that his work was *their* property."

"Are your designs based upon his work?" Sims' rich baritone voice asked.

"Only in a general sense, but, yes."

"Was your father working for General Aerospace when he developed those theories?"

"He did work on them in General Aerospace's labs, but he developed them well before he began working there."

"That may not matter. If he signed an Intellectual Property release, anything he worked on in their labs belongs to them." Sims sounded beaten.

"Could there be anything else that precluded that?" Sandy offered.

"Hell yes! Jock, your father was working at General Aerospace labs under Naval orders. I issued those orders! They did not employ him; he was on loan to them from the Navy. Even if he did sign such an agreement, it would not be enforceable. Everything he developed, physical and intellectual, is the property of the USF Navy."

"That may be true, Admiral, but they could still bankrupt us with appeals." Sims countered.

"They can't bankrupt the United Space Force Navy!" The Admiral's voice had a way of booming even at low volumes.

"There is another option. Ron, what if we filed a wrongful death suit against them?" Sandra quietly asked.

"Well, if we have proof of any unusual occurrences or irregular procedures, we could claim gross mismanagement of government funds. They would have to open up ten years of financials and other company records. The loss of your father to Starclan and to you would be huge. If the Navy joined the suit, even General Aerospace couldn't survive the attorney's fees, let alone the punitive damages."

Jock drummed his fingers on the table for a moment.

"Admiral, what do…"

"Hold on, MacAlister! This involves your private company, even though you're partnering with the Navy. I have zero experience here. I'm not qualified to advise you."

"Understood, Sir! Ron, file the wrongful death case. Do it. Today."

***

Chrysler Building
55th Floor
New York City
Standard Earth Date May 9, 3449

"THEY'VE WHAT?" The fist slamming down onto the polished wood desk punctuated the question.

"They've filed a wrongful death suit, sir, against General Aerospace Developments, for the death of Nial MacAlister. The suit was filed May 5th." The tall, balding man had lost a touch of his usual grace at the outburst.

"You waited four days to tell me?"

"We wanted to run an analysis of the suit to see what their chances of winning were, and have The Board's recommendation for you, before we informed you, sir."

"And?" Sheldon Malone's voice gained considerable control at the possibility of losing the suit.

"They will likely win. The Board recommends a settlement." The tall, balding man's jaw tightened imperceptibly in anticipation of the onslaught to come.

"If they win, what happens to General Aerospace?"

"IF we go to trial, and MacAlister wins, there will be no more General Aerospace, except as a wholly-owned subsidiary of Gravitas Propulsion."

Sheldon sat for a moment, very still, very quiet.

"What do they want?" he asked after the uncomfortable pause.

"Control of G.A.D. Fifty-five percent of the company, exactly. And exactly sixty percent of any future stock issues. And that we forego all claims of any patent infringements, past, present, and future."

Sheldon Malone slumped backwards in his massive chair. He hated this job very much.

***

L-2 Shipyards Orbital Dock
Construction Jig Alpha
Heavy Cruiser CA-1
Standard Earth Date May 9, 3449

"Is there a hero in the house?" the sweet voice boomed over the comms at much too high a volume level.

"Sandy?" Jock looked up from the technician he was watching, "Nice work, Jenkins! Keep it up! Next time, though, make sure the readout isn't installed upside down? You're finish work is top-notch, don't ever change it."

"Aye-aye, Sir! And, thank you, Sir!" Jenkins replied from under a console.

"Jock, it's the lawsuit..."

Jock activated his personal comm unit as walked into the corridor towards the captain's quarters. He had appropriated the suite for himself until the ship was far enough along to turn over to the naval crew.

"Hold on a second, I'm almost to where we can talk." He jogged the last twenty yards and slid into the ready-room. "OK, go ahead."

"Did I make you all out of breath?"

"Not since I've been up here. I was just hustling to keep you all to myself."

"Jock, they settled."

Jock sat down hard. Somehow he hit the chair; he was unaware of it.

"Jock?" Sandy's voice held a touch of concern. "They agreed to all of it."

"Oh, my."

"So, handsome, what are you going to do now?"

"Give it to Dennis. He needs a pension, and they won't be able to bullshit him."

"Good thinking; it was his idea anyway. I'll have Sims draw up the papers."

"What? It figures! Gunny sees through bullshit like no one else. Oh, get a sitter for tonight."

"What?"

Jock smiled as he heard the change in her voice.

"We're having the special at Giovanni's."

"Who?"

"You and I. Tonight. Giovanni's. The restaurant our rehearsal dinner was at, remember?"

"Jock, you're in lunar orbit!"

"Yeah, well, I'm taking some personal time. After dinner, I think you should get me all out of breath. In person-like."

***

Chrysler Building
55th Floor
New York City
Standard Earth Date May 10, 3449

"The room is cleaned now, Mr. Malone. It's all yours." The butler's much too stuffy voice declared.

100

"Was that a joke, Jamison?"

"Not that I am aware of, sir." The faintest of smiles flash on Jamison's face for the briefest of instants, more of a twitch than a smile.

Sheldon Malone walked over to his desk, and looked around on the floor, on the desk, and even up on the ceiling. His eyes lingered on the boxes taped shut. *Boxes full of my things. Packed up as an eviction notice!*

"The cleaning crew did nice work. Tell them to stay around a bit." Sheldon hit a button on his comm as he sat down behind the desk. "Mr. Stack, if your dogs are not too fatigued, I have someone they would like to m-e-a-t." A grinning Sheldon chuckled at Jamison, enjoying the butler's face growing pale at his words.

***

United Space Force Academy
United Space Force Academy Hilton
Cape Canaveral, Florida
Standard Earth Date June 22 3449

Jock looked carefully at the image before him. He studied it intensely, searching for any flaw, any piece of the picture out of place. Finally satisfied, he turned on his heel sharply and walked out of the hotel room.

This was the third time. The first time, there were a few graduates and a cadet there. They formed an honor guard for him, though he doubted they knew why he was there. Still, it was a kind gesture of respect.

I wonder what I'll find this time? Probably no one, I hope. Two hundred and forty six graduated this year, Jock thought as he walked through the night. Spotless Dress Whites; he'd been lucky last year, as the driving rain seemed to stop the second his foot hit the sidewalk outside the hotel.

Last year the entire graduating class, all in Dress Whites, was lined up along the path to the chapel. All of them, an honor guard waiting for him. *Why? Thankfully the Academy Commander was receptive to discouraging the formation of an impromptu honor guard this year. We'll see if it stuck.*

Jock started up the path to the chapel that bore his Great-Great Grandfather's name. He had the card, and the flowers. *I wonder what they do with these after I leave?*

Jock stopped for a moment. He looked to his left, towards Mama Rooney's. He looked down briefly, and then began walking to the chapel.

Just outside the doors, he looked up at the inscription above the doors; "MacAlister Chapel". His head bowed again, and he gently placed the flowers and card to the right of the steps. He froze for a moment, and swallowed hard, remembering that night at this spot. Tears welled up and blurred his vision, but he was not seeing with his eyes. His heart saw Sharon there, nervous as he took her hand and led her into the chapel that night.

Jock stayed in the chapel a little longer this year. He came out as the campus clock chimed midnight, nearly fainting at the sight before him.

On the edge of the path was a line of graduates, each in spotless Dress Whites, each holding a single flower. As Jock watched, a graduate would walk up, remove their hat, and place the flower next to those Jock had brought.

Jock didn't have to count the number of those single flowers. He just knew it would be two hundred and forty six.

***

AG-1 Thistle
Asteroid Belt
Standard Earth Date August 2 3449

Captain Jock MacAlister stared at the target in the center of the small cluster of asteroids on the bridge's viscreen. The ship seemed familiar in some ways, but United Space Force had upgraded and expanded nearly everything. *Gunny would never recognize her,* Jock thought.

His attention came back to the matter at hand. The Space Tug Thistle had been purchased by the USF to serve as a weapons testing platform. This allowed the few ships in service to remain at their posts while new weapons were developed, allowing the new class of ships to be built faster and construction started sooner. When building a new class of cruiser, the first few ships always took longer to finish than the rest of the class. There were always bugs to be worked out, unforeseen problems, and unintended consequences of building with advanced designs, no matter how thorough the planning had been.

The Thistle was a great choice, as she buzzed with excess power whenever she wasn't towing a barge. Her engines were overhauled, enhanced, and updated, her gravity docking clamps were modernized, upgraded and modified to hold modular weapons platforms, and her crew accommodations were expanded considerably. Her shielding was also increased in anticipation of applying energies unknown.

Jock's attentions were focused on the three-mile wide asteroid roughly in the center of the cluster. The test was set here for a reason; the cluster would tell them as much, if not more, about the weapon's value than the target would.

"Detonation in ten seconds." The familiar surroundings kept Jock waiting for "dear!" or "handsome" to follow, but Sally had been retired; Jock suspected Dennis had her installed as his house's domestic control system. The new computer's voice did sound like Sally, but only if she had settled down and had a few kids, and had started taking sedatives regularly. *She would bore Dennis to death,* Jock laughed to himself.

"Five. Four. Three. Two. One. Detonation."

Jock mentally counted down the four-minute delay for the light of the event to reach the Thistle. Waiting was the worst part. Oh, he *knew* the device would work. Well, *should* work. Probably. *Maybe.* The nature of the device dictated the great distance from the test. Jock *knew* they could be safe a lot closer. *Maybe.*

Four minutes can be a long time. Jock looked around the bridge at the four crew members there; Lieutenant Charles Walker at the nav/helm, Lieutenant Theresa Long at sensors station one, Lieutenant Commander Haja Zafy at sensors station two, and Commander Mat Musa Wan who operated the test weapons. These were high-ranking people for so small a crew, but these were important tests. Earth's survival may depend upon their success. While a lot of information about the Bug's home world and intentions had been deciphered from the system on board the alien scout ship, details such as the number and composition of vessels that would be sent against Earth was not there. *They'll have to wait until they receive the scout's message,* Jock thought. *I'm glad I recruited the best brains for this. BBs, Sharon would have called them.*

"Approaching visual Sir."

"THERE!" Lieutenant Walker pointed at the screen all eyes were glued on.

"My God!" Jock watched the target flash briefly, then collapse into itself at a rate that increased as it became smaller. But the effect of the weapon did not stop. The nearby asteroids began moving, slowly at first, then with ever increasing velocity towards the shrinking target. More and more began falling into the target, which had begun to glow from the heat. Every asteroid within ten miles of the target fell into the glowing ember of compressed hellfire, while outside the ten-mile boundary, nothing moved.

"Coming up on the three-minute mark, Mister MacAlister."

"Thank you, Mister Musa. Any local effects?"

"Only a slight variation in the background gravitation, Captain." LC Zafy's cool voice reported. "Sort of like a wave passed us."

"Was that anticipated?" On Jock's ship, with these men, a question not directed at a specific crewmember, it was directed at every crewmember. But you had better have an answer with value if you replied to it.

"What was the time delay, Mister Zafy?"

"None measurable, Captain."

Communications!

"Captain, are you thinking of using this as a communications system?"

"Let's see what the data tells us, Mister Musa, but yes, that was my thought. You're the Wizard of Waves, do you think we can modulate it?"

"Easier than modulating old style radio waves, I'd say, Sir."

"Okay, people, let's keep focused on the test we're running. Charlie, ET since activation?"

"Elapsed time since device activation is twelve minutes and forty seconds, Captain."

"Almost there. How is the data stream, Miss Long?"

"Solid Sir. We're getting feeds from every sensor, and monitored data is centered on predicted values."

"Okay, don't let up, people, stay sharp. We're almost there. Mister Walker, engine status?"

"Reactors hot and ready, engines purring like sleeping panthers, sir."

"Heh, thanks for the colorful visualizations, Charlie. Time?"

"Coming up on scheduled shut down, Sir."

"There it is! Right on time! Readings?"

"Background gravity, nominal. Background radiation, nominal. It's off, Sir. You did it!"

"HOO-RAH!" The four on the bridge let out the ancient cheer.

"Okay, Mister Walker, take us in closer to the target. Mister Zafy, send to Admiral Alimonte: GravTorp testing completed. We have a weapon! "

"Aye-aye, SIR!"

"Well done, everyone!" Jock smiled at his crew.

***

West Lake Road
Skaneateles, NY
Standard Earth Date April 7 3466

"This is good." Sandy MacAlister sighed as she held up the glass, gazing at the fire's flickering through the ruby red liquid inside. Her head rested on her husband's lap as he smiled at her, absentmindedly stroking her long blond hair.

"The wine, the fire, or the company?" The contentment in Jock's voice carried his smile with the question.

"Yes. Yes. And yes." Sandy snuggled just a little closer as she sipped the tangy Baco Noir. "Oh, Jock, this is so nice. Are you sure you don't want to retire? We could spend every night like this."

"Not yet. As soon as the ships come out at a fast enough pace, I'll retire. I would do more good at Starclan in R & D then."

"Hmmm. You being home every night. That is such a wonderful thought."

"That it is, Lass! That it is." Jock took a sip from his glass and set it down, his expression falling from serenity into concern.

"Sandy, have you made the plans for picking up Jack at the end of the year?" Jock's voice reflected the apprehension his face displayed.

"What's wrong, dear? That's the third time this week you've asked me that. Every thing's all set."

"I have to stay a day past graduation, two days past his last class." Jock stopped stroking Sandy's hair, placing his hand on the rug next to her shoulder, as if bracing himself.

Sandy sat up, and turned to smile gently at her husband.

"Yeah, so? Why is that a problem?"

"I need to tell you why." Jock lowered his eyes as he spoke.

"Oh, the flowers for Sharon? You're worried about that? Of course you're going to leave them this year. I scheduled it into your trip," Sandy stated simply.

"You, how, what, you know about that? You, you don't mind?" Surprise and relief fought for control of Jock's voice. *I don't deserve this woman.*

Sandy leaned close to her husband and kissed his lips with that gentile passion that always sent tingles up his spine. She knew it drove Jock mad.

"I've known about it since your first trip." Sandy curled a lock of Jock's hair with her finger as she spoke.

"It doesn't upset you?"

"Jock, you loved her. I know that. I know you love me, too." Sandy dropped her eyes to smile at the proof of her statement. "And Jack. And Mary. And Corrine. And Alistair. And Alexander. And Allison. You give Earth, and everyone here, most of yourself, you time, your entire life almost. You give me, you give *us*, everything you have left until this is done. Then we, I will get you all to myself." Sandy leaned in and kissed Jock again. He moaned a little when she broke the kiss. "I can give Sharon's memory one day a year. Because it means so much to *you*, it means a lot to me. Because you need to go. So, go, my darling. But not tonight; tonight I need you to show me how much you love *me*!"

Sandy leaned in again and Jock pulled her to him. This time when the kiss broke she moaned. Neither of them worried about the spilled wine.

***

Chrysler Building
55th Floor
New York City
Standard Earth Date May 20, 3466

"Mr. Trap will see you now." The Bronx twang of the receptionist drifted to the dark clad figure seated on the bench opposite her desk.

The figure rose, and walked silently past the receptionist and into the huge office.

"Hello, Mr....?" Dennis Trap stood and walked to the figure with outstretched hand.

"My name is unimportant. You may call me Elathan if you feel the need to label me. You are nearing retirement, yes?" The heavily accented Celtic voice reminded Dennis of the sounds made when scraping hides to make leather.

"Aye, and I've been told you can help with that?" Dennis looked up and down this figure dressed in black pants, a charcoal grey turtleneck, a loose-fitting black jacket, and a large black Panama hat. Dennis couldn't make out the features of the figure's face, only that there were dark glasses under the hat's shadow somewhere. He shivered as he suddenly felt a chill. *Did someone lower the thermostat in here?*

"I can...facilitate a useful transition for you. Aye."

"I see...May I get you something?"

"Yes, you will."

"Okay, well, eh, have a seat and fire away! Name your poison."

"Let me share this apple with you." Elathan hissed.

***

West Lake Road
Skaneateles, NY
Standard Earth Date June 25 3466

"Mom, I need to talk to you." Jack MacAlister leaned against the doorjamb of his parent's bedroom, staring at his shoes.

"What is it, honey. Is everything Okay?" Sandy looked up from folding clothes, a little alarmed at the serious tone of her son's voice. *How grown up he looks, so handsome!*

"Mom, I'm worried. I, I think Dad is cheating on you. I think he has another woman at the Academy." Jack choked on the words. "When I was in Dad's hotel room, I saw flowers, and a card. Her name is Sharon."

Sandy gave her oldest a faint smile as she walked over and placed a hand on each of his shoulders. "Jack, ask your father about this. It is time you two talked about it. It's important to both of you. He'll be home soon. You wait for him in the study, and I'll send him in. And stop worrying; it is NOT anything like what you fear." She reached up and cupped his face with her right hand and kissed his forehead. "Now, relax."

Jack was very confused. Mom seemed unconcerned with what he had said, and that confused him even more.

"I never worry about your father doing anything like that. Jack, since the moment I first met him, I have known exactly what he was thinking. I can't explain it, it only happens with him; all I have to do is think of him, and I know his thoughts, and also what is much, much deeper inside him. And sometimes I see what is going to happen, in a general way, around him. So, I never worry about him that way. Now, go into the study and *relax*." The tall Space Force Cadet walked to the study to wait. *This is just too bazaar.*

A few minutes later he heard his father come home. He heard him talking to his mother. *They aren't yelling, that's good, but Dad sounds upset. I wish I could hear…*

The door to the study opened. Jock stepped inside, and closed the door behind him without looking at Jack. He walked over to the cabinet behind the desk, unlocked it and took out a bottle of 25-year old Glenfiddich and two whiskey glasses. He poured a dram in each and carried them over to the couch Jack sat on, holding one glass out to his son while he sat down next to him. He looked at Jack for the first time since he entered the room. Jack was surprised by the look in his father's eyes.

"Take it, Jack. Sip it. Savor the tastes, try to separate them in your mind, and think about how they fit together. Life itself is distilled in a glass of good Scotch." Jock took a sip of the amber liquid, savoring the comfortable smoothness of the heat sliding down his throat, the familiar warmth spreading throughout his chest.

Jack looked at the whiskey glass as he took it from his father. *Another strange ritual I have to 'experience' before he'll explain anything to me,* Jack thought. *Okay, I'll give him this. But the explanation better not be anything freaky.*

Jack took a small sip. The texture of the golden liquid was surprisingly thick, almost like olive oil. The whiskey burned Jack's tongue even as he tasted honey, caramel, vanilla, and something else he couldn't quite define. The gentle burn on his tongue and down his throat spread out into a warmth that lingered a bit before fading with the flavors. Jack looked up and turned to face his Dad. He started to tell his dad about what he had seen, but Jock raised a hand to delay him.

"Jack, I have to tell you about your birth mother," Jock began. "First, I have to tell you about my father's death.

"Your Grandfather was a brilliant engineer, a talented physicist. He invented the gravitic propulsion systems we're installing on those ships up there," Jock raised his glass as if to point, then took another sip before continuing, "He was on assignment, working for General Aerospace Developments on the drives, when the lab exploded and he was killed. The Marine Guard came and told me ten days before I was to leave for the Academy.

"Jack, my father was my best friend, my best teacher, my idol. Everything I wish I could have been for you. These preparations for the Bugs, the alien invasion, have taken me from you, and I'm sorry about that.

"Your adoptive mother, Sandy, was my high school sweetheart. We had hinted at marriage to each other, I sort of assumed it would happen. She seemed to know it would. When they told me my Dad had died, I shut them all..." Jock took another sip, "I shut them all out. My friends, Sandy. Everyone except Mom. But she was too crushed to help me deal with it. My friends let me be alone; they wanted to help, but I wouldn't let them. Then, before I knew it, I had to leave for the Academy.

"The first day, I met Angie, Pat, and Sharon." Jock took another small sip of Scotch.

Jacks eye widened at the name, and this time he sipped his whiskey along with his father. *That's the name. Is she there now, waiting for him? He's never talked with me like this before. This is hard for him. But he'd better not be cheating on Mom.*

"The three of them made me forget about losing Dad. It was like entering another world, leaving all that pain behind, pretending it never happened. The four of us did everything together. Pat kept hitting on Sharon, Angie kept hitting on me, all in a half joking, kidding kind of dance. Then Mom died. And I shut everyone out, Sandy, Don, Aggie, Sharon, Pat and Angie. They all wanted to comfort me, but I denied them that closeness. As for my friends here, I was so ashamed about not contacting them that I wouldn't contact them after my mom died. Before I knew it, I had graduated. The day after, my USF friends and I had received our assignments. The four of us went to dinner together, then we each got this," Jock pulled his polo shirt off and turned his right shoulder towards his now wide-eyed son.

"Pat and Angie went off together, to plan their future. I asked Sharon to marry me, and she said yes. We walked around the campus, not really paying attention to where we were going. We ended up in front of the chapel, and we went in.

"My flight was the first to leave the next morning. The four of us went together. I was waving good-bye..." Jock finished his Scotch and stood up. Jack downed his fast to catch up to his Dad, and winced at the burn. Jock walked to the cabinet and stood with his back to Jack, pouring a second dram.

"They were hit by a bus as I waved to them. I couldn't stop the tram, or even go back. I couldn't even call from the ship or the lunar base, too classified. My LC helped. A lot." Jock walked back and sat beside his son, handing him the whiskey as he sipped the Scotch. Jack followed suit as he watched a tear roll down his father's cheek.

I've never seen Dad cry. He's always been so strong, like a rock, except with Mom.

"The turret I was stationed on was a two-person rig. The other operator was already there, halfway through her shift. Her name was Shannon Malone. Jack, she was Sharon's twin sister." Jock downed the rest of the Scotch, but couldn't feel the burn or taste the sweetness it carried.

Jack took a small sip. *How do you deal with that? This hurts him. A lot.*

"Shannon helped me finish the development of the gravitic drives. And…" Jock set his empty glass down looked into his son's eyes.

"Shannon proved to me that my father was murdered. And she proved that the bus that killed her sister and my friends was meant for me. Then she took me to her bed. I was dazed, half numb. She revived me, made me start to live again.

"Jack, Shannon Malone was your birth mother."

Jack stared at his father for thirty seconds.

"Dad, where is she?"

"She went into the intelligence service when she returned from the Turret. After you were born, she brought you to Don and Aggie, to keep for Sandy to take care of. Like she knew we would end up together. Then she went off mission; she went after the one who killed my father and her sister. She found him, and she killed him. It was her father. She died with him."

Jack downed the Scotch in his glass. It could not penetrate the numbness, the confusion of the weird story he'd just heard. *How do I deal with this?*

"Jack, talk to me, tell me how you feel. Don't shut me out like I shut out my friends."

"Dad, I, I don't know what to say, what I'm supposed to say. I mean, I don't know…"

"I came back and found Sandy here, waiting for me. She waited all that time, without ever hearing from me. She showed me you, and told me that she loved you, because you were a part of me. I can't imagine why, Jack, but she still loves me. And she loves you."

"I know she does, Dad. Too much, sometimes, I think. Dad, how do you deal with all of this?"

"Jack, at first I dealt with it by withdrawing. Don't do that; it's more

110

painful, and it just draws out the sorrow and emptiness. Let your loved ones share your pain, they can lessen it a lot. Your pain, it's a part of you. When you share it, the good memories become stronger."

"So, what's with the flowers and the card?" Jack's eyes drifted to the tattoo on his father's shoulder again.

"I should have let her into my life sooner, Jack. With Sandy, I was lucky. I got another chance. With Sharon, I didn't. So, I do what I can to remind myself, every year on the night after graduation, where we promised each other before God. It's not much, but I need to do it." Jock leaned towards his son, "Don't wait, and don't shut out the people who love you."

"Dad, what was my birth mother like?"

"Jack, Shannon Malone was a smart, and unique lady…" Jock smiled as he refilled their dram glasses with the fine single malt. He handed the glass to Jack, and then pressed a button on his desk. A soft, nasal wail came out of the speaker system:

D'ya hear that lonesome whip-poor-will
he sounds too blue to fly.
The midnight train is whining low.
I'm so lonesome I could cry…

***

Chrysler Building
55th Floor
New York City
Standard Earth Date November 26, 3466

Dennis Trap looked around the huge room. He walked over to the thermostat and checked it again. *Eighty five and it's still cold in here. It's been cold in here for six months. What the hell am I doing?*

"The papers are ready, Mr. Trap." The nasal twang of his receptionist's Bronx accent only irritated him more. And he'd been in a constant state of irritation lately.

The receptionist's overdone hip sway as she left the office was absurd, Dennis thought. *Much better to have Sally.* He looked down at the documents that Elathan had said would save Jock. It didn't make sense!

If I sign this, Jock is locked out of Gravitas and General Aerospace. Elathan

111

will be the richest man on Earth, and I'll be the most tortured. Jock's left me no
choice. The fool! Leaving Gravitas, and General Aerospace vulnerable like this!
The only way to save him is to sign! Thanks be to that son of a bitch Elathan!

Shivering, Dennis picked up the pen, and began writing on the papers. He initialed and dated each page of the document that would transfer all of General Aerospace Developments and Gravitas Propulsion to Elathan. He signed his name at the bottom of the last page, just above where his receptionist had signed as a witness.

Dennis placed the pen back into its holder, pushed his chair back from the desk, and stood up.

So cold!

He turned and walked over to the center of the long wall of windows. He reached up with his left hand and touched the frame. He was gazing out across Manhattan when he felt the bloodlessly cold fingers inside his chest, moving through his very core as if searching for something. They wandered around in his chest, burning him with their frigid touch, until they reached their beating goal. The inhumanly cold, dark fingers froze his breath, his soul as they closed ever more tightly upon his heart. Then Dennis saw, for that fleeting moment that his life remained, the truth of what he had just been tricked into doing; by signing the papers, he had ripped the companies from his friend as these frigid fingers now ripped his life, his heart, his soul from him. Dennis' mouth opened in silent agony as he fell to the polished floor, his now hollow body quivered a brief, feeble protest against its emptiness.

***

Mars L-2
J. Wadsworth R & D Station
Commander's Quarters
Standard Earth Date December 23, 3466

"We've run autopsies and tox screens. There is nothing there. It was a heart attack, simple as that." Ronald Sims' face and voice explained over the comm. Sandy sat behind him and off to one side, eyes red and tired.

"I'm sorry, Jock. But, it's all gone. Dennis signed the companies away just before he died. Everything he was in charge of is gone.

"So, what's left, Ron?" Jock asked.

"Well, there's the StarClan Engineering firm. That's still there. Of course, they can't use any of Gravitas' patents. The physical equipment and name of Gravitas Propulsion are for sale. It looks like they only wanted the intellectual property and the patent infringement agreement."

"Yeah, property from the minds of my father, Shannon Malone, and me. Okay, Ron," Jock let out a huge breath he didn't remember taking in, "buy everything of Gravitas that's for sale. Those employees didn't ask for pink slips. We'll take care of them. We'll keep StarClan separate. I want it in a trust for the family, managed by your law firm." Jock looked at Sandy's smile and returned it.

"Jock, that will stretch you a lot more than just a little thin. Are you sure?"

"Ron, USF will need someone to handle everything General Aerospace can't. That will be Gravitas Propulsion. Make it happen."

***

United Space Force Academy
United Space Force Academy Hilton
Cape Canaveral, Florida
Standard Earth Date June 15 3470

Jack MacAlister knocked on the hotel room door. He absentmindedly rubbed the dull ache in his right shoulder through his Dress Whites as he waited for the answer. He was a little tired after graduation, and all the activities after. There was one more he was participating in, but something he had to do first. After a few seconds the door opened.

"Jack! Come on in."

"We have to hurry, Dad. There is, well, something extra this time." Jack said as he walked into the hotel room. As he entered the room, he stopped in the doorway, holding open the door.

"Dad, there's someone I want you to meet."

Jock smiled before he turned around. At six feet, four inches, Jack stood two inches taller than his dad, and just as well muscled; sliding out from behind his son was the smallest set of dress whites Jock had ever seen. His eyes swept over the four-foot, ten-inch cadet, taking in the long jet-black hair, the dark olive skin, her full lips and perfect nose before settling on her fiery green eyes. There was something there that broadened Jock's grin into a full-blown smile.

"You must be Kesa. I am so happy to meet you. Jack has told us nothing about you!"

"Dad!" Jack laughed, "Please!"

"I am honored to meet you, Captain MacAlister! Jack has told me so much about you, even if he has kept my existence secret from you!" The small cadet's voice carried immense confidence.

"Dad, Kesa is first in her class in GPA, including graduate physics and thermodynamics." Jack beamed his pride.

"I see. So, that is the most important thing about Kesa you want to tell me, that she is hard-working and smart?" Jock was enjoying setting Jack up, wondering if Kesa would catch on.

"Well, no, Dad. The most important thing about her is that I love her."

Jock walked up to Jack and grabbed his son in a big hug.

"I'm glad you finally figured out what is important, Jack." Jock stepped back grinning, and turned to Kesa. "I am so glad to meet you. Jack has told us so much about you. You must come with us tonight."

"I am honored at your request, Captain, but is it my place in such a personal remembrance of yours?"

"This night has also become a tradition for graduates, and to Jack that means he wants to remember you."

Jack looked at his father with widened eyes. *How does he know this? Can he see my mind like Mom sees his?*

Jock turned to his son with a raised eyebrow, "Have you?"

"Not yet."

"When?"

"Chapel."

"Understood. Kesa, I insist you come with us. When we reach the chapel, please allow me a few moments alone inside. When I come out, you and Jack may go inside."

"Yes, Captain. I am honored to be included in your family traditions. Fortiter, Sir!"

Jock's head moved back and his eyes widened with his smile.

"Come, it's time to go."

The three walked out of the hotel and across the campus, passing many graduates on the way. When at last they came to the chapel, there was a line of graduates and some cadets there.

Every year it gets bigger, Jock thought. *They're so young, so full of dreams. They're here to pledge something to each other, lovers and friends. Sharon would like that, I'm sure.*

One of the graduates turned and noticed Jock, and whispered to the girl in front of him. She turned and whispered to the graduate in front of her, and soon the path to the chapel was clear, every graduate and cadet looking at Jock.

Jock slowly walked up to the spot near the steps, bent down and placed the flowers and card there, among the dozens of single blooms already there. He stood, teary eyed, and walked into the chapel.

Jack and Kesa walked up behind Jock, Jack placing the single flower next to the bouquet his father had placed in remembrance of Jack's aunt. The two waited patiently for several minutes, and finally Jock came out of the chapel. The other graduates had formed an honor guard along the path, standing at attention saluting the Captain's devotion.

Jack and Kesa slipped into the chapel unnoticed by all except Jock. At the end of the honor guard he stopped, turned sharply, and saluted the graduates lined up. Then he stood at ease, centered between the lines of graduates, waiting for his son. He could not suppress the grin that crept onto his face as his voice snapped out, loud enough for only those outside of the chapel to hear, "Hold position, AT EASE!" *How many Dads get to do this for their son? He has no clue that I had spoken to Kesa last week. She has no clue Sandy helped him pick out the ring. And I had no clue he would do it tonight, but it's perfect. Perfect.*

The doors to MacAlister Chapel opened and Jack held them for Kesa to pass. Jack froze when he heard his father's commanding voice echo across the campus.

"ATTENTION!"

Two hundred and sixty graduates snapped to attention with the easy flawlessness spawned by innumerable repetition. As Jock snapped a perfect salute to his son, the honor guard, now celebrating one of their own, snapped their salutes to Jack and Kesa.

Briefly a touch of panic flashed through Jock's mind; *could she have said 'no'?* As his eyes caught the glints from Kesa's ring, the flush of her cheeks, and the light smiling in her green eyes, Jock released his salute and stood at ease. The impromptu honor guard followed his lead, breaking into applause and moving in to congratulate their friends.

Mars L-2
J. Wadsworth R & D Station
Commander's Quarters
Standard Earth Date May 4, 3473

"I know, Sandy. Soon, I'll be back on leave. Jack and Kesa too. We leave in three days." Jock waited for the time delay. These vids were great, but the damn time delay for the laser feed to go from Mars to Earth and back slowed down conversations.

"Jock, I can't wait. I'll see you soon, honey. Stay safe." Sandy's image faded from the viscreen in Jock's ready-room. He sat back, contemplating his travel.

"Ding-DING!" his door chime called. *Who could that be at this hour? Research shifts ended two hours ago.*

"Come in."

The door opened and Jack, Kesa, Lieutenant Rhonda Rhodes, and Commander Haja Zafy stumbled over each other entering the room.

"Okay, everybody. Sit down and relax." Jock commanded. The youngsters were highly excitable, and Haja tended to reflect the emotions of those around him.

When the four had sat down, Jock looked at each of them.

"Okay, what's up?"

"Well, the special resistance numbers…"

"Gravitic Friction to spatial fabric distortion…"

"The moderation of the GravTorp field limiter can let us stretch out…"

"QUIET!" Jock commanded. "One at a time, please! Haja, go!"

"We have FTL, Commodore," Commander Haja Zafy said simply, "and more!" Jock looked into the faces in front of him. Jack and Haja he could read like a book, Rhonda he had an idea, but Kesa he had no clue about. *They're excited, not giggling. Damn, they've really got it!*

"OK, what do you mean by that. Haja, simple, concise answer, please."

"Admiral, simply put, the modulator that limits the gravity sphere in the GravTorp detonations can also stretch and compress points in space. By compressing the space a ship occupies and the space along a straight, one-point thick line to the destination, we can achieve nearly limitless velocities. Tests indicate transit rates on the order of dozens or even hundreds of light-years per day." Haja stopped to let his CO digest what he'd just said.

"You said there is more. Go on."

"A slight adjustment to the quantum frequency turns the same modulator into a drive that acts directly upon the fabric of space. Essentially it is a 'fuelless drive'. The combination means our ships can devote all of their volume to payloads, civilian and military."

"What are the energy requirements for this?"

"That's the best part, Sir. We have the gravitic generator design working as well. By holding an electron and a proton in close proximity, while preventing the electron from orbiting or colliding with the proton, we get huge amounts of energy, hundreds of times as much as the plasma generators make. More than enough to power the drives, and a lot more." Rhonda's breathless voice beamed with pride as she explained the progress.

"Where did you get the theories for this?"

"They're yours, Dad. The ones you and Shannon worked on. One hundred percent Space Force owned research!" Jack confirmed.

"What stage are you at with this?"

"Drone tests have run flawlessly. We have a manned ship ready, the Thistle."

"When is the test scheduled for?" Jock looked at his son and daughter-in-law.

"May 7th, Sir. Three days." Rhonda chimed in with a grin.

"I see. And, do you have a crew for this test-drive?"

"We have a crew, Sir, but we need an experienced command officer." Kesa's musical voice sparkled.

"What route have you geniuses mapped out?" Jock sat back. He was trapped, and he knew it.

"We first considered an outward route, but we finally settled on an inbound route, Mars L-2 to Lunar L-2. We figured the trip will take, oh, like, twelve seconds." Jack explained, barely able to contain his excitement.

"OK, well, I had better start packing then, I guess." Jock smiled and added, "Well done, everyone. Great job. Now, I've got some arrangements to make, so if you'll excuse me..."

"Sir, there are two more things. Commander Zafy has asked that we transport some equipment with us, Sir."

"What equipment, Rhonda?"

"Gravitic wave communication transponders, Sir. Drones have confirmed that Commander Musa's design works perfectly. Real-time communication anywhere in the universe."

"The second?"

"Gravity stealth; your designs to apply the light bending tech from the stealth probes to large ships using gravity waves works. We've made the Thistle invisible!"

Jock shook his head as he watched them file out of his office. *Well, I'll be damned! We're gonna make it!*

Chapter Five

"Are we ready for this?" Haja Zafy grimly asked his companions. "He's going to be angry, you know."

"Kesa, he's going to be frightened. Of losing you." Jack explained.

"He'll get over it." Admiral Bucktooth declared. "I'll order him to. All right everyone, stick to the plan!" Jericho reached up and hit the door chime.

"Come in!"

The door opened at the call of the voice, and Lieutenant Commander Charlie Walker, Lieutenant Rhonda Rhodes, Lieutenant Commander Jack MacAlister, Commander Haja Zafy, Lieutenant Kesa MacAlister, and Admiral Jericho Bucktooth nervously crowded into the small office.

Jock walked out of the living quarters and into the office portion of his suite, and stopped dead when he saw the collection of people in front of him.

"What's going on?" Jock asked in a grimly quiet voice.

"Relax and sit down. We're here to discuss the Needs of The Fleet." Jericho said, understanding Jock's apprehension.

"Commodore, I've asked for a transfer four times this past year, and you've denied me each time. I'm asking again, Sir." Kesa began.

"Kesa, I need you here. I can't replace you." Jock's lame plea did have a ring of truth to it.

"Dad, you mean you need her here, where you can keep her safe. You mean that you can't replace her as a daughter-in-law." His son's words hit Jock with the hammer of truth.

"Kesa, Jack, I..." Jock took a big breath and exhaled his fears slowly. "I guess I didn't realize that. Now that you say that, Jack, I, I don't know what to say."

"Commodore, I've asked for transfers as well, twice in the last six months. So have Charlie and Rhonda." Haja added.

"Dad, you've been a great CO for all of us. Now you need to be a

119

great mentor." Jack added.

"Jock, these officers have given you more than you could ask for. It's time you let them grow. It's time you grew. It's time for you to focus on what The Fleet needs, what Earth needs, and put it above what Admiral Jock MacAlister wants." Jericho Bucktooth's last few words brought surprised glances from everyone in the room.

"Jeri, what…"

"Here it is, straight and simple. Fleet has hundreds of new ships. We need bright competent officers to command them. Fleet needs bright, competent Admirals to lead them.

"Jock, Admiral Alimonte is retiring. I'm being selfish here, but since I've been tapped to take his place, I want the best damn people I can get supporting me.

"That means that as of today, Charlie, Rhonda, Haja, and Kesa have been transferred to Fleet Command Line, and will leave for Ship Command Orientation tomorrow; Rhodes and MacAlister will be promoted to Lieutenant Commander. Walker is promoted to Commander and Zafy to Captain. Upon successful completion, each will be assigned as Executive Officer under an experienced Captain.

"Jack will be promoted to Commander, and has accepted assignment as Commander, R & D. Jock, you're coming with me. You should know that Musa has been promoted to Rear Admiral along with you. You will report tomorrow to my skiff, and accompany me to Earth. There we will meet with and organize our command staff and structure. Any questions?"

Everyone in the room was stunned by the promotions and clear visions described by Admiral Bucktooth. Twelve eyes stared at Jericho for several silent seconds before he broke the meeting.

"Very well. Dismissed. No one leave yet." Jericho leaned back in his chair slightly. "I believe our new Rear Admiral has some fifteen year old Scotch he would like to share?"

***

Chrysler Building
55ᵗʰ Floor
New York City
Standard Earth Date September 11, 3476

"So, we have a unanimous vote then, ladies and gentlemen. I will inform our new Principal this evening. Thank you." The tall bald man's elegant voice informed The Board.

"What of Mr. Elathan?" A lone voice quivered out the question no one else dared to bring forth.

"Mr. Elathan prefers to remain in the…background. He will be available if…required. Nothing else? Good. Adjourned."

***

United Space Force Academy
MacAlister Chapel
Cape Canaveral, Florida
Standard Earth Date June 19 3477

"It's weird, that's all. It's just not logical." Corrine MacAlister frowned.

"It's sweet. Imagine a love so perfect!"

"Yeah, then imagine it's *your* Dad and *not your* Mom. It's weird!"

"What does your Mom say about it? Have you talked about it with her?"

"She's fine with it. She tells me she can read Dad's mind. I don't know what to think of that. It's not like she's crazy or something. She's always so logical and practical, except…"

"Except when it comes to your Dad. Geeze, Corry, get a clue, will ya? Your Mom and Dad are gaga for each other! I've seen them together for what, fifteen–plus years? This thing isn't weird, it's sweet, and your Mom knows it. Why don't you?"

"Tracy, the whole thing just doesn't make sense to me."

"I know, it won't fit into that neat, perfect little package you demand of everything. Maybe you're just over…anal…yzing…Oh, my!

121

Will you look at that!" Tracy Singh grabbed her friend's arm tight enough to make her gasp. Corrine MacAlister just didn't feel it. All of the eighteen-year-old prospective cadet's senses were focused on the tall, dark haired marine cadet striding confidently their way.

"Hello, ladies. May I be of assistance to you?" Cadet Michael Halsey's smooth, deep voice vibrated around the two girls as he tipped his hat in greeting. *She is absolutely gorgeous!*

"W-what? Excuse me?" Corrine asked as Tracy sighed dreamily. *Gorgeous?! Me?*

Look at the fire in those eyes! I wonder what ignites her? Hold on, slow down buster! Remember who her father is!

"Well, miss, the Admiral asked me to escort you two ladies around the campus, to help you understand what your life would be like should you decide to come here next year."

Tracy broke her death-grip on Corrine's arm and looked at her friend.

Ignite me, indeed! Corrine thought. "Dad! OK, so he thinks *we* need a chaperone, like I haven't been here a *dozen* times *already*! Well, okay then 'Prince Charming', lead on!" *Did I say that out loud? And am I really hearing what he's thinking, or has Tracy got my head all turned around again? Still, he IS VERY tall, taller than Jack. And handsome. Like Daddy, only better...*

"Please, call me Mike. Now, ladies, this way please!" Mike held his arm out to Corrine. The touch of her hand sent a small shiver through him. *Oh, my. She is something special. Something very, very special!*

Corrine smiled as she took his arm. *Special. He thinks I'm special! And gorgeous! His arm is so hard. Like steel. I wonder if...*

Tracy stared at the two walking away from her. The pretty blonde called out, "Hey, what am I, chopped...oh, never mind!" As she caught up to them, she saw Corrine blushing heavily. *Well, well, maybe my friend the Ice Princess is melting! That's one show I just have to see!*

***

"She's doing *WHAT?!*"

"Relax, Sandy. I've checked him out; he's a good cadet, solid grades, and good character. Plus, he knows my rank, and Tracy and I will be there. They'll be fine!"

"Well, you'd better hope so, mister, or you'll have a lot of explaining to do!" *Should I tell him? That I can feel this boy's thoughts, just like I feel his? No, can't let him in on that just yet.*

"Yes dear." Jock grinned. "He'll be here soon, so I'll let you go now."

"Good-bye, darling." *He's almost as nervous as she will be right now.* Sandy thought as she cut the comm link.

Corrine and Tracy had begged to come and see the academy when Jock went this year. *I think it was more Tracy's idea than Corrine's.* Jock thought.

"DING-ding".

"Corry, are you ready? He's here!" Jock shouted through the half-open door to the girl's suite.

"Just a minute, Dad! Let him in, please."

"It's just dinner in the hotel restaurant downstairs. Why are she and Sandy making such a big deal about this? What is taking her so long?" Jock muttered as he checked his tie. "Like Sandy on our first date, we almost missed the movie she took so long getting ready...Oh!"

When Jock opened the door, he was a little surprised to find Marine Cadet Halsey in his Dress Blue-Whites. The young man snapped to attention, a crisp salute held awaiting Jock's reply.

"At ease, cadet. For the entire evening, please!" Jock replied as he returned the salute. "Come in. The ladies are almost ready. I hope."

"Thank you, Sir!" The tall cadet walked into the suite as Jock closed the door.

"Have a seat, Mr. Halsey. It could be a long campaign."

"Thank you, um, yes, Sir."

"So, I take it you had a nice time with the ladies this afternoon? My daughter insisted that you join us for dinner. That is highly irregular."

"Your daughter is a highly unusual girl, eh, lady, Sir. Unique, er, different, um...Special! Sir." *Sure, Cadet, ram that foot just a little further down your own throat.*

"Relax, cadet. Tell me a little about yourself, son." Jock leaned back, hoping to relax the young man a bit.

"Well, Sir, my family has served in the military for over 1500 years. I grew up on the USF Naval Starbase at Salt Lake City. It just seemed natural to go to the Academy."

"I can understand that, cadet. Now, about Corrine..."

"Oh, Sir! I have only the best intentions..."

"Relax. That's an order. You wouldn't be here if I didn't believe that, or if Corrine didn't believe that. Do you know this is her first date?"

"Sir? But, she's coming to the academy next year, Sir. I don't understand. She's never dated?"

"I never understood it either, son. Her mother seems to, or so she claims. Corrine always said it would be a waste of time, and cruel to the boy she went on a date with. She has me miffed. Oh, well, you're here, so you must have made quite an impression."

"Mr. MacAlister?" Tracy's voice sang from the door.

"Tracy, are you two ready?"

"Yes, Sir." Tracy said as she opened the door all the way and walked into the room. She looked stunning in a simple green dress with a pearl necklace, white handbag and matching shoes. Jock caught a hint of perfume.

"Tracy, you've met Mr. Halsey. You look lovely, dear."

"Thank you, Mr. Mac." She smiled her response.

"A-hem!"

The three turned to the doorway at the cough. Jock's mouth hung open. He had never seen his daughter like this before. Oh, she'd gone to proms and dances, with Tracy or stag when Tracy had a date, but Jock had never seen his little girl as... as a woman. A very stunning woman. *Sandy, at our Senior Prom.*

Her long blonde hair flowed freely to just above her hips, yet was pulled back from her face. She wore just the slightest hint of lipstick and eye shadow; the blush on her cheeks was natural, as it intensified just a bit when she looked at Mike. Her dress was a stunning bare-shouldered pink and silver, cut close to her waist and loosely around her hips.

"I think I may be underdressed!" Jock broke the tension.

"Don't be silly, Father. You look fine." Corrine said, as her gaze

124

remained fixed on Michael.

"Where did you two get these outfits? Don't tell me you packed them?" Jock whispered to Tracy.

"Really, Mr. Mac. A girl must *always* be prepared!" Tracy whispered back.

"Okay, people. Let's go. We do have reservations! Mademoiselle, s'il vous plait?" Jock said as he offered his arm to Tracy. He smiled as Mike followed his lead with Corry. *I don't know why, but I like that kid. Maybe that's just because she likes him. Good enough!*

***

Mars L-2
USF Dreadnought
Flag Bridge
Standard Earth Date December 3, 3478

Rear Admiral Jock MacAlister surveyed the people at the virtual meeting. Each ship's Captain was logged in, along with those present in the room; the four Commodores, Rear Admirals Musa and himself, and Fleet Admiral Bucktooth. He felt confident in this group, and in the fleet they had equipped and assembled.

"Gentlemen, Ladies, at ease. This meeting is to review and confirm our training operational plan before we put it into effect tomorrow at 0600 hours, SST. Admiral Musa, will you please review Operation Black Smith."

"Thank you, Admiral Bucktooth. This fleet is presently comprised of one hundred and thirty eight ships; sixty-two light cruisers, thirty heavy cruisers, sixteen battlecruisers and twenty battleships. We will deploy the fleet into battle formation as illustrated here..." The Admiral indicated the viscreen where a diagram showed the ships arranged in roughly a disk shape.

"Each battleship will have one heavy and two light cruisers as escort. They will comprise Task Force Anvil.

Ten of the battlecruisers will be escorted by one heavy cruiser and one light cruiser each; this will form a Task Force Hammer.

The remaining ships, six stealth battlecruisers each escorted by two stealth light cruisers, will form our reserve force, task Force Nail.

Anvil will form a disk deployment at the Earth side of the

formation, with the Hammer ahead and to the center. The reserve squadron, Nail, will support Hammer as needed.

"The plan is to set Anvil in the path of the Bugs, to cross their 'T', and use Hammer to pound anything still moving after crossing the Turret line into the Anvil. Any questions?"

"Sir, what if the Bugs try to move around the Anvil?" Captain Rhodes of the heavy cruiser USF Nili Patera asked. *She knows the answer,* Jock thought, *but she also knows others here don't! Smart officer! No wonder her ratings are so high.*

"Rear Admiral MacAlister will explain. Admiral?" Admiral Bucktooth selected Jock to answer due to his role in hacking into the alien computer system.

"Thank you Admiral. The Bug computer system contained a wealth of information on the Bug society and military; these are essentially one and the same. The Bugs are like a hornet nest; they seem to blindly attack, without strategy or planning. Their only method of attack is to enter a system at roughly one-half light speed, and to rapidly decelerate only when near the target planet. This target planet is always the most heavily populated world in the system; they ignore outposts, stations, and bases in the initial wave. The tactics outlined in their computer system indicated…" Jock swallowed hard, "just over twelve thousand Invader class ships in an average attack. The colonizing vessels follow only after confirmation of victory.

"They have little maneuverability when entering a system. Their ships just don't have it built into them, and their attack plans preclude it."

"What are their ships like, Admiral?" The viscreen indicated Commander Kesa MacAlister, Commanding Officer of the heavy cruiser USF Bear Mountain Bridge had asked that question. *Again, she knows the answer; she's just making sure the rest of the team does too. I'm glad I couldn't talk her out of this command. I was wrong and selfish trying to keep her in R&D. God, what a team we have here!*

"The Bugs attack ships are oval in shape and are roughly a kilometer long. The structure is similar to that of the bugs themselves. Their ships are thick-skinned and hollow, entirely one monocoque structure. One large room inside the twenty-meter thick outer hull. Penetrate the hull, and every Bug on the ship dies. They carry two main weapons on each ship; a dense projectile carried external to the hull, as we see on the viscreen here, and a powerful beam-type weapon mounted near the midships region. They have a blind spot in front of and behind their ships, as well as to the side opposite the beam projector. Next question?"

"How will they attack, Sir? What tactics do they use?" Captain Charlie Walker of the battleship USF South Carolina asked.

"Their attack tactics are simple, enter the targeted system at half of light speed and in tight formation, release the projectiles before decelerating hard. The projectiles clear a path to the targeted planet, taking out any mines or missiles along the way; then they impact the planet, in most cases destroying it. They then use their beams to mop up.

"We will use their plan to our advantage. We have seeded the predicted paths with millions of tons of sand and fine asteroid ore tailings, a passive micro-minefield that is dependent upon the Bugs high velocity attack profile to be effective. Further in-system, our ADS systems, or Turrets, have been reactivated, updated, enhanced and expanded. The Turrets are much further out from Earth, the target, than the Bugs plan on being when they release their projectiles. They are now armed with Super High Velocity Railguns, plasma lasers, extended range gravitic grapples, Shrike nuclear missiles, and GravTorps. But the Turrets biggest assets are their new reactors; the Gravitic Nuclear Opposition Reactors on our Turrets have twelve thousand times the power output of a Bug Invader ship. The Turret lasers carry fifty times the energy of the Bug beams, and the average Turret has forty-four installed. The twenty gravitic clamps in each Turret complex have enough power to divert the Bug ships as they pass, forcing a premature deceleration. They also have enough range to overlap with the next closest Turret. So do the lasers.

"The plan is for the Turrets to launch their Shrikes and GravTorps to wait in the Bug's path, while attacking with multiple SHVR rounds. The railgun rounds will be a grapeshot derivative; each round consisting of ninety-six one-kilogram lead balls designed to spread out and create a large kill area;" *as long as they get past the projectiles,* Jock thought, "between the five Turrets covering the projected path, the SHVRs will kill any Bug ship within a twenty thousand kilometer area. The Shaver rounds will arrive first, followed by the Shrikes, then the GravTorps. Then we grab any ships that are left by the gonads, using the G-clamps, and hold them as the lasers cut them up.

"Anything that makes it past the Turrets is ours. Our battleships and battlecruisers carry the same lasers the Turrets do; the heavy and light cruisers lasers are one half and one third the power of the battleships respectively; still much more powerful than the Bug beams. Our ships will also be firing Shrikes, GravTorps and Shavers. Tens of thousands of them. We will meet them with the Hammer just inside the Turret line; the object is to drive them into the Anvil.

"Anything that makes it past us has to deal with Admiral Seymour's Beta Fleet; three hundred and ninety eight heavy cruisers.

"We have the tools. We need to learn how to fight them. These exercises are designed to teach us how to maneuver our ships in formation at FTL relative speeds; how to pursue and overtake the Bug ships, to destroy them before they destroy Earth."

Jock sat down. He thought about a lot as a few others asked peripheral questions. *It is a good plan. A very good plan. It's the best we can do. I have no doubt of that. Is it good enough? We do have the tools, if we can learn to fight them.*

***

Chrysler Building
55th Floor
New York City
Standard Earth Date December 3, 3478

The tall slender woman leaned back in the oversized leather chair and stared out at the Manhattan skyline below. Her dark brown hair almost hinted an auburn tint in the sunlight. She turned back to her desk and picked up a datatab. She opened the file 'JOURNAL' and began talking, the words appearing on the screen as she spoke.

"I have seldom left this room during the past fifteen months." Her pretty face frowned, and a single tear tried to form in her eye. "How different 'life at the top' really is from what I used to dream of. I'd planned to do so much good once I got here, and to enjoy it. How did I come to be... this? People have been destroyed, people have... died. So I could move on. And up. How had I changed so much? When? Now..."

"Bong-bong-bong!"

The comm signal snatched her attention as swiftly as it evaporated her tears.

"Go!" Her hard, cold voice commanded.

"We have the Bug computer database. It's being analyzed as we speak. Preliminary examination shows that we should have many useful items we can patent. And much useful information on your *other* line of inquiry."

"Good. Your payment will be deposited today. Your bonus will be paid when I have something I can use. Dismissed." She abruptly cut the comm link.

Something I can use.

"Chaos and unrest brought me to this position," she told the datatab, "and they will take me where I have to go."

***

First Marine Logistics Training Unit
Near Mars Orbit
LCPA-44
Standard Earth Date December 3, 3478

"Close up, Halsey! You're drifting out again!" Marine Captain Tony Constantine's voice blared in Michael's ears. *Dammit! Why does it drift like that?*

"Aye-aye, Sir! She seems to drift a little."

"They all do, Halsey. Slight variations in thrust alignment, load distribution, local gravimetric variations, and a billion other anomalies. Compensate. Pay attention!"

"Aye-aye, Sir."

The collection of eighteen blunt-nosed, boxy landing craft seemed to shimmer as the cadet pilots struggled to keep their ships in formation with the auto dampers off. The exercise was a little advanced for this point in their training, and Tony hoped it wouldn't kill anyone; space didn't give you a lot of second chances.

The unit was out there to support the Fleet's combined maneuver exercises. The first FTL maneuvers by large numbers of ships ever. There just weren't enough dedicated SARAs, or Search And Rescue, Armored ships built yet. *These kids could do a search & rescue if they had to; they are all good pilots. Might as well get in some formation training while we're waiting out here!*

"Williams! Stay on line!" Tony snapped out. *I'll have to watch them closely this trip, or they may not come back.*

USF Dreadnought
Flag Bridge
Standard Earth Date December 3, 3478

"Target away, Admiral. Velocity zero-point-five light speed."
Lieutenant Alvarez announced.

"Countdown until Target is in position." Jock directed.

"One minute, Admiral."

"Give us a five-second countdown over Fleet Comm, Lieutenant."

"Aye-aye, Sir."

"Open Fleet Comm please."

"Fleet Comm open, Admiral." Ensign Jason Bennings confirmed
from the comm station.

"Rear Admiral MacAlister to Hammer; Target is away. We will
execute maneuver "Hammer Strike" as the Target passes. Look sharp
people, focus, and trust your training."

"Five. Four." Bennings' voice cracked just a bit, "Three. Two."
Bennings' voice finished solid and strong, "One! Target passing!"

"Execute Hammer Strike!" Jock calmly ordered.

The ten battlecruisers each with their two cruiser escorts engaged
their FTL drives at the same instant, closing the gap with the Target
asteroid within a few seconds. Task Force Hammer spread out into the
attack formation designed to give maximum firepower exposure to a
Bug fleet.

Everything moved in synchronized orchestration as the Target
approached the Anvil.

"Rear Admiral MacAlister to Hammer; prepare to disengage.
Execute Turn Alpha."

Ten giant battlecruisers and the twenty escorting cruisers turned
ninety degrees port and accelerated away from Task Force Anvil's
position. *It looks good*, Jock thought.

Then the heavy cruiser Nili Patera drifted slightly sunward as
alarms rang out on the Fleet Comm. The drift increased as the ship
began a wobble. She moved further off course at tremendous velocity
until she struck the South Carolina. The impact broke the Nili apart and
caused the massive South Carolina to collide with her escort, the heavy
cruiser Bear Mountain Bridge. The cruiser broke into three large pieces
at the impact, each drifting in a different direction.

A hollow feeling grew in Jock as the ships collided. He feared a snowball that could involve most of the fleet. But their training had been solid; commanders and crews responded instantly with appropriate maneuvers to keep the collision localized. No more ships were damaged, but the formation ended up spread over an immense area of space.

"Damage report from the South Carolina, Sir!" Bennings' voice cracked his announcement. Jock listened to the bad news as he looked at the Dreadnought's Captain, sitting ashen-faced next to him. Charlie Walker had trained an excellent crew; his ship would survive, and he already had boats launching to look for survivors. Jock was more worried about his flagships' CO right now.

"Charlie, are you OK?" Jock asked quietly on his private comm link.

"Gridley, report!" He snapped.

"Yes, Admiral. I'm fine. Sorry, Sir."

"Charlie, she could be all right. She could be dead." Jock whispered. "You and I will talk about this later. For now, box it and concentrate; your crew needs you here."

"Aye-aye, Jock. Thanks." Chuck Gridley replied over the private command link. His voice rang out over the ship's comm; "Damage report! Talk to me people!"

The bridge crew that had been briefly stunned by the collisions now moved with a new focus.

Jock began skimming the reports streaming onto his datatab.

***

First Marine Logistics Training Unit
Far Mars Orbit
LCPA-38
Standard Earth Date December 3, 3478

"Attention! This is not a drill! Repeat, this is not a drill!" Captain Constantine's voice clamored like an alarm over the comms of the eighteen landing craft. "Emergency verifications now people!" Tony watched as eighteen green lights flashed on his Commander's Heads Up Display. *Damn, that was fast.*

"We have multiple collisions with breeched hulls in the immediate proximity. We are to proceed on SARs duty to the following coordinates. This looks bad, people. Trust your training, and stay focused, don't rush things. Use formation Delta from our briefings. Thrust levels ninety. Go!"

***

USF South Carolina
Flag Bridge
Standard Earth Date December 3, 3478

Charlie Walker blinked. Then he blinked again. His eyes wouldn't clear. He was looking through a red blanket whenever he opened them. *That must have been some party last night, judging from this hangover,* he thought. *What was it for, anyway? His promotion? Yeah, that had to be it! Promotion to Captain, flagship Captain! What's that racket? It sounds so far away…*

Charlie tried to sit up, and found he couldn't move. Something was covering him, something heavy and hard. And cold. He reached up to touch it…

"Don't move, Captain. Help is coming, just hold on, and for God's sake don't move!"

I know that voice. Ensign Derek something. Why is he giving orders?

"Ensign, report!" Charlie managed to get out.

"Sir, the Nili Patera collided with us. We collided with the Bear Mountain Bridge. Damage to the SoCar is moderate sir; the bridge took the worst of it. Captain, Admiral Musa is dead, sir. So is most of the bridge staff." Charlie heard the Ensign gulp. "We are cut off from the rest of the ship for now, Sir. Damage Control parties are on their way. Captain, I'm not a doctor, Sir, but I think it's important that you don't try to move, Sir. You've lost a lot of blood, and you've got a structural beam pinning you down."

"My eyes, Ensign, I can't…"

"Here Sir" Ensign Derek Thorpe found a piece of cloth and wiped the blood from Captain's eyes. "Try it now, Sir."

Captain Walker, moving just his eyes, he looked around at the wreckage of his bridge. The first thing he could focus on was the Nav Station; random sparks flashed at irregular intervals around the pile of debris there. He could see a leg and a bloody arm sticking out, the new diamond that Lieutenant Osborne had proudly displayed that morning,

132

shining on a pale bloodless finger. Charlie snapped his eyes shut at the thought; it was the only way to keep the bile down.

He felt it all spinning. "Ensign, are, is the ship stable?"

"We are dead in space, Sir. The Rescue Teams are almost here, skipper. Stay with me Sir!" Despite Thorpe's pleas, Charlie felt everything spinning away from him, growing dimmer and dimmer in the distance...

***

West Lake Road
Skaneateles, NY
Standard Earth Date December 3 3478

The empty feeling washed over her so fast she almost fell.
Jock!
Sandy ran for the comm station.
"Ding-DING-DING!"
"Corry, what is it!" Sandy was breathless from running and...
"Mom, it's Michael." Corrine sobbed through the link.
"Calm down, honey. Tell me what you feel." *Oh, God, please! This family has suffered enough!*
"He's OK, mom, but he's...he's looking for...Kesa. Mom, something's happened to Kesa!"
Sandy sat down with a thud on the sofa. Her world started to spin. *Jock!* She refused to let herself go there. She started to put up her stonewall again, the one she had used to imprison her pain when she had felt Jock meet Sharon. But she couldn't use that now. Her *babies* needed her!
"It's okay, baby. Tell me more."

***

LCPA-44
Standard Earth Date December 4, 3478

There has to be something out here! Halsey thought as he squinted at

133

the sensors. *My eyes hurt; my lips are dry…What time is it? Only thirty hours. Slow down a little, don't miss it…*

"HALSEY!" His comm snapped his mind around.

"Here, Captain!" Mike thought his voice sounded much better than he felt.

"Halsey, you sound like shit, and your vitals are off specs, too. You need to head in, son." Captain Constantine's voice sounded reasonable and soft to Mike. That worried him a bit.

"I'm fine, Captain. I have another ten hours of fuel, air and water, Sir. I need to use them." *I'd never be able to live with myself for quitting.*

"Eight hours, Mike. Then you come in. That's an order." *Every damn one of these kids, the same friggin' story. Damn, I'm proud of them!*

***

USF Nili Patera
Wreckage
Standard Earth Date December 4, 3478

Rhonda Rhodes looked at the three survivors of her first command bridge. Ensign Fran Thomas would be OK, if he got to a hospital soon. At least they had stopped the bleeding from the stump of his leg. Lieutenant Randy Chalk had a bad head wound and unknown internal injuries. He likely would not live much longer. Ensign Tamera Epps was in pretty good physical shape, but now that they had done everything they could, she looked emotionally fragile to Rhonda.

I hope no one was hurt on the South Carolina. Damn lousy time for a Gravitic Drive Control Unit to fail. Should I have run more tests, drills? We ran twenty percent more than regs called for. I was happy with the ship, so was Ed. He was one damn hard to satisfy engineer, too.

She was used to the spinning now; it wasn't all that fast a spin, anyway. And there was no way to stop it.

Rhonda looked around again, and did some quick math in her head. *Maybe an hour of air left. Maybe. It's already so cold in here. What is that light?…*

***

LCPA-44
Standard Earth Date December 4, 3478

"OK, Halsey. Fifteen more minutes. But, that's it; you go in with me. Clear?"

"Clear, Cap. Hey, what's that?" Mike's adrenalin surged him awake as he centered his sensors on a faint glint of light…

THERE!

"Captain, this is LCPA-44. I have a large contact, Sir! Looks like about a quarter of a heavy cruiser. She's got some power…moving in now."

"Halsey, don't ram the damn thing. ST, did you get the coordinates?"

"Roger, Captain C. We have coordinates. ETA twelve minutes."

"I'll be here, Tugs." Mike sat back in his chair as he set his LCPA on station keeping. *Someone is alive in that wreck!* He went over the exterior of the ship and came upon part of a name; "USF Bear Mou". *I've found her! She must be in there! For Corry's sake, please Lord, let her be in there!*

***

West Lake Road
Skaneateles, NY
Standard Earth Date December 5 3478

Sandy snatched on the comm almost before it rang. "Yes?"

"Mom, Mike's found a big piece of Kesa's ship. She could be there! I had to tell you!"

"Thank you, baby. I'll call Jack."

USF Dreadnought
Admiral's Quarters
Standard Earth Date December 6, 3478

"That's the last report, Admiral." Jock sat back in his chair, looking through the image of Jeri Bucktooth on his viscreen. No more reports, no more orders, no more coordination to be done. Just the healing now. Contacting the nine hundred and forty families to tell each of them that their children were not coming home.

But first he had to talk to Chuck Gridley. He had taken it hard. When Rhonda was found so badly hurt, it seemed to deflate him. He needed to have Chuck back, to keep things together while he went to see Jack.

He had to see Jack. But he had to put those nine-forty ahead of his own. And, he needed Gridley back before he could take care of them.

"DING-ding" Jock's door chimed.

"Come."

The door opened and Admiral Bucktooth walked in. He strode right up to Jock's desk and stopped; Jock knew that this stride, this look his friend and mentor wore now meant, 'Just do what I tell you. No argument. No discussion.' Jock's exhausted eyes looked up.

"Go see your son. That is a direct order. Period." Jericho raised his right arm and pointed to the door, to the tired marine cadet pilot standing there.

Jock stood up, slanted his head to one side. His mouth opened, but the logical protests he had halfheartedly formed evaporated before he could give them any voice. Instead the hoarse whisper came out quietly: "Thanks".

Michael Halsey watched the two Admirals look at each other for a few more seconds. Jock walked over to him and simply said, "Let's go, Cadet!"

***

Chrysler Building
55th Floor
New York City
Standard Earth Date December 6, 3478

"We have what we need to begin. Do you approve of the campaign?"

The brown haired lady stared out the windows until the messenger almost repeated himself. Just before his words came out, she turned and spoke.

"We will begin the campaign in four days. There will be news soon that will help us if we time this correctly. Go. Now." She turned back to the windows as the messenger left.

***

Mars L-2
J. Wadsworth R & D Station
Commander's Quarters
Standard Earth Date December 6, 3478

The two men stared at each other for a moment before they embraced. Mike Halsey stood nervously nearby, wondering if he should stay or wait in the hall. Finally Jock stepped back and called to Mike over his shoulder, "Come in, sit down. If you're going to be part of this family, start now."

What does he mean, 'part of this family'? I haven't even told Corry I was thinking about that! Mike thought as he sat down on the far side of the room.

"Over here, Marine!" Jack half-laughed his insistence as he indicated a chair near the desk.

Jock sat down near Mike's new chair as Jack poured the Glenfiddich.

"You've seen the tattoo. Do you know what it means?" Jack asked as he handed Mike the whiskey glass.

"Fortiter means, 'To Go Boldly Forward', Sir. The tattoo is the Crest of the Highland Clan MacAlister. " Mike replied, looking at the whiskey as if he had never seen the like of it before. "When I asked Corrine about it, she wouldn't speak to me until I had proven to her that I could explain it."

"Well, that's her mother in her. And cut the "Sir" in here. This is family time, Mike."

"Yes, sir, eh…"

"Heh!" Jack smirked. "You look like I felt the month before I asked Kesa to marry me." Jack was almost having fun now.

"You'd never looked as nervous, as you did that week!" Jock's tone softened as he continued, "How is she?"

"They tell me she'll be OK. She's mostly shook up about losing her ship. I'm leaving tomorrow to see her."

"Jack, how are *you* doing?" Jock continued to the real reason he was here.

"Dad, I was pretty shaky. But what you went through, and what we talked about, helped keep me grounded. Knowing you *can* get through something helps a lot. Mike, do you know the story, the *real* story behind the tattoo, the flowers, and my birth mother?"

"I, uh, the flowers, the girl you were engaged to, Admir, er, Mister MacAlister, was killed. Corry explained that to me. The rest, no, sir."

Jack poured another round as Jock told the story. When he finished, Mike sat back and asked the question burning his gut.

"Why did you need to tell me this?"

"Because you're almost ready to join my family." Jock's larger than life presence filled the room, "Before you commit to that, you needed to know everything about us. My wife and my daughter will fill you in on the rest of it. You will be spending the holiday break with us, am I correct?"

"Yes, sir."

"Good. You will talk with my wife then. Mike, welcome, should that be your choice. We think very highly of you."

"Thank you sir." *Man! Talk about pressure!*

"Now, gentlemen," Jock raised his glass seriously: "To those who died so Earth may live!"

The three glasses clanged and the men downed the Scotch.

Jack poured another round, and raised his glass.

"To Admiral Musa: we miss him greatly, as we are blessed to have known him."

"To Admiral Musa!"

Again Jack poured. Again Jock raised his glass.

"To Rhonda: Thank You Lord, for allowing her to stay with us a little longer!"

"To Rhonda!"

Jack poured again, and Jock raised his glass again.

"To Charlie: Thank You Lord, for allowing him to stay with us a little longer!"

"To Charlie!"

As Jack poured the last of the bottle, he stood and raised his glass a little higher.

"To my wife, Kesa, and my child: Thank You Lord, for allowing them to stay with us a little longer!"

"To Kes..." Mike's voice stopped. Jock looked wide-eyed at Jack. A few seconds passed until Jock's lips slowly curled up into a fierce grin. He raised his glass to his son's.

"To Kesa and child!" The three men toasted.

Chapter Six

United News Network
Times Square Studios
Standard Earth Date December 10, 3478

"Tonight, in our sights is the leaked analysis of the Bug society; what it means for Earth's future, and what we should do about it.

"Hello, every one, I'm Donald Derringer. Welcome to Straight Shot!

"With me tonight to discuss the anonymous leaking of the Bug's plans for Earth is Professor Wendell Urth of the Universal Guaranteed Liberties Institution, on my left, and Major Roger Heeley, from the Earth Life First Society. Welcome to you both.

"Major news today is the release of the analysis of Bugs plans for the destruction of Earth. Just in case you've been living under a rock these last thirty-five years, the USF captured an alien space ship crewed by creatures that have come to be known as 'Bugs'. Since then, half of our economy has been directed into building up defenses to defeat the Bugs and save the Earth. Yesterday, the classified analysis of the computer system on that alien ship was released, just days after a tragic training accident which killed almost a thousand of our brave star sailors.

"This analysis seems to show that the Bugs intend to wipe out Earth completely. They see us as a threat, and are moving to exterminate that threat. Your reaction, Professor?"

"Thank you, Don. Obviously, the Bugs think we are a threat. If we show them we are not, then of course they will leave us alone. We should be disarming instead of..."

"Are you INSANE? The Bugs kill EVERY civilization they encounter! It's all in the ANALYSIS! READ IT! They MUST be EXTERMINATED!"

"Now, Roger, please don't interrupt again, or I will mute your feed. Professor, you say, what?"

"Thank you, Don. The Bugs are intelligent, so they must want what we want. To be left alone in peace. It was likely our first nuclear explosions that drew them here to investigate us. If we had welcomed them with flowers instead of lasers, perhaps we could have a peaceful trading partner instead of an invading horde!

140

"But, thankfully there is still time! If only we would scrap all of our weapons, our young men and women need not die in training accidents brought on by the corrupt leaders of this Military Indus…"

"YOU ARE NUTS! Here is an alien that has done NOTHING but kill, and you want to bare Earth's throat to them? Don't you get it? Once they slap us, there will be no 'other cheek' to turn! I say, kill them ALL before they kill ALL of US!"

"That's all the time we have for this segment. Thank you both for coming into our sights! When we come back, can the Planned Extinction of an intelligent alien species be a GOOD thing?"

***

Chrysler Building
55th Floor
New York City
Standard Earth Date June 1, 3479

"The latest public opinion polls are in. Our efforts have had the desired effect. 68% now feel that extinction of the Bugs is our only option."

The brown haired woman turned her aging head slightly towards the viscreen. "We need more. Keep the pressure up until they attack, then we add revenge into the formula. Dismissed." She cut the comm link and turned back to the windows.

"So, now I've sunk into speciecide. The Great Exterminator."

She thought back to happier times of her youth.

"I was going to cure disease. End hunger. Eliminate poverty, crime, hate…it was all so important, it hadn't mattered how I got here, what I had to do."

She took in a big breath and let it out slowly.

"Could it be that the only thing that matters is how you get there?"

She lifted her glass and gulped down a large swallow of fifteen-year-old Knappogue Castle.

Yeah, maybe how you get there is all that matters in the end.

United Space Force Academy
United Space Force Academy Hilton
Cape Canaveral, Florida
Standard Earth Date June 20 3479

Jock MacAlister looked around the hotel suite. Next year it would be quiet. *I don't know if that's good or not.*

This year he had a real crowd; Alistair, Alexander, and Allison. The triplets had been a handful almost from the moment of conception, and that did not lessen with time.

The three may have a tough time when Fleet splits them up.

"Dad, after Mike graduates tomorrow, can we go out with him and Corry?" Allison batted her lashes at her father from the doorway to her room. "Please?"

"No. The night is for the graduates and their dates." *And Sharon.* "You three are stuck back here."

"Do we get a dreamy escort, like Corry did?"

"Allison! You need a cold shower, girl! Besides, do you think your brothers would let anyone near you?"

"Oh, Daddy!" *I know exactly how to distract those two!*

"Ding-DING-ding" Jock shook his head as he walked to the door. "Michael! Where's Corrine?"

"Sir, I came alone to see *you*, Sir." Michael swallowed hard as he stood at attention. *I finally got it! The reason they teach you attention is to give you a familiar posture when you're nervous as hell.*

"Come on in, Son." Jock turned to hide his smile from Mike. As he walked past the door to Allison's room, he gently pushed her head into her room and closed the door. *Tomorrow night. He wants to know the spot.*

Jock motioned to one of the chairs next to the small desk. "Have a seat."

Michael sat down and brushed his pants, then looked around the room as if searching for a possible escape route. Jock looked at him until Michael's eyes finally met his. After a few seconds, Mike's mouth opened. Jock spoke before Michael could get a word out.

"It's fifty yards due west of Star's The Limit Body Art."

Mike stared at the father sitting in front of him. He swallowed hard, and then it sunk in. *The spot he asked Sharon!*

"Mike, this will be the plan. I will take Corrine on a tour. We'll eat at Mama Rooney's and talk about your assignment. After dinner, you'll go to the chapel, and I'll take Corrine to the Star's The Limit. We'll go inside, where I'll show her the tattoo. They keep a running tab on how many they've done. When we come out, I'll lead her to the spot, you'll be there. I'll take the Triple A's with me. You have forty minutes to ask her and get back to the chapel."

Mike just stared for several moments. "Sir, that won't work. She'll know. Don't ask me how, but it's like she can read my mind..."

"Ha-ha ha! Oh, son, are you in trouble! Okay, don't come to dinner. I'll make some excuse blaming Marine traditions. You have to concentrate, hard, on some technical manual. Over and over. Meet us outside the tattoo shop per the plan, alright?"

Michael stood, smiled and saluted.

"Aye-aye, Admiral!"

Jock heard a creak and a giggle.

"Allison, close that damn door!"

***

Mama Rooney's Bar And Grill
Cape Canaveral, Florida
Standard Earth Date June 21 3479

"Admiral! I have your table here! Follow me, please. A large group this year!"

"Yes, Wanda. You look as beautiful as ever!" Jock gave the lady a kiss on her forehead. "When are you going to retire, Wanda?"

"I retired years ago, Admiral. I only work one night each year, when a certain hansom, romantic, big tipper comes in." Wanda continued in a quiet voice, "I loved the Four Musketeers too, you know!" She turned and followed her cane to a large table. When she motioned for them to sit, Jock leaned in close to her.

"Wanda, would you be kind enough to change to a sporting channel please? I can't eat with another "kill the Bugs" talk show on."

The lady smiled and said, "Anything for you, Mr. Mac."

Jock set his bouquet of flowers down and motioned to the triplets to sit on one side of the table while he escorted Corrine to sit next to him. Alistair held the chair for Allison while Alexander held Corrine's chair.

"OK, now let's eat!" Jock declared as food started arriving.

"Dad, we didn't order yet!" Alex protested.

"They bring the same food every year, squirt." Corrine said darkly.

"Are you all right, sweetheart?"

"Daddy, he should be here!" Corry managed to both whine and pout.

"I'm sure he'll find a way to join us as soon as he can, Corry." Allison tried to comfort her big sister.

After dinner, the five walked to the tattoo parlor and stood outside. Jock began to explain the tattoo on his right shoulder that he got here, but Allison interrupted.

"Dad, can we get the tattoo now?"

"Not at this place, pumpkin, not until you graduate. It's the only tattoo they'll do on *this* night, and they won't do it unless you've graduated or..."

"Then why is Corrine inside?"

Jock turned and saw his middle child sitting on the chair as the robot needle drew the pattern on her right shoulder. It took seven minutes before Corrine's tattoo was done. She stood up and pulled out her credits, but the shop owner pointed to Jock, and refused to take her money. Corrine became quite animated, but the owner held fast. A few other graduates had formed a line to wait their turn, and they urged Corrine to end her display. Finally, she walked out.

"Corrine!" Jock snapped.

"Dad, you never told me it would hurt that much!" Corry pouted.

"Hey, how come you got the tattoo? Dad said you could only get it when you graduate!" Alistair whined.

"If you had let me finish; if you graduate or if you are engaged to a graduate. You're...not...en...gaged!" Jock said. *Yet! Oh crap, she played us! She knew!*

"Excuse me, ma'am."

"Michael!" Corrine gasped as she ran to him and jumped into his arms.

"Alex, Alistair, Allie, come with me. Now." The image of the Triple A's as toddlers, Allie riding Jock's shoulders, hands on his forehead, and a boy on each arm flashed through Jock's mind as he led his three youngest away towards the chapel. *Even though she knew, she's still having an unforgettable experience tonight. How do I top this for the next three?*

144

West Lake Road
Skaneateles, NY
Standard Earth Date July 4 3480

"Really, Ron, you can't be serious!" Sandy sat in her living room across the coffee table from Ronald Sims. She set her tea down and leaned back. "Why me?"

"Sandy, you are the smartest person I know, and you have a great moral foundation. You stick to your principles no matter what. The people need you in office, Sandy." Ron took a sip of his coffee, and then continued; "Many of us are worried about this "Kill All Bugs" movement. Quite frankly, we see it as taking mankind down a dark and evil path, where we become like the Birds and the Bugs. Sandy, we need to counter this, to shine the light of morality on the evil foundations that support all hate. You are that light, Sandy."

"Ron, you're already writing the speeches! Look, the kids are gone, and it's finally quiet around here." *Too damn quiet!* "What you're asking could keep me from seeing Jock. You know that is the single most important thing in my life now."

"Mom, you know Ron's right. Everything you and Dad have taught me cries out for you to do this." Mary MacAlister said from her seat next Ron. "Since I've joined the firm, we've seen this movement grow like a cancer in every aspect of society. Mom, you can do this. Dad would want it."

"Talk it over with him, please. Consider it. Humanity needs you, Sandy MacAlister." Ron urged her again.

"I'll think about it." *Something does have to be done about this. It's pure evil to willfully exterminate an entire species without even considering if it's necessary.*

***

"Gentlemen, we are here to discuss the post invasion plans." Fleet Admiral Jericho Bucktooth announced.

"What are the plans, Jeri?" Jock asked as he looked around the room. Only the four Admirals were there: Jericho, Mark Gordon, Karen Seymour, and Jock.

"As you all know, there has been a large push of public opinion to preemptively attack the Bug's home world and annihilate them before they attack us. Countering that is a movement to completely disarm and hope the Bugs just shake our hand when they get here. Then there is a third movement towards a balanced outlook that defends the Earth while taking measured responses to any invasion.

"Our plans will include *follow up* strikes on the Bug homeworld to be executed after they invade; one plan will be to destroy the Bugs technology. The second will be to destroy everything." Admiral Bucktooth gave that a few minutes to sink in.

"Killing every Bug, do we have the right to do that?" Karen asked.

"If we do it, are we any better than they are?" Mark added.

"Isn't there a plan to try and reason with them, to negotiate their surrender? That seems to me to be the best course." Jock offered.

"I have been ordered to prepare only for the two options I've outlined. Gentlemen, Ma'am, there is no indication the government is preparing any negotiation tactic at all."

"That is the most foolish stand they could take! Jock, do you have any insight? Sandy being in the Assembly now, and all?" Karen frowned as she contemplated possible answers to her own questions.

"Just what Jeri has said, officially." Jock shook his head. "They will likely ask us to kill them all." Jock's baritone voice was often most powerful when it was quiet. It was both here.

"Jeri, how do we respond to that?" Mark asked.

"Does this situation meet the standard of Orders Demanding Immoral Action?" Karen added her apprehension to the group's tension.

"What about war is moral? That is the question we would have to

146

answer. Why is it moral to kill Bugs in our system but immoral to kill them in their system? We need to answer that before we can refuse those orders." Jock pointed out. "I don't think we have enough information to decide that here and now."

"Jock is right." Jeri sighed as he sat back. "We need to know the situation in more detail before we can decide that question."

The four of them stared silently at the same empty point in the center of the office table for a long time after that.

Eventually Mark and Karen left. Jock decided to stay on a bit.

"Jeri, what do you do if negotiations are offered by the Bugs and the orders are to destroy them?"

"I don't know, Jock. I just don't know. The more I think about it, the more I come back to my duty about following orders."

"Jeri, you're my friend. You saved my soul a few times over. I have to tell you to do the right thing."

"What the hell is the right thing any more? We serve the leaders people elect. We are a reflection of society. They need us to follow orders."

"Damn it, Jeri!" Jock stood up and walked around the office, running his right hand through his hair. "Listen to yourself. You're defining right and wrong in terms of elected officials who spin the definition to fit the moment. Right and wrong do not change with each swing of the public opinion polls. Jeri, can't you see that? What does Jericho Bucktooth think is right and wrong in this situation?"

"Jock, what are you telling me to do? Disobey orders? Stage a coup d'état? What is so right about Treason?"

"Jeri, think about right and wrong as your foundation. I'm not talking about stupid but lawful orders here. If the order is illegal, do we follow it? That is entirely different from a military coup and you know it." Jock walked over to his friend and stood over the sitting older man. *He looks tired, worn out. He's been beating himself up over this for some time.* "Jeri," Jock's tone softened considerably now, "what did *you* decide is the right thing to do?"

"Jock, I can't disobey an order from the Commander in Chief, but I can't stomach wiping out a species that wants to surrender. Even the Bugs deserve that chance."

"Jeri, in that case, it is the order that is wrong, not your decision on what to do about it. Take strength that you are grounded in a stable moral foundation." Jock reached his right hand down to his friend.

Jericho Bucktooth took Jocks hand and stood up. "Jock, you're right. That order, under that circumstance, would be wrong. I would not be able to carry it out. I would refuse on moral grounds. Publicly. Very, very publicly. Thank you my friend."

"Jeri, should that come to pass, understand that I will be standing right next to you."

***

Asteroid Defense Station 1437
CIC
Standard Earth Date March 29 3488

"PROXIMITY ALERT!"
"PROXIMITY ALERT!"
"PROXIMITY ALERT!"

The computer's alarm rang throughout the station. Within the Combat Information Center, alarm indicator lights flashed red along with the announcement, and then stayed red to indicate the threat.

"Report, Mr. Wilson. What have you got?" Commander Corrine Halsey slid into her command station.

"Three bogies at sensor edge inbound at high velocity. Course projection brings them into our fire zone in three-two minutes, Commander." Edison Wilson gave his report as concisely as he could. Commander Halsey was always on him to communicate efficiently, and drill after drill had improved his ability to do so significantly. But he still never seemed to get it good enough to satisfy her, even though she frequently praised at his efforts.

"Weapons status?"

"Forty of forty-four plasma lasers have a firing angle on the bogies course at closest pass. All report charged and ready." Lieutenant Jane Jones reported.

"Sixty of seventy-eight SHVRs have firing solutions viable for four minutes. All report loaded and charged." Lieutenant Parker Yamamoto added. Super High Velocity Railguns were known as Shavers for short.

"Three hundred GravTorp tubes loaded and standing by." Lieutenant Troy Hicks gave his report.

"Twelve hundred Shrike missiles hot in tubes, yields set to three Kilotons." Lieutenant Stewart Montgomery reported.

"Forty-four gravitic grapples ready, Commander" Elsa Armstrong added her report.

148

"Screens at nine-nine percent and now passive." Lieutenant Kevin Alvarez finished.

"ID status yet, Mr. Wilson?"

"Bogies match Target Delta drone configuration, Commander."

"Yamamoto, fire four Shavers on each target when ready. Jones, stay alert. Hicks and Monty standby."

"Aye-aye" echoed from each weapons station.

"Shavers away, Commander. Target intercept ETA twenty seconds."

"Ready another round, Yamamoto. Hold fire on it."

"Aye-aye, commander."

"Shaver impact in: Three. Two. One. Impacts. Screen clear, Commander. All bogies destroyed."

"Thank you Mr. Wilson. Computer; time from bogie detect to target destruction?"

"Elapsed time for this Class One Exercise is fifty-two seconds."

Cheers erupted throughout the CIC as the computer announced a new USF record.

"Okay, people. CIC combat staff to my ready room in five for debriefing. Good job, people. The record is now twelve seconds shorter. Don't get cocky."

"Comm, open tight channel to ADS 1284, attention, Commander Tracy Singh. The record is now fifty-two seconds. Repeat, FIVE TWO SECONDS. C. Halsey 1437." *Oh, how I wish I could add, 'Hugs and Kisses, Corry.'*

A second round of cheering broke out on the CIC as Corry stood and walked to her ready room.

She left the door open as she walked into the office and looked around. This room did it to her every time. She'd seen the upgrade plans; this one room used to be the two crew quarters. She could be standing where her brother Jack was conceived.

I can't imagine two people locked up in the small spaces this used to be. Now we've got thirty-six on a station sixty times the size, with hundreds of times the power. From here Dad captured that Bug ship. Unreal.

The commotion of the CIC staff walking in brought her mind back to the work at hand.

"At ease everyone." Corrine began. "Good job. You busted that record. You busted the hell out of it.

"Edison; concise reports. Perfect.

"Parker; good shooting. Data indicates eleven of twelve Direct On Target. What is the Fleet record at this range, Mr. Yamamoto?"

"The current Fleet record is eleven of twelve, Commander. The previous record at this range was eight of fifteen, Commander." Yamamoto stood as he reported in an emotionless voice.

"Parker, your section's performance is again outstanding. Keep it up!

"Jane; great readiness. Keep it up.

"Troy; great job. Don't let up.

"Stewart; great work, as usual.

"Elsa; great job, again.

"Kev, great job. You always squeeze a little more out of those screens.

"People, this is where I usually give you goals for your improvement. Today, I want you to give me goals for my improvement. You've shown me that you *are* the best, and as such, you deserve the best commander. Talk to me." Corrine sat down and waited. The staff looked around at each other for a few seconds. Then Edison stood up.

"Commander, we need a name. Sir."

"I don't understand, Lieutenant."

"We need a name for our Turret. 1437 just won't do. Sir." Edison sat down.

"What do you have in mind?"

"The crew picked it, Commander. We took a poll, and everyone sent in the same name. Sir."

"Well, what was the name?"

The entire group stood up and came to attention. Kevin answered his commander.

"Turret Halsey. Sir."

***

Chrysler Building
55th Floor
New York City
Standard Earth Date March 29 3488

The woman was staring out the window when the messenger's footsteps echoed across the huge room. *Forty-Four steps,* she thought. *Such a short distance, yet I am so far removed from Humanity.*

She ignored the messenger's presence for several long seconds before she looked up at him. *He will be enjoyable refreshment.*

"What do you have for me?" the words slithered like a snake over his ears.

"The, eh, the progress report. Our objectives are, um, within reach, even with the unforeseen surge from MacAlister winning the Senate seat. We have ramped up both sides, so that people are either for total disarmament or for total extermination of the Bugs. The ultimate choice does not matter, since we know the USF's analysis was correct; the Bugs will continue to attack, mindlessly following their instincts. When we defeat them, the 'Evil of Humanity' campaign will depress everything, and the ensuing chaos will allow our power to expand as planned."

Mindlessly following instinct! If this fool only knew, he'd run screaming for his mother!

"Good. Now…" She stood up, her long brown hair falling in frizzled waves to the floor. She took a creaking step towards the messenger, and reached a wrinkled hand up to caress his face, flakes of her dead skin floating in the filtered light.

"Now, I think you are terribly overdressed…"

He shivered as she ran a wrinkled finger along his jaw line. He was suddenly naked without having moved. Terrified, he stood frozen in place. *They told me she was thirty-four years old. She looks and smells three times that. What is she?*

The messenger's screams echoed and died as his footsteps had. Forty-four times.

The woman sat down, crossing her long, shapely legs. Youthful legs. She licked a small drop of blood from the left corner of her cheek as she admired her young face in the mirror. Now she buttoned her jacket and quickly straightened her skirt before she began brushing her long, silken brown hair. *It would not be proper to look unkempt when the cleaners came to remove the mummy of that messenger. This job does have its perks. Listen to yourself! Pure evil.* Part of her loved that thought…but part of her was repulsed by it…

***

Asteroid Defense Station 1437
Landing Bay Alpha
Standard Earth Date March 30 3488

Has it been over forty years? Jock looked around the strange structure. Other than the name, not much of the Turret remained as Jock remembered it. He stepped off of the LCPA and walked to meet the greeting party.

"Permission to come aboard, Sir!" Jock asked the Officer of the Deck.

"Permission granted. Welcome aboard, Admiral." Lieutenant Parker Yamamoto replied. "Admiral on the deck!"

"Admiral!" Corrine Halsey walked two steps toward her father, "Dad!" before running the last five.

"Corry! Nice to see you, pumpkin! Is my Turret ready for inspection?" Jock gave her a hug.

"Dad, no 'pumpkins' or hugs in front of my command, please!" Corrine whispered, then she said loud and clear, "And, yes, Sir!"

"Sorry, Commander! I believe you know my security escort, Captain Michael Halsey?" Jock turned to indicate Mike, but instead saw the flash of the big marine going by and lifting his wife into his arms. "Oh, eh-em! Well."

The crowd of two-dozen marines and sailors that had accumulated on the deck burst into applause as their CO blushed in her husband's arms.

Mike set her down, and stepped back with a smart salute, "Pleased to see you, too, Commander!"

"Yes, well, Hmm. Follow me, gentlemen. And Marine!" Corry returned his salute and turned to her command, "At ease!" She rolled her eyes before she turned to her father and said, "Admiral, would you care to begin your inspection now?"

"Absolutely. Oh, Tracy sends her love and a message."

"Message?"

"A weird one. Just, 'five-zero'. Any clue what it is?"

"It's a soon to be *old* record." *DAMN!*

"Which way to the mess? I'm starved. Lunch first, then inspection."

"Follow me."

After lunch and an hour in their quarters to 'freshen up', Corrine

152

brought Jock into her ready room.

"The place has changed a bit. Corry, are you sure you're okay with being stationed here?"

"Admiral, you've asked me that every month for two years. Yes, it's fine. The only thing that gets me a little-and it is just a little-is coming into this room, where you and Jack's mom…"

At that moment Mike walked out of the bedroom door, wearing only a towel and drying his hair.

"Corry, do you have a hairbrush or a comb or…" Mike froze as he spotted the Admiral.

"Ha-ha, ha, ha!" Jock started laughing. "It didn't get you *that* much! Corry, now I'm the one spooked by visions in this room!"

Corry started laughing even as her face glowed crimson. Mike just stared at the two of them, scratching his head. Then the alarms sounded.

"PROXIMITY ALERT!"

"PROXIMITY ALERT!"

"PROXIMITY ALERT!"

"Admiral, this drill my crew will run without me. I want to see how they react. Here, we can watch on this viscreen." Corrine indicated the viscreen over the conference table as she and her father sat. Mike joined them after dressing in record time.

The viscreen showed the CIC. The commander's station remained empty. Not only that, but the Commander was not in the CIC, and that was not a usual occurrence. The crew took only a half second to recognize it and rotate around. Wilson manned the command station.

"Every time we've run this drill without me at the command station, I've been standing on the CIC watching. I want to see how focused they are."

Corrine and Jock watched them run through the exercise with amazing efficiency; four inbound bogies.

"Sensors, talk." Wilson commanded.

"Four inbound bogies, configs match Mark III Target Drones, Sir." Lieutenant Thomas Kowalski had rotated into the sensor station to pull double duty with his comm assignment until the replacement comm officer arrived. She came in just as Tom finished his report.

"Shavers status, Parker?"

"Locked and ready, Sir!"

"Fire at will. Four rounds only. Laser status?"

"His commands flow easily, the crew has no problems following his orders. Good, Corrine. But four Shavers? Protocol calls for four on each target…"

"Admiral, Eddie's found something here. By checking status in the weapon-of-choice, he was able to fire about ten seconds sooner." Corrine's proud voice carried the compliment to the Admiral.

"See that you tell him that, Commander."

"Oh, I was planning on it, Sir."

Twenty seconds later the exercise ended when all four Shaver rounds destroyed the target drones.

"Computer," Corrine opened her comm to the CIC, "time from bogie detect to target destruction?"

"Elapsed time for this Class One Exercise is forty-two seconds."

"PROXIMITY ALERT!"

"BATTLESTATIONS!"

"PROXIMITY ALERT!"

"BATTLESTATIONS!"

"PROXIMITY ALERT!"

"BATTLESTATIONS!"

The CIC staff never skipped a beat as they drove right into their tasks. Corrine, Jock and Mike made it to the CIC before the computer announced the third alert.

"Admiral on the Deck!" Wilson announced as he vacated the command station just as Corrine slid into it.

"Talk to me, Wilson!" Corrine's command easy and level voice removed half of the tension from the CIC.

"We have sensor…shit! *Four thousand* contacts on predicted Bug path. Configs match Bugs, Commander" Edison's manner slipped back to pure professional mode after the momentary slip. "ETA weapons range four-point-three hours. Velocity zero-point-five light speed. Now picking up a larger group behind. It looks like another sixteen thousand ships, same config."

"Comm, get me Fleetcomm. Send 'Paul Revere'."

"Message sent, Commander"

"Admiral?"

"Fight your Turret, Commander." *What the hell happened to our picket ships? They must have been destroyed, jammed, or bypassed.*

"Aye-aye, Sir. Comm, station wide."

"Open."

"This is Commander Halsey. This is not a drill. Repeat, this is not a drill. This looks like the real deal, people. This is what you've been preparing for. You have the tools. You have the talent. You have the damn guts. Trust your training and stay focused. Turret Halsey, lets squash some Bugs!"

Jock swore he could feel the entire station shake with the "HOO-RAH!" He shot a quick glance at Mike, recognized the pride he saw there. *I'll never look at my little Corry the same way again!*

"Commander, Taclink with 1284, 1157, 1389 and 1621 online and four-by-four. Designation 1437 Command Flag unit."

"Roger, Comm. Admiral, the station to my right is now your area command link."

"Thank you Commander. Comm, open link to Fleet and ADS on Taclink."

"Open."

"This is Admiral MacAlister. You know what needs to be done. You are trained for it. You have the tools. You have the training. You have the ability. You have the drive. You have the plan. Now you have the opportunity. Trust your training, trust yourselves, trust each other. The ADS units on active Taclink are now designated Star Castle Shannon. Godspeed and good hunting."

Jock heard the roar of the ancient cheer, "HOO-RAH!" one more time. *Revving them up is the easy part. The waiting is the hard part.*

"Weapons, talk to me, Taclink numbers" Corry's voice refocused her crew.

"Three hundred forty Shavers with firing solutions. Outlyings window opens in one hour, forty minutes, center window, ours, in one hour, fifty-five." Yamamoto read his stats like an accountant.

"Fifteen hundred GravTorp tubes loaded with twenty reloads each." Troy Hicks clicked off his assignment.

"Six thousand Shrikes in silos. Ten reloads available each silo. Yields set on max at Fifteen Kilotons." Montgomery's accent calmly delivered his information.

"Two hundred Gravitic grapples ready, projected to be in range of bogies at pass-through." Elsa's voice was as calm as the rest.

"Two hundred lasers charged and ready." Jones took a deep breath after reporting.

"Defensive screens at one-zero-seven percent, now passive." Kevin Alvarez reported.

"Tactical Plan Beta for the ADS on Taclink; GravTorps and Shrikes launch round one for standby stealth mode. Shavers ready for rapid, sustained fire. Lasers keep your targeting locks. Grapples, stay alert. Screens, go active after initial Shaver fire.

"Fleet, execute Black Smith. Task Force Anvil, Task Force Hammer and Task Force Nail, execute well and keep your eyes open. Admiral

MacAlister out."

Now, we wait.

Chapter Seven

The Battle For Castle Shannon
Ort Cloud
Standard Earth Date March 30 3488

"Sensor update, Commander." Lieutenant Wilson declared.

"Talk to me, Eddie." Corrine Halsey commanded.

"The first four thousand Bug ships have begun decelerating hard. Twelve thousand objects inbound at zero-point-five light speed."

Damn it! Jock thought, *they know about the turrets, and they're attacking them. That's what I'd do, keep them busy. Crap.*

"Course projections. Give me targets, Eddie, and ETA. I need information, and I need it now."

She's damn good. Thinking way ahead. Jock thought. *She could fight this Taclink Grouping on her own.*

"Projectiles are smaller than predicted, more numerous. Target appears to be us, Commander. None are targeted at the adjacent turrets. ETA two hours."

"Commander, they're trying to keep us busy. We'll need to split our Taclink sensors; track the projectiles, as well as the main group." Jock responded. "Comm, is Fleet into Taclink yet?"

"Four-by-four, Admiral."

"Commander, your thoughts?"

"Their vanguard is targeting us. They are ignoring or are ignorant of the other Turrets. First, we hit the projectiles with the Shavers. They're small targets, but Parker can hit 'em. Second, we target their main body with the other Turret's Shavers, and all the combined GravTorps. Third, we target our Shrikes at their vanguard, the other Taclink Shrikes at their main body. Fourth, we use our lasers and grapples against their vanguard, and the rest of the Taclink weapons against their main body." Corrine let out a huge sigh at the end of that.

"Good plan, Commander." Jock took a deep breath. "We'll follow your first and fourth recommendations and target the incoming with one Shaver round per projectile. Lieutenant Yamamoto, you don't have to hit each one, but more than half would greatly enhance our odds of survival."

"We'll do better than half by a bit, Admiral. It's Tuesday, so I'm using both eyes today, Sir!"

"Our lasers will target the rest. On your toes, Lieutenant Jones."

"Fish in a barrel, Admiral." Jane replied.

"All other weapons target the main body. Commander Singh?"

"Here, Admiral" Tracy's voice cracked just a little. *I know where this is going.* She thought.

"Command of Castle Shannon Taclink is hereby transferred to you."

"Admiral," Her voice cracked until she swallowed, "Mr. Mac, I..." The image of Jock cleaning her scraped knee when she was seven years old, drying her tears, her second father, flashed before her.

"You have the judgment, the talent, the guts and the training for this, Commander Singh. You're my best choice." Jock softened his tone a touch, "I need you to do this, Tracy. It has to be this way."

"Aye-aye, Sir!" she snapped a professional response while glancing around her CIC. Every eye was on their own station, giving her a moment to be human. "Admiral, one more thing."

"Yes, Commander?"

"Fortiter, Sir." Tracy unconsciously rubbed her right shoulder as she spoke.

"Fortiter!" The voices of Commander Singh's bridge crew echoed over the comm.

"Fortiter, Tracy."

Damn you, Corry, you'd better come through this okay. And your dad and husband too, Tracy thought.

"Comm, Turret Halsey only."

"Open."

"We're target number one for the Bugs right now. They haven't targeted the other turrets, most likely because they don't know about them. Our mission is to reduce the main force so the Fleet can mop up. We will fulfill that mission.

"I'm asking a lot from each of you. Earth is asking a lot from each of you. Give 'em Hell!"

***

Task Force Nail
USF Lexington
Standard Earth Date March 30 3488

"Comm, direct link to Admiral Gordon." Commodore Rhonda Rhodes did not like what she saw unfolding. Not one iota.

"Open."

"Mark, do you see it?"

"Yeah. They're piling on 1437. Jock's there."

"Damn! Mark, let me take Task Force Nail to support him."

"I can't let you do that, Rhonda. Your twelve battlecruisers and twenty-four cruisers are the only stealth ships in the fleet, and I need them to support Hammer even more now. I don't think the turrets will be as effective as we needed them to be if the Bugs know they're there."

"Mark, let me go stealth and move to 174.224.88. Can you see it?"

"Hold on, let me look…" Admiral Gordon scanned the coordinates position, studying the 3D relationship to Hammer, Anvil, and the Castle Shannon. "Hmm…Nice, Rhodes. Go. And good hunting, Commodore!"

"Aye-aye, Sir!" The invisible ships of Task Force Nail began moving the moment the Admiral uttered the word "nice'.

***

Task Force Hammer
USF Dreadnought
Standard Earth Date March 30 3488

"Admiral Gordon to Task Force Hammer, we're moving to new intercept coordinates. Formation to 174.188.80. Acknowledge."

"174.188.80. Roger That, Admiral," echoed from the thirty battlecruisers and sixty cruisers in the task force.

"Charlie, we're gonna end up in a knife fight here. I can feel it." *At least we'll be in position to help Jock.*

"It's what I'd do, Admiral. Try to disrupt our formations and get in close to use the beams. They have the numbers, about twenty to one."

Charles Gridley replied.

"But we've got speed and maneuverability, and our ships should have superior firepower. I just have to figure out the best way to use it."

***

Chrysler Building
55th Floor
New York City
Standard Earth Date March 30 3488

"What?" The brown haired woman snapped impatiently at her comm. *Why does everything hurt?*

"It has begun."

"Good. You know what to do, so do it." *I feel like Hell! I can't stay like this. It just isn't right!*

***

The Battle For Castle Shannon
ADS 1437 CIC
Standard Earth Date March 30 3488

"Sensors, immediate updates on any changes. Weapons, thirty second notice before Shavers firing point."

"Aye, aye, Admiral!" Wilson and Yamamoto chorused.

"Commander, what do you see?" Jock indicated the large tactical viscreen. *I need to teach here, and not get in her way. I just hope it's not a waste.*

"They need to get in close to use their numbers." Corrine observed.

"Exactly. They're swarming."

"Kill the queen, disorganize the swarm?"

"That may just work if the queen is here."

"She has to be, Admiral."

Jock stared at his daughter in surprise. "Go on."

"They don't have FTL comm. The queen has to be in comm range. Unless it's all preprogrammed."

160

"Right. If the Queen Bug is here, and we target it…"

"Everything moves to defend it."

"And if it is preprogrammed? Doing the opposite of what they expect may just overload the contingencies built into their plan."

"So, we hit their rear, ignore the vanguard and the main body."

"Comm, Fleet Comm One, link."

"Open."

"Jeri, Mark, Karen, Commander Halsey has an idea…"

"New sensor contact, Admiral! Three ships, big…about eighteen kilometers in diameter, roughly egg shaped. Vanguard has ceased decelerating. Main body is now decelerating hard."

"Good work Wilson. Admirals, I think those three big ships are the CIC of their operation. Suggest change to Flying Wedge, use Anvil to punch a hole through their first wave so Hammer can move in and squash the queens."

"I see it, Jock. What about Earth? A lot of ships will get by us…"

"The main body is decelerating hard. That means that they've already released their payloads, and they are committed to protecting the three big ships. Karen, you bring up the four hundred heavy cruisers of Beta Fleet to intercept any projectiles aimed at Earth. Once Hammer has engaged the Bug's VIPs, Anvil will pursue and destroy all main body Bug ships. Beta will mop up and support as the situation allows."

"Any objections? Comments?" Jeri asked. After six seconds, he spoke again; "Mark, Karen, work out the details of what Jack outlined for your own respective commands. Don't ask for approval, just execute it. Anything else?"

"One more thing, Jeri." Jock injected. "Task Force Nail is supporting Castle Shannon and Hammer's position. I have a better use for them…"

***

Task Force Nail
USF Lexington
Standard Earth Date March 30 3488

"Rhodes here, Admiral."

"Rhonda, I need Nail for something special." Admiral Bucktooth began quietly.

"I'm listening, Admiral," Rhonda's reply was challenging, almost a growl. *I hate that calm, quiet voice! It means I'm not going to like this. I will NOT leave Admiral Mac strung out to die!*

"We think that the three large Bug ships at the rear of their formation house the Bug's local command structure. We think that if we take them out, the Bug attack will collapse. Rhonda, these Bug tactics are not what we had prepared for. If we don't adapt, we *will* lose Earth." Jeri paused while he swallowed. He could see Commodore Rhodes swallow with him.

"The new plan is to ignore the Bug vanguard and have Anvil smash through their main body, opening a passage for Hammer to move in and destroy their three command ships. Task Force Nail has a crucial role to play in the overall success of this mission.

"Rhonda, I need your piss and vinegar on this. There is no officer I would rather have leading this mission." *I know what Jock means to her as a mentor, a friend, an idol even. I hate asking her to abandon him, and I sure as hell wouldn't want to feel her wrath on the back end of this after she does.*

"Give the word, Admiral." Her voice carried the pressure of her clenched jaws enclosed in the heat of suppressed tears.

"Here is your assignment, Commodore..."

***

The Battle For Castle Shannon
Turret Halsey CIC
Standard Earth Date March 30 3488

"Thirty seconds to Shaver firing point, Admiral."

"Fight your turret, Commander Halsey." Jock's order came low, not quite under his breath; he had meant it as much for the CIC crew as for his daughter.

"Parker, are you happy with your firing solutions?"

"Give me ten more seconds, Commander..."

"Mr. Yamamoto, you may fire at will." Corrine's voice dripped the easy confidence her crew had come to thrive upon. An outsider only hearing her voice would envision her filing her nails as she spoke.

"Almost...there. Shaver firing commenced."

Jock watched the numbers on his display moving up at a tremendous rate as the auto-loaders kept the railguns firing.

"Tell me when you're happy with the rounds out, Parker. Mr. Wilson, status of the vanguard?"

"They are heading for us at zero-point-two light speed. ETA two hours. Main body has dropped to zero-point-one-five light speed. Main body has dropped sixteen thousand projectiles at zero-point-five light speed. Target projected as Earth. Main body has formed a rough cone around the Three Kings."

"Three Kings, Eddie?"

"Best thing that came to mind, Admiral."

"First round of Shaver firing concluded, Sir. Five thousand rounds out." Parker Yamamoto broke in.

"Good enough for me, Eddie." Corrine confirmed. "ETA, Parker?"

"Twelve minutes, Commander."

"Excellent. They'll see the railguns firing about twenty seconds before they hit."

"Taclink: all turrets, fire all GravTorps. All turrets: target Shavers on Bug main body. Fire at will. Commander Singh out." Commander Tracy Singh's strong, confident voice boomed over the Taclink comm.

"Comm, acknowledge Taclink command, 'will comply'." Corrine directed. "Parker, get ready for round two. Jones, look sharp. Your time to shine is coming."

"Have lens, will burn Bugs, Commander."

"Monty, target your Shrikes per Taclink Commander. Bugs main body."

"Targets set, Commander. Optimal firing time in forty-four minutes."

"Excellent, Monty." *Even though it signs our death certificates.*

"Admiral, Commander!" Eddie broke in, a new excitement coloring his voice. "The projectiles, well, half of the projectiles targeting us have split into six pieces each, and they are decelerating!"

"Corry, they're planning on boarding us!" Jock's voice carried a touch of surprise.

"Comm, station wide."

"Open."

"This is the Commander. Prepare to repel boarders. Repeat, prepare to repel boarders!"

"Commander!" A powerful deep voice came from the rear of the CIC as Mike Halsey stepped up to stand between Admiral MacAlister and Commander Halsey. "I am the ranking marine on board, is that correct?"

"It's all yours, Captain. Go." Jock's voice made it clear that there was no discussion available on this topic. Mike saluted the Admiral, glanced at his wife and gave her a wink as he left the CIC, already on his comm organizing his resources. Corry's eyes followed him, pleading…

"Commander." Jock's voice now exuded a contagious confidence. He continued, much softer, so that only his daughter would hear, "Corrine. Corry."

She shot her father a look, "Sorry. That was too selfish," she said as their shared purpose came back to her in an instant. "What a damn fine group to fight with!" The volume and power of her voice surprised Jock, but the CIC crew took it in stride. The chorused "HOO-RAH! reply shook the core of the asteroid base.

DAMN my daughter is GOOD! Jock thought.

***

Chrysler Building
55th Floor
New York City
Standard Earth Date March 30 3488

"At your service!" the brown haired woman had her eyes closed and trembled visibly as she spoke with subdued, gentle tones.

The Target is in sight. It is very unlikely that he will survive this time. Concentrate on the other matters now.

The voice in her mind died, terminated at the source. She remained trembling for several minutes after that. She looked at her hands, spotted with age, thin, pale and dry. *Am I really this…have I really become this… evil?*

***

United News Network
Times Square Studios
Standard Earth Date March 30 3488

"Good evening. Tonight we have a special show for you. Tonight

164

we have exclusively in our sights the controversial Senator Sandy MacAlister. Hello, every one, I'm Donald Derringer. Welcome to Straight Shot!

"Senator, some have accused you of a dovish naïveté when it comes to handling the Bug threat. Some have called you a war-mongering tool of your husband, Admiral Jock MacAlister. Tonight you have the opportunity to explain and clarify your position before the people. What do you say?"

"Thank you for this opportunity, Donald. I'll get straight to the point; my concerns lay with our actions after we defeat the Bug invasion. As I see it, we will then have a choice to make. Do we attack and wipe out every single bug, or do we open a channel for communications, and offer them a chance to negotiate? That is..."

"Hold on a second, Senator! Breaking news, ladies and gentlemen! Sources have confirmed that the Bug invasion has begun! We now go to Barry Holland for the latest; Barry?"

**

The Battle For Castle Shannon
ADS 1284 CIC
Standard Earth Date March 30 3488

"GravTorp firing point, Commander." Lieutenant Alex MacAlister calmly announced.

"Comm, Taclink."

"Open."

"Castle Shannon, you may fire GravTorps when ready." Tracy Singh's command sounded in each of the five Turrets on the Taclink.

On the hundreds of quarter-mile wide and larger chunks of rock that comprised each Turret, doors opened allowing the GravTorps to slide from their hidden tubes. The bus-sized torpedo was a self-guided, gravitic drive powered drone carrying a Gravitic Implosion warhead. When detonated, each warhead became a miniature black hole, exerting a pull of hundreds of thousands of gravities within a ten kilometer-wide sphere for thirty minutes. The effect was devastating. A ship in contact would be 'sucked-in' and collapse into the warhead, compressed into a dense chunk of matter only a few meters wide.

The GravTorps moved silently out in a predetermined pattern to cover the Bug main body's approach. There they waited until ships matching the configuration programmed into their Artificial Intelligence Systems came into range. When they detected a Bug ship, they would accelerate to that ship and detonate when in range.

"Shrike Launch firing point, Commander."

"Castle Shannon, you may fire Shrikes when ready." *A few more minutes,* Tracy thought as she took a big, deep breath. "Look sharp, Alex."

Ten waves of thirty thousand missiles each streaked from silos buried in asteroids across the five Turrets that made up Castle Shannon. Each of the nuclear tipped missiles accelerated towards the Bug main body at a fantastic rate. Shortly after the Shaver rounds swept through the Bug main body, three hundred thousand fifteen-kiloton nuclear warheads would detonate within the Bug main body formation.

"Shaver firing point, Commander." Lieutenant Alex MacAlister announced.

"Castle Shannon, you may fire Shavers when ready. Exhaust all rounds."

Hundreds of one hundred-kilogram pellets sped silently from each of the hundreds of muzzles every tenth of a second. Traveling at eighty percent of light speed, once at the optimal distance from their target each round opened and ninety-six one-kilogram lead balls spread out. The SHVRs were in auto-fire mode, microscopic targeting adjustments happening in the tenth of a second interval between each round leaving the gun.

Commander Tracy Singh sat back in her command station chair. Her Command Heads Up Display indicated all five Turrets firing as ordered. She let out that big, deep breath. *God help me. I've just unleashed the greatest amount of firepower in Human history. Please, Lord, let it be enough!*

***

Task Force Anvil
USF Victory
Standard Earth Date March 30 3488

"Admiral, Castle Shannon has commenced firing." Lieutenant Allison MacAlister's voice broke the tension the long wait for action had built. "Task Force Hammer reports they are in position and standing ready, Sir."

"Comm, Task Force Anvil."

"Open."

"Admiral Bucktooth to Task Force Anvil. Spit your chews and grab your crotches boys and girls, it is *Game Time*! Execute The Flying Wedge." Jeri let out a huge sigh. *It's in motion, but now we have to sit and wait for it to work or fail. We can't go over three quarters light speed, or the whole plan could be lost. Damn, I hate waiting.*

"All units of Anvil report 'aye-aye', Admiral."

Allie MacAlister is as cool as her Dad. I'm glad she's here. Admiral Bucktooth thought. His eyes moved up to the CHUD floating in front of his eyes. His huge formation of fifty battleships, one hundred light cruisers, and fifty heavy cruisers moving towards the ragged cone of the Bugs main body. Off to the side, he glanced at the Bug vanguard closing on the Turret Halsey…*another one of Jock's kids. There has to be a way to save them. I can't leave them out there alone…*

***

The Battle For Castle Shannon
Turret Halsey
Standard Earth Date March 30 3488

"Shaver rounds impact in three. Two. One. Now, Sir!" Eddie Wilson couldn't contain his excitement. The actual impacts happened some time ago, but the light showing them was just reaching Turret Halsey. The young lieutenant knew Parker never missed. Had the deceleration of half of the projectiles screwed his aim? *We'll know soon enough.*

"Sensors recording multiple impacts…one-third, one-half, two, three…sensor record eighty percent of the projectiles not decelerating hit and destroyed, Commander!" Eddie's voice carried his desire to jump up and cheer at the news.

"Good shootin', Parker! Eddie, any on the decelerating objects?" Corry's spirits were lifted immensely. She knew this crew would run through a GravTorp wall for her, but how good were they really? Would the records they traded with Tracy's Turret translate into competent battlefield performance? This was her first answer, and she loved what she saw in it.

"Jane, stay sharp. Eddie, any news on the main body attack?"

"Not yet, Commander. Reading on the decelerated objects coming in now, Sir. Twenty…forty…sixty percent hits! YEAH!" Wilson's fist shot into the air, to be quickly and sheepishly withdrawn.

"Damn, Parker, leave some for me!" Jane Jones yelled as she punched the grinning Yamamoto's shoulder.

"Focus people. The bar ain't open yet. Parker, good work. Make it better next time!" Corry's ear-to-ear grin lit up the CIC.

"Fortiter, SIR!" The young man exclaimed, prompting a round of "HOO-RAH!' on the bridge.

"Great work, Parker. Don't let up." Jock added, using the powerful baritone to full effect to remind everyone the battle still raged without deflating them too much.

Jock looked at his CHUD, placing Anvil and the Bug main body, as well as the four thousand plus projectiles still heading their way. It looked like only a couple hundred were real projectiles; the rest would be some type of transport. From the size of them, Jock guessed they were two to four-Bug pods. Four thousand of them.

"Shavers magazines empty, Commander."

"All GravTorps launched, Commander."

"All Shrikes away, Commander."

Jane Jones' eyes grew wide as the other weapons stations reported. *It's down to me now. Our lives depend on me…*

A hand gently rested on Lieutenant Jones' right shoulder. She kept her focus on her targeting as she felt a larger than life presence come close to her. A deep baritone voice whispered into her ear, "There is a reason *you* are here, Jones. You were born and trained for this moment in time. It's your turn to shine. I'm happy with that."

***

The Battle For Castle Shannon
Tracy's Turret CIC
Standard Earth Date March 30 3488

"Looks like Halsey's Shavers took a big chunk out of those projectiles, Commander!" Alex MacAlister didn't try to dampen his pleasure at the sensor readings.

"Shavers magazines are spent Taclink-wide, Commander."

"GravTorps are all launched Taclink-wide."

"Shrikes are all away, Taclink-wide, Commander."

"Lasers, grapples, stay sharp. Alex, how long until our volley hits the Bug main body?"

"Looks like ten, no twelve minutes, for the light to reach us, Commander. The fireworks should last a long time, though, Sir. There's an awful lot of lead flying at them." *And not a damn thing they can do about it. We think.*

***

Task Force Hammer
USF Dreadnought
Standard Earth Date March 30 3488

Admiral Mark Gordon studied his CHUD intently. His eyes felt like they would fall out any second. *There has to be something we've missed. There always is. What is it? Where is it?*

The thirty battlecruisers and their escorts which made up Task Force Hammer maintained position well behind Task Force Anvil. The heavier battleship armor and defenses would deal with the Bug projectiles, and then the Bug ships as well. His command would shoot through the gaps like watermelon seeds spit out at a church social. The three Bug command ships were his targets, if he could reach them. They had to get past twelve thousand Bug ships!

"Turret Halsey's Shavers have crushed the Bug projectiles, Admiral! Estimate is eighty-percent hits."

"Good news, indeed. Let's hope their lasers are up to the rest of Halsey's standards. Weapons, do you have a Shaver firing solution for us yet?"

"Solutions plotted, Admiral. Firing position in five minutes. Just make sure none of the Anvil ships move!" Lieutenant Alistair MacAlister reported to his Admiral.

"Our Shaver rounds are different from the grapeshot of the turrets and battleships; we'll be firing solid gravity compressed projectiles in one hundred kilogram chunks at zero-point-nine-nine light speed. We'll be targeting the Three Kings, as they've been dubbed. That should add just a bit more to the chaos we need to create here, don't you think, Charlie?"

"I think the Bugs are going to be hit pretty hard before we start your knife fight, Sir." Captain Charlie Walker agreed. *But, will it be hard enough?*

***

United News Network
Times Square Studios
Standard Earth Date March 30 3488

"Even as we speak, our brave men and women are moving to attack the Bugs; a technologically superior race of intelligent Exoskeletites the military believes are bent on our destruction. Some disagree, using the logical argument that beings so intellectually advanced *must* be morally advanced as well, and therefore peaceful in nature.

"The question in our sights then, is this; how do we know they are going to attack us, and are not simply a trade delegation bringing goods to barter? How can we be sure of this?

"Our military claims to have "broken the code" of the alien computers. How do we know they didn't just open a page from an alien science fiction novel?

"Many now say we should pull back and give the Bugs a chance to teach us their wisdom. Other scream the bloodthirsty cry of "kill, kill, KILL"!

"Do we have the right?

"What do you say? Send in your comments to Don Derringer, care of Straight Shot."

***

Mars L-2
J. Wadsworth R & D Station
Commander's Quarters
Standard Earth Date March 30 3488

"Report, LC." Commodore Jack MacAlister's deep bass voice softly demanded an answer.

"The Thistle is ready, Commodore. Locked and loaded." Lieutenant Commander Peter Stone replied. He was proud of what they had put together, he knew it would work as designed…well, maybe. They hadn't had time to test everything yet.

"What about our 'Babies'?

"Eighteen Fortiter Mod LCPAs, Sir."

This doesn't seem like much. But if what we have on the Thistle works, and the LCPAs can execute their mission, we could make a huge difference. We will see.

"Good, Pete. Let's man the ships. Volunteers to your posts! In twenty minutes we launch Operation Home Field Advantage."

***

The Battle For Castle Shannon
Turret Halsey CIC
Standard Earth Date March 30 3488

"Shaver rounds impacts in three. Two. One. There it is!" Eddie was hoping to be excited by the impacts of the Castle Shannon's Shaver rounds on the Bug main body. What he saw left him nearly speechless.

"Impacts on ships throughout the Bug's main body. A high hit ratio, Sir! It looks like seventy percent of the main body, Admiral, they're just… gone!"

Jock let out a big breath. *This is too good. What are we missing? Where is it?* Jock's eyes flashed across his CHUD, looking for the danger he was certain lay hidden there.

"Corry, there's something we're missing. What is it?"

"Could it be the boarding, Admiral? Are they boarders, or could they be something else?"

"Like what, Commander?"

"What if they were bombs?"

Jock thought about that. If these were bombs, drifting in to explode with, what, nukes? The damage they would do was iffy at best; the turret CICs were under hundreds of meters of iron ore asteroid. The worst they could do was knock out some sensors…

"Comm; Fleet Command Channel STAT."

"Open."

"Jeri, these boarding pods could be EMP warheads. The same for those headed your way!"

"Understood, Jock. Think 'Shrikes'. You give 'em Hell, son."

"Aye-aye, Sir! Understood."

"Corry, those warheads need to be priority targets over the ships."

"Roger that, Admiral. Jane, you heard the man! Target accordingly."

"Already on it, Skipper!" Jane's hands flew over her console.

"Monty, are any of your Shrikes near the pods?"

"About two dozen, Admiral. It could be enough…"

"Taclink orders have them targeted on the main body, Admiral" Corry reminded her father.

"Eddie, is the main body going to pass in range of these Shrikes?" Jock indicated thirty missiles on his CHUD, relayed and displayed on Wilson's HUD.

Eddie took a deep breath as he ran the data.

"No way, Admiral. Not even close." He let out the air in his lungs. *We just may make it.*

"Admiral's decision. Monty, run these Shrikes into the pod formation and detonate. Target and detonate on your judgment."

"Aye, aye, Admiral." Monty's hands were already adjusting the movements of the missiles.

"If they're EMP bombs, we'll fry them first. If they're boarders, we'll fry them in their own fat." Jock said to no one in particular. *If they have fat.*

***

Task Force Anvil
USF Victory
Standard Earth Date March 30 3488

"We have sensor data on their projectiles now, Admiral."

"I see it, Lieutenant. Good job." Jericho Bucktooth scanned the visuals on his CHUD. *It could be here. Whatever it is that we've missed.*

"Admiral, eleven thousand of the projectiles are decelerating hard. Five thousand are earthbound." Lieutenant Allison MacAlister's voice carried her excited apprehension.

"Shavers, target projectiles not decelerating. Expend all ammunition." *I see a pattern in the ones slowing down. It looks like something I've seen before…where? What is it telling me?*

"Aye, aye Sir. Shavers targeting now."

"Admiral, Hammer is ready to ship their packages."

"Admiral to Anvil, maintain formation while Hammer delivers its mail."

"Anvil ships reply 'will co', Sir."

"Admiral, Anvil's Shavers targeted."

"Fire at will."

"Anvil Shavers firing Sir. ETA return images of first rounds impacts in ten minutes."

"Hammer reports all packages have been sent."

"Jeri, that pattern…" Captain Haja Zafy rubbed her chin as she thought out loud. "Do you remember old blue-water naval history? How they hunted submarines?"

"That's it, Haja! It's a depth charge pattern! It's meant to cover us with…what? They're not boarding, that pattern won't work for that. Explosions won't hurt us, no shock wave, just…EMP!

"Comm, Fleet-wide."

"Open."

"Bug projectiles decelerating are likely EMP weapons. All units use maximum radiation shielding. Anvil, prepare for GravTorp salvo, standby for targeting. Bucktooth out.

"Johnson, give me a GravTorp dispersal pattern that will crumple those EMP warheads."

"I'm on it, Admiral."

"I'm starting to feel a little better about this. Not much, but a little."

***

Task Force Hammer
USF Dreadnought
Standard Earth Date March 30 3488

"All Shaver rounds away, Admiral."

"It'll be awhile before they're on target. Lasers, GravTorps, Shrikes, Grapples, prepare for close range engagement. Charlie, when Anvil engages their main body, I want to accelerate through the fur ball." Mark Gordon had twenty thousand things on his mind right now, and sixteen thousand were the ships of the Bug main body. Getting to those

Three Kings with enough firepower to take them out was his only goal. Almost.

"Just say when, Admiral." Charlie Walker had several routes of attack visualized in his mind. His crew was well trained, so the Dreadnought's helm and nav stations had them plotted as well without any communication past the experience of extensive training as a team.

Ninety ships. Thirty battlecruisers, thirty heavy cruisers, and thirty light cruisers would have to pass through the four thousand surviving Bug ships, and then attack the three Bug command ships; if that was what they were. The Bugs sure seemed intent on protecting them. Fifty battleships, fifty heavy cruisers, and one hundred light cruisers would clear their way. Two hundred ships against four thousand...

"Admiral, we have fixes on the Bug projectiles targeted on Earth."

***

The Battle For Castle Shannon
Turret Halsey CIC
Standard Earth Date March 30 3488

"Shrike detonation in three. Two. One. Now." Monty's light British accent almost made the countdown to one hundred and twenty megatons worth of nuclear explosions sound elegant.

"I'm reading secondary explosions throughout the pod formation. High EMP levels...range outside our danger zone! We made it!" Edison Wilson's relief rang throughout everyone in the CIC.

"Stay focused, Lieutenant! We've still got those ships headed for us, and the rest of the projectiles. And some of those pods are still coming, too. They could be boarders as a follow up." Corrine Halsey's listing of their potential executioners' assets brought the CIC back to work.

"Good work, Monty. Eddie, anything more on the remaining pods?" Jock wanted to build them up a little after Corry had dashed their 'high'. Not too fast, but enough to boost their confidence and focus.

"There are still just under a thousand pods converging on us, Admiral. It's funny, though..."

"Wilson, talk to me." *Analytical thinking here, and he's not afraid to offer it. Corry has led them well.*

"Well, Admiral, they're headed right for Landing Bay Alpha'

exterior doors. That's the only place we *could* be boarded, Sir, unless they could move through twelve hundred meters of asteroid. It's like they know where to go."

He has a point. But, how could they know? We can't have a spy, could we? Good grief!

"Good thinking, Lieutenant. Keep it up. You've got a point there, but other than preparing to be boarded through the landing bay, I don't know how it will help us." Jock was thinking out loud now, trying to allay any fears Wilson's analysis may have engendered.

"I've already deployed with that as the most likely method of attack, Admiral." Marine Captain Mike Halsey's deep voice sounded from the entrance to the CIC.

Admiral Jock MacAlister smiled. He'd bet that any Bug getting into that landing bay was in for a world of hurt.

***

Mars L-2
J. Wadsworth R & D Station
AG-1 Thistle
Standard Earth Date March 30 3488

"All systems go, Commodore."

"Course set for ultra high Earth orbit."

"Very well. One thing left, Pete."

"Yes, Sir."

"Then, as senior commanding officer present, I hereby commission this ship...The USF Jeremiah Wadsworth."

"Jack, look at viscreen three." Kesa smiled.

Jack MacAlister tilted his head to look at the indicated screen. The view was an external shot of the refurbished space tug/weapons testing platform/space sweeper. Bright green letters spelled out the new name.

"Do you know the story, Pete?" Kesa Macalister asked from the weapons console.

"What story?"

"The Jeremiah Wadsworth was an ore carrier, mining heavy metal ore from Jupiter's moons," Jack spoke while adjusting his controls. "They were just leaving Jupiter's orbit, hauling a load in, when the Birds landed. The captain burned their ion drive at max, way, way past

175

specs, until they were pushing three-quarters light speed. Just as they neared the Bird fleet, they blew their core, turning themselves and their ore into shotgun pellets. They wiped out the Bird fleet. Earth was saved. The captain's name was Joel MacAlister."

"Fortiter!" Kesa exclaimed.

"Full speed ahead Peter. Let's sweep us some sky."

The huge, ungainly looking ship moved slowly away from the research station. As it moved clear of the station, eighteen LCPAs moved in very close to the ship's body, nestling in behind the huge radiation shield. Originally designed to protect the crew from the old style reactor's radiation, the shield now protected the LCPAs from anything in front of the Jeremiah Wadsworth. The gravity clamps locked onto the smaller ships, holding them fast.

The old tug moved lazily for a few more seconds. Then, the Jeremiah Wadsworth vanished as the column of space in front of the ship instantly shrunk, sucking the ship forward at four times light speed.

***

United Earth Senate
Montreal
Standard Earth Date March 30 3488

"Madam President, we can *not* withdraw our forces at this crucial moment!" Sandy MacAlister slammed her fist on the polished wood table.

"Senator, please try to leave your feelings for your family members out of our debates! We must withdraw now to protect the Earth! I'm ordering the immediate withdrawal of all of our ships back to high Earth orbit, where they will be better positioned to defend the Earth. That is their mission, after all."

"Allowing the aliens to regroup and plan an attack after they have seen our forces almost assures the destruction of Earth! Surely you can see that!"

"Senator, your love for your family is admirable, but it is clouding your judgment. I will order the withdrawal...I will order...I will..."

"Madam President! Someone call the medics! The President isn't breathing! She has no pulse!"

176

***

Task Force Anvil
USF Victory
Standard Earth Date March 30 3488

"Task Force Anvil, accelerate to zero-point–five light relative twenty seconds from my mark. Mark."

Twenty seconds later the two hundred United Space Force ships moved as one to engage over four thousand alien ships.

"Bucktooth to Fleet. We will soon be engaged in Earth's second ship to ship space battle. It is our task to make sure it's not Earth's last. This is the biggest big time there will ever be, so let's shine tonight!" *I sure wish I was better at this rah-rah stuff.*

***

The Battle For Castle Shannon
Turret Halsey CIC
Standard Earth Date March 30 3488

"Corry, you've got four turrets to provide covering laser fire. We should be able to cut the odds down a bit."

"Thanks, Tracy. We still don't know why they're ignoring the other turrets. Best we can figure, they knew this one was here from the captured scout, and they just can't deviate from their plans."

"Corry, good luck. Tell the old man he owes me one. I really want him around so I can collect."

"Commander, Bug vanguard coming into range." Wilson's voice broke in.

"Let's go to work!"

"Projectiles in laser range in twenty seconds." Jane Jones announced. *Fish in a barrel.*

"Firing lasers. Laser fire form Castle Shannon supporting, but they have crappy firing angles." The normally silent Jones kept up the running commentary as her hands flew across the controls almost faster than the eye could follow.

Nearly a thousand projectiles silently flew towards Turret Halsey at half of the speed of light. The turrets' plasma lasers reached across the vast distances and vaporized the projectiles they hit squarely. Even the vaporized projectiles were dangerous; microscopic particles at that speed still carried a lot of energy.

Many projectiles were hit with only a glancing blow. Some of these continued on, courses unchanged, while others veered off on a new trajectory.

Turret Halsey was about to get pounded.

***

Chrysler Building
55th Floor
New York City
Standard Earth Date March 30 3488

"What do you mean, the President is dead?" Anger, fear, panic and desperation all fought for control of the brown-haired woman's shriek.

"She suffered a massive heart attack while debating the Senate Space Policy Committee."

"And the Vice President? Where is she?" She practically screamed into her comm.

"She is on a suborbital transport, en route to Montreal from Bombay. Her ETA is two hours. She cannot be reached for at least an hour and a half."

The woman cut the comm and slammed her fist onto the unyielding wood of the desk. *I can only hope that I don't need her help. Just in case,* she pulled the plasma blaster from the desk drawer and set it on her lap. Then she turned and stared out the windows.

***

The Battle For Castle Shannon
Turret Halsey CIC
Standard Earth Date March 30 3488

"Attention, all personnel. Prepare for low atmosphere operations.

Repeat, prepare for low atmosphere operations." Corrine's voice carried throughout the station, signaling everyone to get into his or her pressure suit.

"Projectile impacts in twenty seconds." Eddie kept his voice cool and calm as he shot a sideways glance to Jane. *Lord, let her shoot well tonight!*

"Let me know where they hit, Eddie." Corrine said quietly. "As best you can."

Turret Halsey was made up of eighty asteroids in a rough pyramid formation, flat base pointed Earthward. The second largest asteroid in the group housed the crew, most of the sensors, the main shields, a few gravity grapples and several plasma lasers. The remainder of the weapons, sensors, and shielding were spread out among the other asteroids. There were a lot of targets, but only the station was critical. That is where all the people were. The railguns, Shrike silos, and GravTorp tubes were spent, so losing them would not affect the turrets combat effectiveness. Losing the lasers or the grav grapples would leave them defenseless.

"Impacts detected. Beta shielding is gone. Beta GravTorp station is gone. Beta Shrike station is gone. Beta grapples are gone. Beta lasers are half gone. Alpha stations are all gone. Delta stations, all gone." Eddie took a big breath. "Theta station is gone except..."

The CIC rocked violently for several seconds. Almost as soon as it stopped, it began again. Six times the station shook violently before the motion stopped.

All eyes look to Admiral MacAlister when it seemed the seventh impact wouldn't come.

"We're still alive, so let's look the part, people!" Jock was surprised to hear his own voice say.

"We have three lasers still firing on Theta station. We've lost seven lasers on Home Plate. And all of the grapples."

"Eddie, that wasn't a full projectile that hit us; what was it?"

"Best guess, Admiral, is that we got hit by plasma dust, the remnants of projectiles Jane hit square on. By the way, Jane hit eight hundred forty six out of nine hundred eighty four projectiles. Covering Castle fire took out another seventy three."

Jane didn't hear the stats, nor did she feel the awed gazes of the CIC crew. Her exhausted gaze was fixed on her targeting station. She took several deep breaths, and then came back to life as she began her resource inventory to assign targeting priorities for the following pods. After about ninety seconds, she stopped, looked at Lieutenant

Yamamoto and simply said, "Told you I was good." Parker winked at Jones as she went back to work.

***

The Battle For Castle Shannon
Tracy's Turret CIC
Standard Earth Date March 30 3488

"Sensors, talk to me, Alex."

"They got hit hard, Commander, but Home Plate's relatively intact. They lost a lot of lasers and all of their grapples, and they're off of Taclink. Direct laser comm only." *Thank you, Lord!*

"We have three shuttles in Alpha bay, don't we, Alex?"

"Yes, Sir. And each of the other turrets has three more."

"Twelve shuttles. Comm, Castle Shannon."

"Open."

"Turret commanders, ready two of your shuttles for ferry operations…"

***

Task Force Anvil
USF Victory
Standard Earth Date March 30 3488

"Damage assessment on 1437." Jeri had seen the strikes on his CHUD. *Maybe it could be better than it looked. Maybe.*

"1437 is off Taclink. Most weapons and sensor stations are gone. Home plate looks like it was hit…She's still firing lasers, Admiral."

Admiral Bucktooth closed his eyes for one second while he gave thought, *Thank you Great Mother Atahensic!*

"Admiral, twenty seconds to Shavers impact on the Earth bound projectiles."

Ultra High Earth Orbit
USF Jeremiah Wadsworth
Standard Earth Date March 30 3488

"We're in position, Jack"

"Thanks, Kesa. Peter, are you ready?"

"As much as I'll ever be."

"How are our 'presents'?"

"All wrapped up and ready to go."

"Kesa?"

"Field generator charged and ready, Jack."

"Bertha?"

"Stand-by mode. Jack, that's never been tested."

"Okay, one last thing. Comm to Admiral Seymour."

"Seymour here. Who, Jack? Commodore, where are you?"

"Right between Earth and those projectiles, Admiral. I've brought a broom to your party."

"What?"

"We have a gravity net projector fitted to the Jeremiah Wadsworth. It will be effective at FTL speeds, so I can make multiple passes. The net will snare the projectiles, and I'll drop them off away from Earth. Admiral, your force is free to support Operation Black Smith."

Karen Seymour was known for making snap decisions under pressure. That part was easy enough. What set her apart was that her snap decisions were always the spot on right ones. She pondered the situation at hand for a few seconds.

"Jack, make one pass, then I'll decide. I'll prepare for either outcome. Good hunting."

"Thank you, Admiral. Oh, Admiral, I have another 'surprise package'."

***

The Battle For Castle Shannon
Turret Halsey CIC
Standard Earth Date March 30 3488

"Here come the pods, ten seconds to firing range." Eddie's excited voice was back.

"I see 'em, Wilson. If I get 'em all, you owe me dinner."

"Your place or mine, gorgeous?"

Jane was tunnel-visioned in on her job, but Eddie caught the slight upward curve of the corner of her mouth. Right now Jane was focused on killing Bugs. *Like fish in a barrel. Or, Bugs in a pod.*

"The Bug vanguard is closing also, decelerating hard but overtaking the pods." Wilson looked at Jones, willing her to see the new threat.

"Got it Eddie. Thanks love"

Lieutenant Wilson blushed as he turned back to his sensors.

"Corry, this IS an invasion. The vanguard will get here first, soften us up, then the pods will arrive and board us."

"That's the way I see it, Admiral."

"That's what I'd want if I was leading the boarding party." Mike added.

"Targeting Vanguard ships. Not enough lasers for both." Jane yelled.

***

The Battle For Castle Shannon
Tracy's Turret CIC
Standard Earth Date March 30 3488

"Castle Shannon, fire at will. Target anything Bug that you have a shot at." Commander Tracy Singh barked out her orders over the Taclink.

"We're getting hits, Commander. There are a *lot* of targets."

Four thousand Bug ships swooping in ahead of twelve hundred Bug landing pods made a lot of targets, but the lasers did not have great fields of fire.

182

"Keep it up, Castle Shannon, keep it up!" *How the hell did I end up as a fucking cheerleader! I feel so damn useless right now.*

***

The Battle For Castle Shannon
Turret Halsey CIC
Standard Earth Date March 30 3488

"No return fire from the bug ships yet, Commander." Lieutenant Wilson said with a mixture of surprise and dread.

"Keep hitting them, Jones! We out range them. The more we take out now, the fewer hits we take." Commander Corrine Halsey worked her voice, trying to keep her crew calm, focused and optimistic.

Since the Bug ships were hollow monocoque structures, each laser hit on a Bug ship tore a huge chunk out of it and effectively destroyed the ship. But, there were a lot of ships to destroy.

"Castle supporting fire and our lasers are taking out Bug ships, Commander. Looks like they're down to three thousand and falling." Wilson reported. "Bug ships in firing range in three minutes."

Admiral Jock MacAlister watched the laser officer work, amazed at her stamina. Jane Jones had been firing for nearly fifteen minutes, between the projectiles and the Bug ships. The most grueling training simms never lasted over four minutes. She had three more minutes of extreme concentration and stress, and then the Bugs would be shooting back for another ten minutes or more.

"Parker, Elsa, Monty; now would be a good time." Jane said calmly.

"Linked." Monty said.

"Linked." Elsa confirmed.

"Linked. We've got you covered, Jane." Parker confirmed.

Jane sat back in exhaustion, threw her head back and closed her eyes, arms hanging limp at her sides to get some blood flow back into her spent muscles. After thirty seconds, she snapped back into action.

"Commander?" Jock quietly asked his daughter. "What are they doing?"

"It's a little something we've come up with. The simms we've run out here typically last an hour or so. We've figured out that to get maximum efficiency out of any weapons system over that long a time frame, the primary weapons officer controls it for the first twelve to

183

fifteen minutes, then we add secondary officers as available to reduce workload. It maximizes talent use while keeping workloads manageable."

Jock stared at his daughter for several seconds, an eyebrow raised and his head tilted slightly. *Will she ever stop amazing me?* A small grin crept onto his face. "Good job. Keep it up. And next time, let Fleet know about such things *before* the battle starts please."

"Commander, Castle Grapples have pulled a group of Bug ships out of formation. They've just fried them! They're pulling another group out!"

"Leave it to Tracy to find a way of using her resources for best effect." Corrine whispered.

"Eight new bogies detected near turret 1284."

What the hell is it now?

***

Task Force Anvil
USF Victory
Standard Earth Date March 30 3488

"Shaver impact in three. Two. One. Now."

Admiral Bucktooth watched the flashes on his Command Heads Up Display. Hundreds, thousands of flashes all at once. Visually, it gave an overall view of the battle, but it was too large for a numbers assessment.

"Talk to me, MacAlister."

"Two thousand six hundred hits, Admiral. Twenty four hundred still Earthbound."

"Bucktooth to Anvil, good shooting. That was a tough angle. Stay focused and get ready for the Bug ships."

***

Beta Force
USF Albany
Standard Earth Date March 30 3488

"Two thousand four hundred projectiles Earthbound, Admiral."

"Comm, get me the Jeremiah Wadsworth."

"Open."

"Jack, you've got twenty four hundred inbound. I'm sending you the path and coordinates since you don't have Taclink." Karen nodded to her comm officer. "You are free to engage in five minutes."

"Aye, aye, Admiral. Sweep will commence in five minutes."

***

Task Force Hammer
USF Dreadnought
Standard Earth Date March 30 3488

"Halsey's getting hammered, Admiral. They just don't have enough firepower left against those numbers." Lieutenant Alistair MacAlister frowned as he spoke.

"They just have to hold out long enough. ETA to special packages delivery, Lieutenant?" *Stay focused son.*

"ETA is twenty minutes, Admiral."

***

United Earth Senate
Montreal
Standard Earth Date March 30 3488

"Senator, the Vice President's suborbital shuttle is ten minutes overdue."

"Thank you, Mary." Sandy sighed heavily. *Such chaos and confusion!*

This can't be good.

"Mom, Chancellor Campbell is the next in the line of succession. He's sympathetic to your positions." As she spoke, the lights went out. "What...what happened?" Mary MacAlister groped around, trying to find a flashlight or datatab, anything with light.

"I still don't like this whole situation. Not one bit." Sandy said as she kept trying to open the now immoveable door.

***

The Battle For Castle Shannon
USF Jeremiah Wadsworth
Standard Earth Date March 30 3488

"Course plotted and set, Jack. Gravitic Screen charged." Peter Stone announced.

"Thanks, Peter. All we can do now is wait." Jack replied.

"Shouldn't we say a prayer or recite an inspirational saying or something?" Kesa's nervousness was obvious in her voice.

"I said my prayers when we left Mars. I can't think of anything inspirational. How about you, Pete?"

"Inspirational? No. Jack, Kesa, how do you two feel about leaving Ranald on Mars?"

"Well, I couldn't bring him with us! If there were someone else to take this mission, you know I'd be at Nili Patera with my son. My second choice is to be at the side of my husband." All nervousness had left Kesa's voice.

"If I could, I would keep them both safe. Nili Patera has a good history. It was overrun during the Bird invasion, but an infant boy was found alive in the archeological dig there, next to the bodies of his parents. They had transferred the last of their air to him. The search team found him when he had about ten minutes of air left. So, I like the history of the place. What about you, Peter, why did you volunteer?"

"Just bored doing research, I guess. I wondered what using these toys we invent would be like." *And to see if I had the balls to use them.*

"Countdown to light speed, three. Two. One. Now."

The Jeremiah Wadsworth vanished as the column of space in front of the ship shrunk, sucking the ship forward at four times light speed for the second time in a matter of hours. Humanity's first military use of Faster Than Light drive was by an old Space Tug.

***

Task Force Hammer
USF Dreadnought
Standard Earth Date March 30 3488

"Admiral, priority comm from Admiral Seymour."

"Private line."

"Open."

"Karen, what's bugging you?"

"Funny, Mark. I've got Jeri on the line too. You have an USF ship moving towards you at four times light speed."

"Ah, what?"

"Mars R & D came up with a gravity sweeper they say will clear the Earthbound projectiles. I'm giving them a pass to see if it works. If it does, I'm headed for 1437 at FTL myself."

"Karen, I need more details. Talk to me." Jeri didn't sound happy, but he wasn't PO'd either.

"Jack MacAlister flew the Thistle, recommissioned as the Jeremiah Wadsworth, out from Mars. Admiral, he has a gravity field that he says should sweep the projectiles up. He also has eighteen LCPAs he's modified to board spaceships. After he clears the projectiles, he plans on making a FTL run at the Three Kings and boarding them. With your permission, of course, Sir. If you agree. Sir."

Talk about asking forgiveness instead of permission! "Admirals, I ordered you to execute your plans, not ask permission. I haven't changed that order. Thanks for the heads up, Karen. Mark, don't get in Jack's way; no 'own goals'."

"Aye-aye, Sir!" echoed from the two Rear Admirals.

***

Task Force Anvil
USF Victory
Standard Earth Date March 30 3488

"Admiral, GravTorps are in position. Contact with EMP pods in five minutes."

"Very good. ETA Bug main body contact with Castle Shannon's GravTorps and Shrikes?" Fleet Admiral Jericho Bucktooth wanted confirmation of the information on his CHUD.

"Ten minutes, Admiral." Lieutenant Allison MacAlister replied.

"Admiral, I have a Priority Comm from President Campbell, Sir!"

"President, Campbell? What the…put it through, my private line."

"Open."

***

The Battle For Turret Halsey
CIC
Standard Earth Date March 30 3488

"They're still coming, Commander!" Eddie Wilson's strained voice was barely audible over the pressure loss alarms in the Combat Information Center.

"Landing Bay Alpha is open to space. All their weapons have been concentrated there, Sir!"

"I'm out of operating lasers, Commander." Lieutenant Jane Jones sat back at her now useless station, her sweat-drenched hair visible through her combat pressure helmet. All weapons stations were off-line, either out of ammunition or out of operational equipment.

"Mike, where are your marines deployed?" Admiral Jock MacAlister's mind was racing, searching every bit of information for that one edge he may have missed, that one flaw in the enemy's plan or execution that could keep them all alive.

"Eight at the outlet from Landing Bay Alpha. Six at the junctions leading here. Six in the corridor outside, Admiral." Marine Captain Mike Halsey finished his report, then bent and opened the two lockers

188

he had brought in earlier. He began handing the Mark VII carbines out to the CIC crew.

"The last Bug ships are gone, Commander. Bug pods ETA is two minutes." Eddie looked up from his sensors for just a moment to take his carbine from Mike, load a round into the chamber, and stow his weapon within easy reach.

"Thanks, Eddie. Good job, as always. Every one of you, you've made me proud to command you all." Commander Corrine Halsey started to say more, but her husband handed her a carbine, leaned in and touched his helmet's faceplate to hers, pursing his lips in a mock kiss.

"Okay, you love birds, there'll be time enough for smooching later. Mike, I'll bet you've got some surprises rigged for our 'guests'?"

"We have L-17 grenades rigged as mines throughout the corridors. I have Mark II laser auto-turrets set up covering four junctions. It will be very costly for them to reach us, Admiral."

**

Task Force Anvil
USF Victory
Standard Earth Date March 30 3488

Fleet Admiral Jericho Bucktooth dug the fingers of his left hand into his armrest. This was the single most distasteful order he had ever given, he could conceive of ever giving. He counted the eyelets on his hand-polished shoes twice, and then he lifted his head.

"Comm. Taclink. All units." The Admiral's words rolled out low and gritty, as if they had come along a dry gravel road.

"Open."

"Fleet, this is Bucktooth. I," Jeri swallowed hard, "I have been given orders by our Commander In Chief to break off all attacks on the Bug forces and return at best speed to high Earth orbit. These are lawful orders. Therefore, I," another swallow, his fingers dripping blood from his nails cracking as he gave the orders, "I hereby order all mobile United Space Force vessels on Taclink, Task Forces Anvil, Hammer, and Beta, to disengage from all combat operations and to return to Earth orbit immediately. All ADS units will continue their duties without interruption. This is the order from the Commander In Chief and is not open to discussion. Bucktooth out." The last word sounded like a comm being run over sandpaper.

Jeri looked around the silent bridge, not bothering to wipe the tear rolling down his cheek. Everyone stared at him, frozen.

"Damn it, you heard me, now DO IT!" His words exploded within the bridge, sending crew into a flurry of activity.

Jeri's jaws clenched tighter as his eyes came to Allison MacAlister. The young lieutenant was busy at work, running the sensor arrays, keeping busy. *Not thinking about how her Godfather had just condemned her father to death.*

Jeri ignored the comm lights indicating calls from Mark and Karen. He didn't feel human enough to talk with anyone right now.

***

Chrysler Building
55th Floor
New York City
Standard Earth Date March 30 3488

The brown haired woman rocked slightly as she stared out the windows. She thought about walking to the temp control and turning it up, but she didn't move. Her rocking had taken on a life of its own, it would seem. *And, what took my life, then? This chair, this room, these windows? It's always so cold in here now. What kind of an evil creature have I become?*

You have done well, my dear. Our goals are almost within reach now. Just a little more…

"A little more what!" She shot to her feet, rage turning her paled, wrinkled face into a crimson façade. "I used to be good inside. I'm sick of being evil! How many more must die before you have enough power? You are pure evil! I reject your evil! I will not be your tool any…ahg… "

The brown haired woman collapsed to the floor. A few moments later the custodians came and cleaned the room. Again.

The Battle For Turret Halsey
USF Jeremiah Wadsworth
Standard Earth Date March 30 3488

"Jack, something's not right." Kesa's tone caught Jack's full attention.

"Talk to me."

"Beta Fleet has withdrawn. They're headed to Earth. And, if I'm reading this right, Task Force Anvil and Task Force Hammer have also changed course, and are Earthbound at four times light speed. Jack, they're running away!"

"Get Admiral Seymour on the line."

"I'm trying, Jack. They aren't responding. I've tried Bucktooth and Gordon. No answer. What's going on?"

"I don't know. Peter, can you get any news broadcasts?"

"Not now, we're moving four times faster than the broadcasts are. And, we're ten seconds from projectile sweep. Should I abort?"

"Negative. I can't think of anything good coming out of letting those rocks slam into Earth."

"Here we are, Commodore!"

Jack expected to feel impacts, shaking, something to tell him they've trapped the projectiles, even though he knew the science said he wouldn't.

"How many?"

"Jack, we have them all!"

"Is our course still true for the main body?"

"Right on the dot, Jack."

"Without orders to the contrary, we will proceed with the plan. Maintain four C velocity."

Chapter Eight

United News Network
Times Square Studios
Standard Earth Date March 31 3488

"We have breaking news at this hour. Sources confirm that the USF fleet battling the Bugs has withdrawn and is heading for Earth. Unconfirmed reports indicate that an ADS station, known as a "Turret", was heavily damaged in earlier fighting and has been over run by Bug soldiers. The assumption is that all hands there, including Admiral Jock MacAlister, have perished.

"In our sights for expert analysis tonight is retired Lieutenant Commander Jay Thorpe. We attempted to contact Senator Sandy MacAlister to hear her side of this story, but the Senator's office has not yet responded to our requests. Lieutenant Commander, what do you make of this "redeployment" of our ships?"

"I can't say that it looks good, Don. The only reason to fall back like that is if we've had our butts kicked, if this was a complete royal screw-up. I would suspect that if we survive this encounter, there will be repercussions for many of the high-ranking brass running this operation."

"And, Commander, who would that likely be? Admiral Jock MacAlister has been extensively involved in our efforts..."

"That's Lieutenant Commander. Exactly. Admiral MacAlister has managed to get himself promoted, and to arrange cushy jobs for friends and family members for forty years. Remember, it was Admiral MacAlister who started this war by attacking the alien emissary ship. He's even managed to parlay this manufactured conflict into a Senate seat for his wife and several lucrative business deals for himself and his friends."

"But, Commander..."

"Lieutenant Commander, Don."

"Sorry. Lieutenant Commander, are you saying that Admiral Jock MacAlister created this entire conflict for personal gain?"

"I'm just reviewing what we know, Don. Your viewers are bright enough to draw their own conclusions."

"And there you have it, Ladies and Gentlemen. What do you say? I'm Don Derringer, and this is Straight Shot. Stay tuned, we will bring you more as it becomes available."

***

The Battle For Turret Halsey
Landing Bay Alpha
Standard Earth Date March 31 3488

The last alien boarding pod streaked silently along the surface of Turret Halsey's control station asteroid. Every few seconds it would pass a glowing pool of molten metal and rock that had been a plasma laser site, sensor array, gravitic clamp, or a shield generator. The pod had limited maneuverability, and used what it did have to arrive at a preprogrammed destination, the gaping hole that used to be Landing Bay Alpha.

The three alien soldiers sat motionless inside fluid-filled keratinaceous cells. As the pod slowed and drifted into the landing bay, the fluid drained away and the soldiers became active. When the pod's motion stopped, the three soldiers straightened their armored legs and shattered the travel cells as well as the pod's structure with their armored backs. The last pod's shell fell in shards onto the landing bay floor as the three soldier Bugs it carried joined the eleven hundred already there.

As if of one mind, the soldiers now lined up and began moving towards the door leading into the station, plasma projectors moving side to side, searching for a target...

***

The Battle For Castle Shannon
Tracy's Turret
Standard Earth Date March 31 3488

"Commander, ten seconds to 'special package' delivery." Lieutenant Alexander MacAlister reported.

"Thanks, Alex." *At least they couldn't recall those.*

"Impact in three. Two. One. Now. One hit seen. One of the Three

193

Kings is gone, Commander, one appears damaged!" Alex's eyes pleaded with Tracy through the cheers in the CIC, carrying the question he couldn't ask out loud.

"Alex, ETA for GravTorps and Shrikes on main body, please." She gave him one sideways movement of her head.

Alex turned back to his sensor array. "GravTorp contact in three minutes. Shrike contact in one minute."

"Shuttle ETA on Halsey's Turret?"

"Fourteen minutes."

***

The Battle For Turret Halsey
CIC
Standard Earth Date March 31 3488

The CIC crew all stared at the door as the banging started. Four bangs, pause, three bangs, pause, one bang. Corrine Halsey signaled ready and Jane Jones hit the control opening the door. Jock, Mike, Elsa and Monty slid through and Jones resealed the door.

"All the connections are made. We use the Laser controls to activate." Jock walked over to the makeshift barricade and looked back at the door. "Captain, are you happy with the set up here?"

"Happy, Admiral? No. But I think this is damn good considering what we had to work with."

"Commander, do you agree?"

"Yes, Admiral. I don't see how we could do any better." Corry replied.

"Hmm…" Jock walked along the barricade, stopping near one end. He moved a chair an inch to his left. "There. Much better, don't you think?"

Everyone stared silently at Jock. After several seconds, he broke into a childish grin, and the entire crew began laughing.

Then the alarms went off.

"Movement into the corridor outside Alpha. High energy readings flashing sporadically, consistent with energy weapons fire."

"Boyd to CIC. The Bugs are breaking out, hundreds of them. We've fried dozens, but they keep…" Static. Then silence.

"Boyd! Harlow! Report!" Mike ordered.

194

"There is no comm signal on the other end, sir!"

"Marines, this is Halsey. Fall back to the CIC. Repeat, fall back to the CIC. The corridors should limit their speed."

"Fire Team Delta, Aye-aye."

"Fire Team Gamma, Aye-aye."

The doors opened when the marines banged the code. Jones closed them immediately.

"When are you going to activate your toy, Admiral?"

"When as many Bugs as possible are in the corridors. We'll only be able to use it once. Until then, I want as much carnage out of the L-17s and auto turrets as possible. Eddie, do you have anything on those eight bogies?"

"I couldn't get a fix on them before our last sensors went out, Admiral."

"Okay, let's focus on what we can do something about. Corry, who are your best shots with the carbines?"

"Jones, Hicks, Yamamoto, Elsa, Monty, Kevin, myself, and Wilson, in descending order. We're all within zero-point-five percent of each other, and zero-point-one percent ahead of the marines. We're all damn fine shots in here, Admiral."

"If you're down at number six, I don't doubt it. Lieutenant Jones, how does my daughter handle finishing sixth best?"

"Sir, Commander Halsey hates to lose, Sir!" Jones said with a tiny grin. "But she does tell us how proud she is of us, Admiral. Every time."

"Jones, did you know that the Commodore here was the National Intercollegiate skeet shooting champion? Twice?"

"Da-ad! Eh, Admiral, shouldn't we be concentrating on the Bugs?" Corry's face was bright red.

"I think we'll have our fill of Bugs very shortly, Corrine. I was only pointing out that we have a room full of exceptional marksmen, and ladies here. I like our odds!" *Yeah, and if you bought that one, I've got a bridge for sale...*

"Explosions in the corridors. Auto-turrets firing. They're on their way."

The Battle For Castle Shannon
USF Jeremiah Wadsworth
Standard Earth Date March 31 3488

"Coming up on 1437, Jack."

"Peter, drop to one-half light speed."

"One half light speed achieved, Sir."

"MacAlister to Jenkins. Releasing clamps. Good hunting, Jimmy."

"You, too, Commodore."

"LCPAs away, Sir. Confirmed twelve on course to 1437."

"Set speed to four times light speed, relative, Pete. We have another delivery to make."

The Battle For Castle Shannon
Tracy's Turret
Standard Earth Date March 31 3488

"Shrikes contact in three. Two. One. Now." Alex gave the countdown in near monotone. "My God!" he exclaimed as three hundred thousand fifteen-kiloton nuclear warheads detonated as one. For a brief instant, a second sun burned on the edge of that star system Humanity called home.

"Damage assessment, Alex. Did we hurt them?" Tracy asked.

"I'm detecting three thousand plus a handful of Bug ships still active. Plus the two Kings. We hurt them a lot, Commander."

"How long until the GravTorps hit?" *This could end here and now.*

"Just under one minute, Commander."

Three hundred thousand GravTorps closed in on the Bug main body ships as they moved closer around the two remaining Bug Super ships.

"GravTorp contact in three. Two. Commander!" Alex shouted.

"Talk to me MacAlister!"

"The Bug ships, Sir! They're...gone!"

***

The Battle For Turret Halsey
CIC
Standard Earth Date March 31 3488

"Steady now, Jones. Steady." Admiral MacAlister whispered as the crew watched the CIC door smolder under the attack of some type of energy weapon. "Now, Lieutenant Jones!"

"Engaged, Admiral!" Jones activated the device, then immediately grabbed her carbine and resumed her firing position behind the barricade.

As soon as Jones hit the switch, a horrendous shrieking wail rose up from behind the CIC door. The lights dimmed for three seconds, then came back up. The screaming from beyond the door died.

"Mike." Jock pointed at the door with his carbine.

Mike Halsey worked the control that operated the doors. They groaned and creaked, sliding open with the loud mechanical protestations of a machine that had functioned for the last time.

The first thing they noticed was the smell. It assaulted them as a great wave of partially incinerated garbage. Smoke was the second thing the crew noticed. Thick acrid and reddish-brown, it seemed to occupy every inch of the corridor the Bug bodies did not. And there were a lot of Bug bodies.

Piled one upon another, with legs sticking out at odd angles and bodies split open as they cooked from the current, the smoldering Bug bodies filled the corridor with a ghastly, odorous smoke.

"I guess your little surprise worked, Admiral. Running the power output from our reactors through the floors and walls of the corridors did a number on them. Eddie, do you have any readings in the station?" Corrine turned her head away from the door and towards Wilson.

"There is movement, but I can't..."

Eddie's report was cut short by a bolt of white-hot plasma passing through his right shoulder. Three more bolts flew into the CIC before the marines began returning fire. Two of the bolts hit Kevin, burning a hole in the center of his chest and abdomen. The third bolt hit Corrine just below her left elbow, vaporizing her forearm.

"Cease fire! Save your ammo," Mike called, even as he leapt across the CIC to his wife. Parker was already applying a bandage to her cauterized elbow, and Jane was binding up Eddie's wound.

"Here they come again!" Jock exclaimed as he began firing into a corridor suddenly alive with squirming legs and snapping jaws behind bolts of star-hot plasma.

***

The Battle For Castle Shannon
USF Jeremiah Wadsworth
Standard Earth Date March 31 3488

"Where the hell did they go?" Kesa screamed at her sensors.
"Could they have FTL?"

"If they had FTL, they would have just bypassed us to attack Earth. But, somehow, they just…vanished!" Jack scratched his head.

"There! Look, they're closer to 1437. They jumped somehow. Peter, get us on top of them."

"On it, Jack."

"Finch, are you ready?"

"Frothin' at the bit, Skipper."

"It could be a rough ride, Otis. Hang on."

"Roger that."

"On them, Jack."

"Kesa, what's the maximum speed of this tub?"

"I can get you there in twenty seconds."

"Do it."

***

The Battle For Castle Shannon
Tracy's Turret
Standard Earth Date March 31 3488

"Alex, what just happened?" Tracy was trying to make sense of the information on her CHUD.

"The Bug main body just moved two hundred thousand kilometers in three one-hundredths of a second. It must be some type of

198

dimensional shift."

"Those GravTorps were our best chance. How could they know they were about to activate? Damn. OK, what about the Bug vanguard units?"

"They're still turning. ETA for their return is ten minutes."

"And we have no weapons that can reach them effectively."

"Commander, we have twelve ships inbound to Turret Halsey. Configurations match Marine LCPAs!"

***

The Battle For Turret Halsey
CIC
Standard Earth Date March 31 3488

"Fall back to the barricade!" Jock's voice called. The sailors and marines pushed back. There was not much room left. The CIC before them was strewn with the bodies of Bug soldiers and dead crew. For the moment things were quiet, thanks at least partially to a pile of Bug bodies that blocked the door.

Damn, Jock thought as he looked around, *Mike, Jane, the marines Johnson and Rodriguez, Elsa and the wounded. Corry, firing with one arm, Eddie, shooting left-handed. And me. Well, losing a leg doesn't hurt as much as I thought it would.*

"Captain, there's movement in the corridor." Johnson announced. The survivors lifted their carbines once more, and waited.

***

The Battle For Castle Shannon
USF Jeremiah Wadsworth
Standard Earth Date March 31 3488

"We're almost in position, Jack."

"Ready, Finch?"

"Give the word, Commodore."

"Clamps released. Give 'em hell, Otis!"

"Hoo-Rah!"

The six modified LCPAs broke away from the Faster Than Light compressed space of the Jeremiah Wadsworth and immediately accelerated towards the two surviving Bug Super ships. The landing craft had special modifications designed to allow them to board the alien ships; high-powered gravity clamps to hold them tight to the Bug ship's hull and a molecular gravity drill to bore through that hull.

The six armored ships only had a few kilometers to travel, but the Bug reaction from the main body ships was swift. Four were vaporized almost immediately. Another was hit in its main drive unit and tumbled away until it was also destroyed.

"Hull clamp active, Major. Beginning to bore." Sergeant Anderson Poul supervised the boring operation. The twenty marines could do nothing but wait until the bore made it through to the single huge chamber thought to be inside the Bug Super Ship.

"We're through, Major."

"C'mon, you Devil Dogs, ya wanna live forever? Down the hole!" Major Otis Finch dropped a stun grenade down the hole, counted to four, and then jumped in himself.

Nineteen marines wearing evil grimaces dropped down the hole yelling, "HOO-RAH!"

The Bug Super Ship exploded before the Major reached the end of the hole.

***

The Battle For Turret Halsey
CIC
Standard Earth Date March 31 3488

"Ready, I think they'll be coming soon. Check your ammo." Mike went down his mental checklist. He looked around, remembering the faces he saw when he first came aboard the station. He looked at his father-in-law, as strong a figure as ever, even after losing a leg to a plasma blot that hit just below his knee. He looked to his wife, and his heart screamed in pain. Others injured as badly, or worse. Jane's voice brought him back to the task at hand.

"Ammo has been redistributed, Captain. Everyone able to fire has thirty rounds, plus handguns and a combat knife."

Damn. That gives us less than a minute of combat. Corry, I'm sorry. Mike looked at the gorgeous face of his wife, caked with the sweat and grime of combat and paled by her injury; he saw her face that night he proposed, his Angel, his life. He saw the tattoo they shared, and looked down at his own right shoulder. *Fortiter!*

"OK, people, there can't be many of those bugs left. Make every round count, and stay focused. Next Tuesday, the first round is on me!"

"There," Jock called, "The door, they're clearing…" Jock raised his carbine and aimed.

"Hello! Hello! Is anybody in there?"

***

Chrysler Building
55th Floor
New York City
Standard Earth Date March 31 3488

"Someone will have to monitor things until a more… permanent solution is decided upon. Your temporary comm station is here. Anything you desire will be delivered to you here, all you have to do is ask."

"What happened to that comm station?" The young man looked at the melted comm station on the right hand side of the massive desk.

"You need not concern yourself with that. Just handle the tasks as they arrive."

"Understood." *I hope!*

***

The Battle For Castle Shannon
USF Jeremiah Wadsworth
Standard Earth Date March 31 3488

"Damn it!" Jack Macalister pounded his fist onto his command console. "One hundred and thirty eight men dead! Damn it!"

"Jack, it was a gamble. We couldn't know they'd react that quickly,

201

or that they'd scuttle their ship rather than let us capture it. Every one of those men volunteered, and you tried to talk every single one of them out of it. Sometimes this crap happens in war." Peter's speech struck a chord with Jack. He was right on every count.

"Maybe, Pete. But it still sucks. I shouldn't have tried this."

"Jack, the chance to capture a Bug Super ship! It was worth the risk." Kesa tried to use her unquestionable logic to comfort her husband.

"Jack, I'm picking up more ships. A lot more ships." Peter's voice was excited, almost panicked. "Jack, there's another Bug fleet coming."

"Pete, get the details to Kesa. Kesa, tight beam it to ADS 1284 and Lunar Command. We're turning around."

"Kesa, I've got six hundred Bug Super Ships headed inbound at zero-point-seven light speed. No smaller ships. Position is… twenty light minutes behind Bug main body."

"Sent. Jack, why send to 1284?"

"Admiral Seymour mentioned that they were commanding Castle Shannon; they'll be on Taclink. The entire fleet will know what they know."

"What's your plan, Commodore?" Peter asked.

"I plan to run the weapons test on Big Bertha."

***

The Battle For Turret Halsey
CIC
Standard Earth Date March 31 3488

"Who goes there?" Mike's bass voice boomed out.

"Lieutenant James Jenkins, USFMC, Nili Patera Station. I've got some marines from the other turrets here as well." Jenkins finished his introduction as he shoved the last Bug body out of the doorway and stepped into the CIC. "Good God!" he gasped as the scene before him hit his senses.

Florescent green was splattered everywhere, Bug blood. The stench of rotten garbage, burned flesh, and fried electronics choked the nostrils. There were Bug bodies everywhere, and a lot of human bodies as well, all of it veiled in a thin reddish-brown smoke.

"This is Marine Captain Michael Halsey. I have several injured people here. Are there medics with you?"

"Yes, Captain. We need to get your wounded stabilized and onto the shuttles quickly though. The Bug vanguard is coming back." Jenkins turned his head and yelled, "MEDICS!"

***

The Battle For Castle Shannon
Tracy's Turret
Standard Earth Date March 31 3488

"Have you got that, Admiral?" Commander Tracy Singh asked Admiral Jericho Bucktooth.

"Hell yes. Hold tight, Commander. Bucktooth out."

"Yeah, 'hold tight'. What hell else can we do here?" Tracy started at the sound of her voice; *Damn, did I say that out loud?* "Alex, anything on the Halsey evacuation?"

"Shuttles are away, Commander. Bug vanguard looks to be in pursuit." Alex MacAlister felt renewed energy. His father and sister were still alive. *If I had a sword, I could whip the whole Bug fleet with it right now!*

"Easy, Lieutenant. Don't get too excited. I need you focused here. ETA for shuttles and Bug vanguard?"

"Shuttle ETA four minutes. Vanguard ETA five minutes. Shuttles will be in vanguard range in three minutes. Vanguard will be in our laser range in two-point-five minutes."

"That's cutting it close."

"Roger that, Sir."

***

Task Force Anvil
USF Victory
Standard Earth Date March 31 3488

"Comm, Task Force Nail grav-burst"

"Grav-burst comm open, Admiral"

"Rhodes, execute."

"Grave-burst sent. Confirmed receipt."

"Jeri, didn't Nail come back with Hammer?" Captain Charlie Walker asked on a private comm.

"My orders were to return every ship and task force on Taclink to Earth orbit. I followed my orders. Nail went off Taclink when they went dark. Rhonda's been sharpening her claws ever since."

"I don't doubt that, Sir." Charlie grinned at the thought of that tiger being unleashed.

"Oh, and Charlie, my orders never specified how long we had to remain in Earth orbit."

***

Task Force Nail
USF Lexington
Standard Earth Date March 31 3488

"Grav-burst coming in, Captain."

"My CHUD. Thanks, Sparks." Commodore Rhonda Rhodes ordered. She read the command, twitching like a cat about to pounce

"Comm, open Nail."

"Open."

"This is Commodore Rhodes. Attack formation Alpha 4. Good hunting Nail!"

The twelve battlecruisers and their escorts moved from silent and invisible in space quickly to full powered maximum drive, hitting three hundred times the speed of light instantly. They stopped amid the Bug main body.

"Lasers, fire at will. GravTorps, fire! Just like practice, gentlemen. Give 'em hell!"

"GravTorps away!"

"Maneuver Rhodes One, NOW!"

Task Force Nail disappeared before a Bug ship could target them. The lasers had vaporized seventy bug ships, and now the GravTorps took out hundreds more.

"Nail reports all torpedo tubes reloaded, Commodore." The Task Force had sped away at three hundred times the speed of light after firing their ordinance. Now they would return and hit the enemy again.

204

"Nail, execute maneuver Rhodes Two, NOW!"

Thirty-six laser spiting USF ships stopped, surrounding the Bug Super ship in the center of the Bug main body. Task Force Nail spent seven seconds pounding it with lasers as they unleashed their GravTorp salvo outward at the defending main body. On the eighth second, Nail was gone again. Another two hundred and forty Bug ships had died.

It took Commodore Rhonda Rhodes exactly sixty-four seconds to reduce the Bug main body to a few confused stragglers.

"Comm, Nail."

"Open."

"Nail, follow me. We're going hunting for bugs. Formation Loyal."

***

The Battle For Castle Shannon
Tracy's Turret
Standard Earth Date March 31 3488

"I'll be damned!" Commander Singh's awed whisper was lost amid the frantic cheering in her CIC. *So, that is what FTL ships can do to a sub-light fleet! I hope they get here in time!*

"Commander, Task Force Nail in position between our shuttle and the Bug vanguard." Alex cheered.

Tracy watched the images on her CHUD. *This is fucking amazing!* "I have GOT to get me one of those ships!"

Task Force Nail came out of FTL in a hemispherical formation, with the light cruisers in the center and the battlecruisers on the rim, to concentrate their firepower on the tightly packed Bug formation. The closest bug ships simply vanished under the onslaught of laser fire, now augmented by the accurate lasers from Castle Shannon. When the Shrikes and GravTorps began hitting the Bug ships, it was all over. In three minutes time, the eighteen ships of Task Force Nail had destroyed over a thousand Bug ships. No Bug ship had managed to fire a shot in that time.

Task Force Anvil
USF Victory
Standard Earth Date March 31 3488

"Comm, USF Lexington."

"Open."

"Commodore Rhodes, superlatives are inadequate to define what you have accomplished. Well done to you and Task Force Nail."

"Admiral, the crews of these ships deserve the credit. All I did was let go of the leash."

"Roger that, Commodore. Status of your Task Force?"

"We are undamaged. Two ships reporting torpedo tube malfunctions, four have silo door failures. Half of our ships have at least one laser battery burned-out from overheating. We are down to five percent stocks on GravTorps and ten percent on Shrikes. We can support Castle Shannon, Admiral, but not for long."

"Understood, Commodore. Your orders are to rejoin Taclink and do just that. Comm, private line to Rhodes."

"Open."

"Rhonda, shut up and take this. I'm proud of you. You did a hell of a lot more than unleash the hounds, you personally sharpened each and every one of their teeth. Well done."

"Admiral, I…" Commodore Rhonda Rhodes sat back in her chair, a tear on each cheek. *USF Nili Patera,* she thought about the crew that didn't survive that collision. And that the two crewmembers that did survive it had demanded that they be assigned to the Lexington. "Thank you Sir," she replied quietly.

"Comm, Task Force Nail general." The Admiral ordered.

"Open."

"Ladies and gentlemen, this is Admiral Bucktooth. Well done, Nail. To each and every one of you, well done. Bucktooth out. Comm, Hammer."

"Open,"

"Admiral Gordon, it's your turn. Target that new Bug formation and destroy them. No-holds-barred, Mark."

"Aye, aye, SIR!"

"Good hunting. Bucktooth out."

***

The Battle For Castle Shannon
USF Jeremiah Wadsworth
Standard Earth Date March 31 3488

"All stop."

"All stop confirmed. Weapon charged."

"Kesa, target status?"

"Locked on the center of the formation, Jack."

"Here goes. Firing." Jack hit the trigger and everything went dark on the Jeremiah Wadsworth.

***

Task Force Hammer
USF Dreadnought
Standard Earth Date March 31 3488

"Forty seconds until firing position, Admiral."

"Admiral to Hammer, look sharp and good hunting!" Mark Gordon swallowed hard. He reached up and ran a finger under his collar. It sure felt tighter than it was!

"Admiral, something…what the hell? Admiral, a huge energy burst has destroyed half of the Bug Super ships!"

Admiral Gordon had seen it on his CHUD, but he wasn't sure if he believed it. Then he remembered…

"Scan the area for a cold ship."

"Got it, Sir! How did you know?"

"It's an Admiral's job to know everything, Lieutenant MacAlister. Can you get an ID from its config?"

"Config matches AG-1 Thistle ninety-six percent, Sir."

"Admiral Gordon to USF Indianapolis, detach and assist USF Jeremiah Wadsworth. Evacuate any crew to ADS 1284."

"Aye-aye, Sir."

"Charlie, you ready for your knife fight?"

Captain Charlie Walker loudly patted his combat knife sheath.

"I never leave home without it."

"Firing position in three. Two. One. Now."

Thirty battlecruisers, thirty heavy cruisers and thirty light cruisers were suddenly on top of the remnants of the Bug formation. Admiral Gordon hadn't had time to put together any elegant battle plans, but he did have information. He had seen Nail's firepower overwhelm the Bug ships. Where Rhodes had needed to stab the Bug fleet with her Nail, Gordon was content to pound this Bug fleet with his Hammer.

The huge blast that had halved the Bug fleet had also disorganized it. There was no return fire for twenty seconds. In that time, eighty-seven Bug ships had died.

The big Bug Superships had considerably greater firepower than the standard Bug ships. Each had four beams that approximately doubled the power of the smaller Bug vessels. Over the next sixty seconds, ten light and four heavy cruisers were destroyed by concentrated firepower from dozens of Bug ships. Four battlecruisers were heavily damaged, but the Bugs were being pounded as well. Another ninety-six Bug Superships were killed.

Then Bug ships started exploding all over space, as Task Force Nail in stealth mode swooped in on the alien formation and hit them from behind. Within forty-three seconds, all of the alien ships had been destroyed.

"Comm, Rhodes."

"Open."

"Nice shooting, Rhonda. I owe you a beer."

"I…" A screaming static hit Marks' ears for a split second before silence replaced it.

"Sir, the Lexington…it, it just blew up!"

***

Lunar Command Station
Hospital Complex
Tsiolkovskiy Crater
Standard Earth Date April 3 3488

"How are you feeling, Jock?" Jericho Bucktooth sat down next to his friend's hospital bed.

"Leg's sore. Other than that, well…"

"We kicked their exoskeletal asses, MacAlister. In a very large part because of your efforts."

"That's not what they're saying back home, is it, Jeri."

"Fuck them." Admiral Bucktooth stood up, frowning. "Damn it, Jock, you saved the Goddamn world! You should be getting a parade, or something…"

"I don't care about that, Jeri. What were the final totals?"

"The formal briefing and analysis will be in five days. The short version is this. We lost too much, Jock. Three battlecruisers, ten heavy and ten light cruisers. Plus ADS 1437, the people there. Six LCPAs. And, Jock…" Jeri sat down and looked into Jock's eyes. Jock knew that look. He'd seen it before, a lifetime ago…

"Jack and Kesa. They fired some super beam Jack had designed, and the kickback fried everything inside that old bucket. Jock, they never felt it."

Jock turned his head, and looked at the ceiling. "Jeri," he said quietly, "I…"

"Oh!"

The thud from the doorway caught the two men's attention. Jeri moved fast to her side, only to find Jock already there, somehow lifting his wife while standing on one leg.

"Jeri, help."

The two of them managed to get Sandy onto the bed. Jock sat next to her, panting, pale, and drenched in sweat.

"I'll get a nur…"

Jeri's voice was cut short by four large black-suited men at the door to the room. Two pushed roughly past him and moved to Sandy.

"Hey!" Jeri reached to grab one, and was immediately held by the other two. Jock stood up on one leg and smiled at the closest black-suit.

"You wouldn't hit a cripple, would you?" Jock pointed to his leg that ended in a bloody bandage at mid-calf. When the suit looked at the leg, Jock swung. He was somehow across the bed in front of the other suit before the first one hit the floor.

"Admiral! We're Secret Service! We're your wife's security detail!" Agent Hiram Abim yelled as he backed away. "Admiral, are you OK?"

Jock waivered, then fell down on the bed.

"I've had better days."

Chapter Nine

United News Network
Times Square Studios
Standard Earth Date April 4 3488

"Hello, I'm Don Derringer, and this is Straight Shot!

"Tonight, we were scheduled to have Senator Sandy MacAlister, the primary challenger to President Clark Campbell, in our sights for an exclusive interview. Unfortunately, as you have just heard here, the Senator's oldest son, Commodore Jack MacAlister, and his wife, Commander Kesa MacAlister, died while fighting the Battle with the Bugs. In addition, the Senator's husband, Admiral Jock MacAlister, lost his leg, and their daughter, Corrine Halsey, lost an arm in the same battle. As soon as she was told this heartbreaking news, the Senator's office contacted us and asked that we reschedule.

"Our sympathies to the Senator and her family for the losses they suffered while attacking the Bug delegation. We will reschedule our interview with the Senator as soon as she is emotionally able to handle it. Whenever that may be.

"Now, we do have tonight another in our series of brief biographies of President Clark Campbell, aptly entitled "Cool Under Fire: When Destiny Calls"...

***

Lunar Command Station
Admiral's Conference Room
Tsiolkovskiy Crater
Standard Earth Date April 8 3488

"Analyzing a battle can be a difficult and painful task. This is the best we have come up with." Jericho Bucktooth stood frowning in front of his senior officers. He wore his best 'shuddup-and-listen' look. "It is imperative that we get this right, gentlemen and ladies. We have orders for imminent action."

Jeri waited until the buzz died down a bit.

"Our plan was as good as we could make it, but it could not deal with the Bugs splitting off such a large portion of their force to attack 1437. Even so, we had inflicted huge losses on their fleet, and would have prevailed, even with the addition of the second Bug fleet, which would have produced significant casualties, had we not been called back to Earth.

"As it was, Jack and his Jeremiah Wadsworth saved our bacon. The loss of so many Superships hurt them badly, and disrupted anything they had planned. They had to fight the rest of the battle looking over their shoulders for that weapon.

"Commodore Rhodes' actions, both in her initial attack, and in her final action, won the day. Thanks to her quick planning and decisive actions, our casualties were one quarter what we project they should have been.

"I have recommended several decorations above what you have forwarded to me. For Jack and Rhonda, I have requested the Medal of Honor, Hero of Earth decoration. In my book, all of our Sailors and Marines were heroes that day."

"Now, to the battle! Are there any questions, comments? Admiral Gordon."

"The Bugs did some kind of warp thing where they appeared to 'jump' from one place to another. What was that, and why did they use it only once?"

"The best guess we have is they used some type of dimensional shift technology to move into a different dimension, and return to our dimension in a different place. We theorize that this takes enormous energies, and that it takes a significant time to 'recover'. That's the good news. The bad news is, given enough energy, it could be used for FTL travel. Next?"

"Why did the Bugs go after Turret 1437, and why were we withdrawn? It looks like someone was out to get..."

"A cynical man would say that the Bug actions, combined with the recall of the ships, could only mean one thing, that the Bugs were after that turret, and they had help. I am not a cynical man, but a practical and loyal man. We will not begin speculating on the motives of politicians, alien or otherwise, in my command. Next?" Jericho looked over the faces, good men and women. They knew exactly what he did. Now, to the real reason they were here.

"I have been directed to draw up plans for an invasion of the Bug home system, and the total annihilation of every Bug outpost, station, and inhabited planet there. This invasion is to begin in ten months. You each have an assignment in this planning that is on your datatabs now. Are there any questions?"

"Sir, do we just FTL in there, drop a few hundred rocks on their homeworld, and leave? Don't we give them a chance to surrender?" Jock stood to speak, still wobbling slightly on his interim prosthesis.

"The idea of offering surrender has neither been included nor has it been excluded in the directive I received. Are there any other questions? Good. Dismissed.

"Jock, hang around please."

***

United News Network
Times Square Studios
Standard Earth Date May 12 3488

"Good evening, Ladies and Gentlemen. Tonight we have a special treat in our sights. Rear Admiral Jock MacAlister himself. I'm Don Derringer. Welcome to this special, *live* broadcast of Straight Shot!

"Admiral, thank you for taking the time to be on our show. What brings you here?"

"Thank you for having me, Don. I'm here for two reasons. First, I have resigned my commission in the United Space Force effective as of nine A.M. this morning. Second, there is some information that I think your viewers need to know."

"Well, ah, Admiral, why have you resigned? What caused this? Was it the deaths and injuries to yourself and your family?"

"Don, I resigned because I can no longer fulfill my duties to the USF. Losing my leg means I cannot operate in space combat effectively. And to create a desk job for me would simply be wasting the taxpayer's monies."

"So, the deaths of your oldest son and his wife, and your daughter's loss of her arm had nothing to do with your resignation?"

"No, they did not. My children are all adults now. Those who have entered USF did so as adults, knowing the risks involved. I am proud of all of my children, Mr. Derringer, as each and every one has chosen a career which serves society."

"I see. Well, what is the information that you feel my viewers need to know?"

"Don, your show has taken some rather curious paths the past several months. So, being a curious fellow..."

"Now, hold on, Admiral, you told my producers this 'information' had to do with government corruption and corporate graft, not this show. Were you dishonest?"

"Not at all. You will see as I go on. And please do not interrupt me again. It only degrades your image.

"As I was saying, a search of public records has revealed certain things that seem to make sense out of otherwise puzzling developments. First, I have found that you have recently purchased a vacation home, paid for in cash, valued at two hundred times your annual income. Second, that you have paid zero taxes over the past year, despite an eight figure income. Third, that you have donated huge amounts to the campaign of Clark Campbell. And fourth, that you have suddenly acquired a large amount of General Aerospace Developments stock.

"Now, viewers, Mr. Derringer claims an unbiased and even viewpoint on his show, but is that really the case? Viewers, what do you say?"

***

United Earth Senate
Montreal
Standard Earth Date May 13 3488

Mary MacAlister fumed as she walked down the hallway to her mother's office. People just didn't DO things like this! Not in the world she grew up in...

Mary walked into the office and headed straight into the inner suite.

"Mom. We need to talk." Mary snapped as she kept walking into the private area of the suite.

Sandy MacAlister looked up from the speech she had been revising with her campaign staff. Her left eyebrow shot up as her eyes followed her oldest daughter's stomping march into her private rooms.

"Excuse me, Dave. I've got to see what this is about." She stood and followed her daughter, not hearing her campaign consultant's reply.

"Okay, Mary. Why all the drama?" Sandy stood in front of the closed door, right foot tapping a beat of impatience upon the floor.

"Goddamn Charlene. Everything was a set up. Damn, damn, DAMN IT ALL! How could I be so foolish!" Mary sat down hard on the edge of the bed, looked at her feet for several moments. Then the floodgates opened.

"Mom!"

Sandy was at her daughter's side, arm over her shoulders pulling her injured child close.

"Oh, baby... tell me what happened."

"She, she, MOM! She went to..." Mary dove into the shelter of her mother's embrace, sniffing and sobbing before she could continue, "she went to the press, about US! She did it to hurt you, Mom, everything was just to hurt you, and I fell for it! She never cared for me at all! I let her hurt you!" Mary broke into a continuous sobbing state, emotions piling upon emotions and overwhelming her senses.

"Oh, baby! I'm so sorry. She didn't deserve you. It hurts, now, I know, but you will survive this!"

"But, MOM! She's hurting YOU!" Mary fell into that most comfortable place of sanctuary, her mother's love.

"Darling, anyone she could convince to vote against me, well, I don't want their vote anyway. I don't need their vote! I do need you to keep being my campaign manager, my moral beacon, to keep me on course. I'll be fine. Mary honey, right now, I'm most worried about you."

Mary buried her head into her mother's bosom and let her broken heart pour out, as one can only do in the arms of their mom.

***

United Space Force Academy
United Space Force Academy Hilton
Cape Canaveral, Florida
Standard Earth Date June 21 3488

The two men walked down the paved path towards the chapel, one wearing a black suit and walking with a noticeable limp, the other in a spotless dress white uniform glowing in the moonlight. Each carried a bouquet of flowers with a note attached. When they reached the plaza before the chapel entrance, the Captain knelt and placed his flowers. He remained there for several minutes, his proud demeanor broken now by escaping sobs. When he seemed near to being overcome, the man in the suit placed a hand on his shoulder, bent near him, and spoke into his ear. Soon after the Captain rose and walked into the chapel, leaving the man in the suit to repeat the ritual as he had so many times before.

Nearby, over two hundred freshly graduated officers knelt with bowed heads, the buzz of their whispered conversations barely audible over the crickets' love calls. They had heard of this moment for three years, but most had not experienced it before this graduation night. Could it really have been going on for over forty years? Many couples huddled closer in honor of the moment and their mutual feelings.

As the man in the suit stood and entered the chapel, the graduates moved out onto each side of the pathway. The honor guard was never formalized. Each year's class seemed to form it spontaneously as tribute to those who had passed before them, as well as those they had struggled, grown and triumphed with these past four years.

The two men exited the chapel as one, in step and eyes front they stepped smartly through the honor guard, greatly moved by the experience.

Captain Gridley spoke quietly to Jock Macalister, "Is it always this way, Admiral?"

"Ever since you and Rhonda watched me that first time, yes. I don't know any more if I do this for me, for Sharon, or for them,"

"Jock, I think you do it for us all."

Sometime after they had left the campus, the line outside Star's The Limit Body Art still stretched around the block. An old woman wearing a waitress uniform, stood patiently among those waiting for the "Starclan" tattoo, politely refusing all offers to move ahead in the line. Her well-worn nametag read "Wanda".

***

United News Network
Times Square Studios
Standard Earth Date October 14 3488

"My esteemed opponent would muddy the waters here a bit. You, as voters, have a clear choice, to vote for the reluctant incumbent whose decisive action in time of crisis preserved our race, or to vote for the 'sensitive' candidate who shriveled at the first sign of difficult times, who's own family can't live up to the false bravado and sham morality they would impose upon us all." Campbell sat smugly back in his chair after the poll-proven optimal amount of applause time had passed.

"My reclusive opponent neglects to include certain details in his impotent attempt to revise recent history. Such as the disaster his order to withdraw our ships was, or how General Aerospace sent directives along with campaign cash to him moments before his ill-timed order, or how the brave men and women of the United Space Force saved all of our asses from the certain extinction his incompetence, cronyism and graft would have doomed us to.

"As for my family, Mr. Campbell, do you want to try and hurt ME by attacking my children here on World Wide Vid? What problem, exactly, do you have with my children, sir?" Sandy glared at her opponent, challenging, demanding him his response.

"Well, the, eh, um…hrumpf!"

"Yes, I thought as much. You, Clark Campbell, you are so slimy I'm amazed that you haven't slid out of that chair! Even being on the same ballot as you is degrading to every decent, patriotic, thoughtful citizen of this world.

"Ladies and gentlemen, your choice is clear. You may vote for the nepatalistic, corrupt, and incompetent Campbell, who owes his power to General Aerospace, or you may vote for a moral, ethical, and common sense alternative. I know which choice I will make, for the sake of my children and yours. Ladies and gentlemen, what do you say?"

***

Chrysler Building
55th Floor
New York City
Standard Earth Date September 3 3488

"This is not going well at all, Abernathy." The young man knew trouble when he saw it, and he knew this election was crucial to the objectives assigned to him. Hell, it was crucial to his SURVIVAL!

"We have all the polling place 'interventions' active that we can have, Sir. We can only wait now." Abernathy shook slightly with apprehension as he considered the likely outcome, even with the best efforts available.

"Abernathy, I want you to understand that "close" is not good enough. Should our side not prevail, there will certainly be a cleansing. Need I point out to you that such a "cleansing" will be one extremely long and tortuous affair?"

"I understand, sir. Everything that can be done is in motion as we speak, sir. Along with some, well, plans for way to *incentivize* a certain individual, sir." Abernathy was now visibly shaking. As if to punctuate the situation, a bloodcurdling howl echoed throughout the huge room.

"Be sure your efforts are successful, for if they are not, I will take a small satisfaction in seeing your penance before serving mine!" The young man spat the words at Abernathy as he turned towards the windows.

"That is all. Go away now."

***

Grand Ballroom
New Hotel Syracuse
Standard Earth Date November 8 3488

"And now I see that Julie Saam has managed to get near the Senator's campaign manager, Mary MacAlister. Julie, take it away!"

"Thanks, Don. I'm here at the MacAlister election night headquarters, talking with Mary MacAlister, Senator Sandy MacAlister's daughter and campaign manager. Mary, what do you see happening tonight?"

"My mother's challenger has tried mudslinging, distortion, and outright lies to win this election. It simply will not work." Mary MacAlister said into the overly auspicious microphone. "There is simply nothing that will distract from his horrendous record of gross incompetence."

"But, what about the revelations of your 'affair'…"

"So he planted a trollop with instructions to woo me for the purpose of embarrassing my mother, and I fell for it. Well, I can tell you that that will NOT happen a second time! You are asking, what does this say about my mother? I ask you, what does it say about her opponent? And, what does it say about you, as a reporter, so eager to be complicit in such dealings that you're practically frothing at the mouth? Well?"

The reporter stood dumbfounded on the ballroom floor, unable to speak for several seconds.

"Right. That's what I thought. Voters, what do YOU say!" Mary emphasized her statement by pointing into the camera, and then she smiled and walked away.

***

Fleet Assembly Station
L-2 Lagrangian Point
Standard Earth Date February 26 3489

"We should be coming into view in a moment, Ambassador. It's just beyond the lunar horizon."

"Thank you, Lieutenant..."

"Lieutenant Kowalski, Admir...eh, Ambassador. Sorry, Sir."

"No apology necessary, Lieutenant. There it is!" Jock MacAlister's voice carried just a hint of the awesome sight before him. Four hundred and sixty heavy ships. Battleships, battle cruisers, light and heavy cruisers in a globe formation around four huge vessels: the Monitors!

"They're quite a sight, aren't they Sir! Streamlined dumbbell shapes with two drive units, each of three Gravitic Drives. They can aim one hundred percent of their thrust in any direction. And the UHRGs, Sir. The crews call them 'Uglies'. Ultra Heavy Rail Guns. Each of the Monitor class carries two hundred SPAD fighters each as well, each one armed with two Plasma cannon and two GravTorps or six Shrikes." The pride and confidence in the Lieutenant's voice stirred Jock considerably, but years of training kept his outward demeanor calm.

"SPADs?"

"Space Pursuit and Area Defense, Ambassador."

The shuttle moved quickly and silently towards the closest Monitor. The huge vessel filled the viewport as they neared it. At two and a half kilometers long, these were the largest ships ever built by far. Begun three years previously, the four had not yet been fitted with weapons when the Bugs invaded.

Lieutenant Kowalski deftly flew the shuttle around the monstrous ship, giving Jock an impromptu tour. Dozens of shield generators, sensors, plasma cannon, and railgun turrets dotted the exterior of the

218

ship, with the exception of the hanger doors. They eventually came upon an open hanger, and flew in to land.

Jock stood in the small cockpit of the shuttle, placing a hand on Kowalski's shoulder. "Thanks, Lieutenant. I appreciated that."

"Yes, Sir! It's not every day I get to shuttle an Ambassador who is also a retired Admiral, and his staff, Sir."

Jock smiled and walked back to the passenger area. "Everyone ready?"

"We're all a little eager to get going, Ambassador." Mary MacAlister answered.

The seven staff members stood and gathered their carry-on bags, then followed Jock to the exit. They watched him stand a little taller as the door opened.

Jock strode smoothly down the ramp and onto the shuttle bay deck, walking up to the OD. He stopped, and had to catch his arm from saluting as he said, "Permission to come aboard, Sir!"

"Permission granted. Welcome aboard, Ambassador!"

***

Presidential Mansion
Montreal
Standard Earth Date February 26 3489

"Dave, it is the only way I can be sure the end result is something I can live with. I don't care about future political ramifications or exposures. You should know that!" President Sandy MacAlister leaned back in her chair, calmly confident in her decision.

"Sandy, it's my job to point these things out to you. You won the special election by a whisker. Campbell's machine will never let go of the 'fixed' angle, their egos won't let them. I agree with sending Jock as Ambassador to the Bugs, he's the only one we could trust with it. But you have to know that if there is a truce, the Press will call you weak and concessionist. If we have to destroy them, you will be called Genocidal, vengeful, and worse. Sandy, there is no road to a win in this for you, only a path to the least amount of damage."

"And that path is the one I intend to follow, Dave. I'm interested in doing what is right for Humanity, what is morally right, not what is good for my political career. We must stay on that path, no matter what."

"That is why so many of us work so hard for you, Madam President."

***

USF Monitor
Admiral's Suite
Standard Earth Date February 26 3489

The decorations in Fleet Admiral Jericho Bucktooth's office consisted of three pictures of his only granddaughter along the left side of his desk. It made it easier to move from his office on Earth to Mars, the moon, or a ship with minimal effort. He reached out and touched her face on the most recent one, from her tenth birthday party just a few weeks ago.

"To protect you, Adsila", his whisper interrupted by the door chime. He stood using the time it took walking to the door to compose himself.

"Ambassador! Jock, good to see you!" Jeri gave his friend a solid handshake before pulling him into a hug. "Two A.M., UHRG loading room six. Alone," he whispered. "How's Corry? How's the leg?"

"Jeri, you look well. I've got a decent fit with this new prosthesis, so it's a lot better. Corry is doing fine. She's taken quite easily to being a full-time mother to Ranald. This ship is something!" Jock smiled as he searched his mentor's eyes for a sign of the problem; *what is it? He'll give no clue just yet, I'll have to wait.*

"We've been able to put everything you wanted into these four ships. We've even added a variation of Trap's sandblaster point defense systems. And, Jock, we've also added Jack's super beam to the bow and stern, with more power and better shielding. These four ships are impressive."

"Are your quarters adequate, Ambassador?"

"They'll do nicely, Jeri. How is the fleet coming together?"

"You know I can't talk about that. I can relay information that may assist you in completing your mission. We will have enough firepower to eliminate six times the forces that attacked Earth. If it's ten, we're even. That's without taking the Monitors or FTL tactics into account. You've been give the classified outline of the plan, take out their military, offer them terms, and see what happens. You have linguists along who think they can talk to the Bugs, I understand."

"Yes, Jeri. My mission is to try and find a solution that assures no further attacks from the Bugs without exterminating them. If possible." *Still no hint. This must be bad for him to compartmentalize it like this. And that classified crap. I'm married to his Commander In Chief! He figures his office is bugged. Damn.* "Are you bringing all four of these Monitors or are you leaving some here?"

"There will be adequate forces in place to protect the Earth. Now, Jock, what can you tell me about this theory that the Bugs wiped out the Birds?"

"As you know, a scout-survey ship was sent to the assumed Bird homeworld. The data they brought back went straight to the President. Jeri, the most likely orbit for the Bird homeworld has only a spreading field of rocky debris in it. Three other regions in the system near gas giants have similar debris fields. Our best bet is that the moons and planets were all destroyed."

"Would Bug bombardment be able to do that?"

"We doubt it, unless they used something much larger as projectiles. Still, it seems the only answer at this time."

"Unless there is someone else out there. Someone who did to the Birds what we're getting ready to do to the Bugs right now."

"Yeah, well. Hrumpf! Would you like a view from the bridge of the departure tomorrow? It's pretty damn spectacular."

"I wouldn't miss it!"

***

Chrysler Building
55th Floor
New York City
Standard Earth Date February 26 3488

The young girl sat shaking in the vast room, thinking that the huge room seemed to close in on her in the dark. The man sat in the corner, silent and unmoving, staring at her with eyes faintly glowing a pale pink. As she stared at the blank comm screen... well, it was not entirely blank; something moved about, touching her senses as a twilight swarm of gnats just on the edge of her field of vision. She had been sleeping at home, in her bed, and then she woke up here. That was four days ago. She swallowed hard, trying to remember the protections her grandmother had tried to teach her as she waited for *IT* to come back...

"Soon. We will know soon, when IT returns..." the man in the corner softly growled.

"I am thankful that I am alive and in health," the girl began, "So, then now do you, Sky-Holder who lives in the sky, do you continue to listen? You next, the nocturnal Orb of Light, our Grandmother, and now also the Stars in many places, do you know that I have made plans to thank you?"

SILENCE CHILD! We have everything in place. IT was back, words booming in her head.

"Then, then, you'll let me go?" She stood up, for her Grandfather had taught her to stand boldly in the face of Evil.

Your Grandfather must live up to his end of the agreement. Only then will you be free of this place. Unless...

"I, I will NEVER join you! You are evil! Stop asking me that! My spirit protector is here, now, so go away!" She imagined herself standing tall with the strong arms of a huge black bear protectively around her. Her faith in her family's teachings was all she had to fight with.

***

USF Dreadnought
Bridge
Standard Earth Date February 26 3489

Admiral Mark Gordon looked around the bridge, watching the crew move about their tasks. *This atmosphere is so different than the last engagement. Everyone was anxious, on edge, but focused and sharp. Now, they're efficient and confident. Overconfident? I need to keep the confidence yet sharpen their focus.* He shot a glance at Captain Charles Walker, catching the man's eye. When Mark moved his eyebrow a fraction of a millimeter, Charlie hit the trigger under his finger, and the alarms shook the ship.

Ding-ding-ding.
"ALERT!"
Ding-ding-ding.

222

"ALERT!"

Ding-ding-ding.

"ALERT!"

"BATTLE STATIONS! Repeat, BATTLE STATIONS!" Lieutenant Alistair MacAlister's voice calmly boomed throughout the ship.

Mark watched the crew on the bridge move efficiently through the routine; they had done this hundreds of times in simulations and drills, and once in battle. He saw no hesitation, no wasted time, just the determined motions of professionals executing their assigned duties with efficient competence.

"Twenty one seconds from initial alarm to 'all battle stations ready', Captain."

"This is the Captain. Well done! Secure from battle stations. That is all."

Charlie turned to the Admiral and winked. Mark looked back, the faintest of grins pulling at his mouth. *That's better than any drill before the battle. I feel better now. Much better.*

***

USF Monitor
UHRG Loading Room Six
Standard Earth Date February 27 3489

Ambassador Jock MacAlister slid quietly through the hatchway at fifteen minutes before the indicated time. He scanned the huge room once for signs of life, then again to take in the immensity of the place. It was a roughly box-shaped area, forty feet to a side and twelve feet floor to ceiling. While the floor was painted a medium grey, the walls and ceiling were painted in an off-white, almost yellow color. Nearly every square inch was filled with massive machinery. Off to his left Jock noticed the huge enclosed ammunition feed housing that fed into the railgun's breech. Just past that the magnetic drivers began coiling around the huge barrel as it disappeared towards the muzzle at the stern of the huge vessel, nearly a half mile away.

There wasn't much room for people in here. This area did not normally have a crew, it was an armored shell housing the automated loading mechanisms. The hatchway was only to allow for maintenance and battle damage repairs. The air buzzed with static charges, a constant humming droning on in the background, the odor of warm electrical circuitry and lubricants further crowding the room.

A noise startled Jock. Something moved behind the driver coils, scurrying along, until it finally ran past Jock and through the hatchway into the corridor.

"Everywhere man goes, mice follow, despite the best laid plans." Jeri stepped through the hatchway and closed the hatch, latching it securely. Then he took out a thumb-sized device that he attached to the wall and handed two earplugs to Jock. He motioned for Jock to cover his ears even as he quickly covered his own. Then he hit a button on the device.

Even through physical and electronic barrier of the plugs and his hands, the high-pitched warbling screech hurt Jock's ears. It seemed to go on for much too long, until finally it stopped and a green light flashed twice on the device.

"Sound will not pass through that hatch, and there are now no listening devices in here. Any people would have run screaming out unless their ears were protected." Jeri said as he pocketed the device.

"Jeri, what's going on?"

"Jock, there are some pretty big leaks in Fleet. Information about our ships and plans has gotten to the press.

"Even worse, we've analyzed the Bug attack. Jock, we are ninety-two percent certain the Bugs primary objective was ADS 1437."

"Jeri, could that have been due to me snagging their scout ship there?"

"That is the official word. The real data suggest something else entirely. Jock, we think they were after *you*."

Jock frowned at Admiral Bucktooth for several seconds, unsure how to respond to that, or what it could mean.

"Did they have agents here? Why would they go after me? What purpose would that serve?"

"We can't get a clue as to communications techniques or motivations. We do know that Clark Campbell became a wealthy man exactly forty seconds after he recalled the Fleet. He hung you out to dry, Jock."

"OK, so what do we do...Sandy! Is she safe? Jeri, is she?" Jock grabbed his friend by the front of his shirt as horrendous images flew through his mind.

"Relax. If assassination was an option, they would have taken you out that way. Besides, we have no indication the Secret Service has been compromised."

"So what do we do now?" Jock exhaled more air than he knew he'd taken in, but he still was nervous about his wife.

"We follow Plan Delta, twelve light cruisers will scout the system, flying in at FTL, stopping for twenty seconds to snap pics, then FTL out. Once we know where their military is, we take them out. Then we move in and offer them the terms."

"And these moles don't know this plan?"

"The plan put in front of them was to fly in and stop in orbit, fight off any attacks while delivering our 'ultimatum'."

"Someone fell for that? Are they that clueless?"

"They think *we're* that clueless."

"Well, we'd better make damn sure we disappoint them."

***

Presidential Mansion
Montreal
Standard Earth Date February 27 3489

"Madam President, we now have word that there are protests organized in two hundred cities. This could be a security threat."

"I want every security officer to have their cams running. I want drones up as well. Pass the word, these cams and drones are to monitor the *police*. I don't care what the protesters chant or curse. How long till air time?"

"Ten seconds, Madam President."

"Okay, here we go."

"Good evening. I am talking with you tonight to announce the departure of our fleet. Their mission is a simple one, to assure the survival of Humanity.

"Their task is not so simple. They will be arriving at the home world of the beings that attacked us last year by sending sixteen thousand asteroids at Earth. This attack, had it not been thwarted, would have ended all life on Earth.

"Our fleet is not traveling to the alien homeworld to conquer or to exterminate those known popularly as "The Bugs", but they will remove the alien's ability to attack us again. In addition, we believe we can communicate with the aliens. Therefore, I have assigned retired Admiral Jock MacAlister to act as Ambassador, to attempt to come to an understanding with the aliens that would allow both of our civilizations to coexist peacefully.

"Some among us think we should not be taking this trip, that we should just stay in our system and hope the aliens don't attack again. I believe it is the right thing to do, to be proactive in this way, to be sure these aliens can never attack us again. Those who will be peacefully protesting this action have the right to do so. They have the right to disagree with me, to disagree with our government. That is our way, and it is our most important ideal that we not lose our way on this point! Rest assured that I will *never* veer from that path, even though it leads me away from this esteemed office.

"On March tenth, I will resign from this office. I will not seek, nor will I accept another office in government, appointed or elected. Ever."

"Our brave men and women of the United Space Force have sacrificed greatly defending Earth. They are putting themselves in harms way yet once more for our sakes. Let us never forget the debt we owe them.

"Good night, and God bless you all, even the protesters. And Godspeed, USF!"

Chapter Ten

USF Monitor
Bridge
Standard Earth Date February 28 3489

Mary MacAlister stood uneasily on the bridge. She was thrilled to spend this much time with her father, yet she was uneasy standing on a warship. She had dedicated her life to peace, in a sense. After following her mother's footsteps and graduating law school she had joined her mother's old law firm, handling pro bono defense cases for those not able to afford quality legal counsel. Something told her she was needed elsewhere, so she had enrolled in theology school. Then her ministry had taken a back seat to her mother's political campaigns. That had been painful for her. Her mother was a good woman and would help those she could, but the campaigns were brutal, cruel, and personally destructive. Now here she was, standing amidst the largest instrument of destruction ever made by Man. With a hidden gun.

Her father had been right, she knew. After what they did to her to try and hurt her mother, she knew that. She also knew no one would dare frisk or scan a priest.

"A penny for your thoughts, Angel." The softness of her father's voice, the love it carried to her nearly made her blurt out, 'Daddy' and give him a hug. She smiled at him instead, shaking her head slightly. *He would understand, then try to tell me why it has to be so. Oh, Father, you pull at my heart so!*

"Ten seconds. Is everyone ready?" Admiral Bucktooth's question elicited nodding heads all around.

"Three. Two. One. Now." Lieutenant Alistair MacAlister proudly counted down for his father and his big sister. As he said the last word, the universe physically changed.

Space in front of the huge ship shrank under the gravitic energies applied by the Monitor's drive generators, even as the great ship's engines pushed upon the fabric of space itself to thrust her ahead. In just three days, the USF Monitor and the rest of the fleet would travel nearly twenty light-years.

To those watching the viscreens there on the bridge, the sight was wondrous. The area directly ahead of them played through a rainbow of colors as it shrank to an immensely bright pinpoint of light directly ahead, while the stars off to the sides began stretching from glowing dots into brightly smudged lines. Mary watched one begin as a tiny dot of light breaking from the central pinpoint ahead, moving up and along the right side of the viscreens surrounding the bridge, changing colors as it lengthened into a long thin line; then it began shrinking rapidly and changing color again as they passed it by.

"Daddy, it's amazing!" she gave in and whispered to her father. *Dear Lord, please help me understand all of this. What is the role you've chosen for me here?*

Jock leaned over and whispered into her ear, "This is nearly as wondrous as I felt the day you were born."

"Well, Ambassador, what do you think?" Admiral Bucktooth beamed.

"I think I could stand and watch this for three days!"

"It usually takes twelve minutes to become 'uninteresting'. Come on, let's have some breakfast. My treat."

***

USF Essex
Achird 12 System
Standard Earth Date March 2 3489

"Sensor report, Lieutenant?" Captain Tracy Singh rubbed her chin as she studied her CHUD. The bright yellow star with an orange dwarf mate made for some interesting gravity fields in the system.

"Just getting readings now, Captain. There are approximately twenty thousand ships moving around the system, mostly in what look to be holding or patrol patterns. There are twelve large stations orbiting the only planet in the habitable zone. Everything seems centered there. I've got Bug comm traffic, but just background level."

"Okay, good work, Alex. Comm: general."

"Open."

"Here we are, boys and girls. Full stealth mode, FTL in, stop for twenty seconds, scan like mad, and FTL out. Our assigned scanning location has the closest proximity to the Bug homeworld. Piece of cake. On my mark, in three. Two. One. Mark!"

The USF light cruiser Essex flew into the star system at twenty times the speed of light with full stealth generators on, and stopped ten thousand kilometers from the Bug homeworld.

"Scanning, full spectrum."

Tracy Singh studied her CHUD as several ships passed close by. *A collision would just wreck my day!*

"FTL engage on my mark in ten. Nine. Eight. Seven. Six. Five. Four. Three. Two. One. Mark!"

The light cruiser vanished at twenty times light speed, on a course following the one she came in on, away from the fleet.

"Coming up on ten light-minute mark, Captain."

"Helm, accelerate to one hundred light speed, then ready course 166.23.220 on my command. Bring us back to the fleet."

"Ready, Captain."

"Ten light-minute mark in three. Two. One. Now."

"Helm, execute."

"Aye-aye, Captain!"

***

USF Monitor
UHRG Loading Room Six
Achird 12 System
Standard Earth Date March 2 3489

"Is it ready?" The officer asked from the shadows.

"I've got the stuff here. On every recording in the fleet it will look like the Bugs begged for peace, and we still squashed 'em. But, what if they do ask for peace?"

"They won't." The officer ducked through the hatchway and strode down the dark corridor.

USF Dreadnought
Bridge
Achird 12 System
Standard Earth Date March 2 3489

"Comm, Admiral Bucktooth."
"Open."
"Admiral, Task Force Alpha is ready."
"Prepare for execution of Hornets Nest on my command."
"Roger."

***

USF Monitor
Bridge
Achird 12 System
Standard Earth Date March 2 3489

"Ambassador, we've got our targets plotted. Once their heavy installations are down, we'll broadcast the surrender terms. After that, everything is upon your orders."
"Understood, Admiral."
"Comm, Taclink up. General Fleet."
"Taclink up. General Fleet open."
"Ladies and Gentlemen, we are about to remove the threat the military might of the Bugs poses to us. After that, we will act upon the judgment of Ambassador Jock MacAlister. He alone will determine if we exterminate the Bugs, or live peacefully alongside them.
"Remember the Lexington! Execute the Hornets Nest."
A slight rumble went through the Monitor as her main Ultra Heavy Railguns opened fire. Huge projectiles sped silently through space at nearly the speed of light, targeted to meet the Bug orbital fortresses in four hours.
The firing lasted only a few minutes, as the fleet waited three and a half hours before it moved at maximum FTL speed to a point outside the opposite edge of the Bug star system. Any Bug ship noticing the

firing of the railguns would be looking at where the fleet used to be.

"OK, Ambassador, the battle has begun. It's time for you to take your position in my ready room." Jeri pointed to the small office just off the bridge where the Bug communication feeds would be sent to Jock.

"Good hunting, Jeri." Jock said as he and Mary moved into the room and disappeared as the doors sealed them in.

"Some SOB once said something about war being intense boredom interrupted by unspeakable horror. Smart SOB." Gridley commented.

Around the bridge, crewmembers killed the waiting time by eating an energy snack or sipping a stim-drink. They also checked, rechecked, and re-rechecked their equipment. Finally the clock ticked down.

"Comm, Fleet general."

"Open."

"FTL: Task Force Alpha to Firebase Alpha. Task Force Beta to Firebase Beta. Execute on my mark. Mark!"

The fleet moved at maximum FTL to a point near the Bug homeworld yet with the orange dwarf star behind them, making them difficult to see.

"Impact in three. Two. One. Now."

Jericho Bucktooth watched his CHUD as the Bug orbital fortresses all vanished in a cloud of plasma. Nearly immediately thousands of Bug ships swarmed to the planet from their patrol routes. Only seconds later did hundreds of Bug Superships rise from the planet in an angry mass.

"Task Force Alpha, weapons free, target ships only. Task Force Beta, weapons free, target ships only. Good hunting!" Jeri took a big breath. Here was his big show.

Firebase Alpha and Firebase Beta were Lagrangian points opposite the Bug homeworld. The USF ships all had stealth systems this time, and even when firing the Bugs could not target them. Minute after minute the Bug ships died by the hundreds. A few random Bug beams found USF ships by chance, destroying six ships.

Then the firing stopped. There were no more targets.

"Comm, Fleet."

"Open."

"Cease fire, defensive mode only. Cease fire. Well done. Bucktooth out. Jock, it's your turn now."

"Roger that, Admiral. Comm, frequency broadcast, translate."

"Open and ready."

"We have destroyed your military. We can destroy you. We would rather live in peace. Will you discuss this?"

"NO!"

The volume of the response almost knocked Jock out of his chair. It was as if millions of voices each had a loudspeaker and screamed at once. To punctuate the refusal, hundreds of powerful beams reached out from the planet, searching for targets to destroy.

"Target those beams. I want them out now." Jeri ordered.

USF railguns pounded the surface, steadily silencing one Bug weapon after another.

Again Jock pleaded for surrender, and again the Bugs refused. This time, the planet seemed to split open as a gigantic ship began moving slowly out of a deep underground lair.

"How big is that thing?"

"Two thousand kilometers. It's going to split the planet with the thrust!"

The giant Bug ship seemed to be moving in slow motion, then it suddenly shot up into orbit. The huge gaping hole in the planet began swallowing up oceans even as the rest of the planet started cracking under the strain.

The giant Bug ship began firing huge beams near the wreckage of destroyed USF ships, killing ten more ships in a heartbeat.

"All ships, fire at will!" Jeri shouted.

Dozens of GravTorps plowed into the alien monster ship. The gigantic vessel began shaking slowly, then started falling into itself. Faster and faster it collapsed until there was nothing left but a glowing super dense ball of matter.

"Bucktooth to Fleet, let's go home." The words dripped off of the Admiral's tongue like sweat off of a spent racehorse.

***

USF Monitor
Admiral's Quarters
Between Achird 12 And Earth
Standard Earth Date March 4 3489

Ding-DING!

"Come in." Jericho Bucktooth was tired. Exhausted, as if every exertion from his entire life had happened just twenty seconds ago. Yet he still had one more task he had to do. He lifted his eyes up to see

Gridley, Jock and Mary standing there.

"Why, Jeri?" Jock asked quietly.

Jeri couldn't tell if Jock was angry or sad. Likely he was both, from what he knew of the man. He had every right to be. He swept his gaze across the trio. He owed them.

"My granddaughter. They have her. She's only ten. I had to." Then Jeri finished his last task, biting down hard on the hollow tooth. He tasted something bitter, and then he felt a slight tingle all over as everything became dark...

***

United News Network
Times Square Studios
Standard Earth Date March 5 3489

"Good evening. I'm Don Derringer. Tonight Straight Shot sets our sights on some good news. Adsila Bucktooth, the Granddaughter of the late USF Fleet Admiral Jericho Bucktooth, was found alive and well today in a forested area of the Onondaga Indian Nation in Central New York State. The ten-year-old girl was frightened, cold, and a little confused, but medical staff expects her to make a full and rapid recovery.

"Admiral Bucktooth, the girl's grandfather, was killed during the attack on the Bugs' homeworld.

"In what authorities are calling an unrelated incident, the body of a tall man wearing black pants, a charcoal grey sweater, sunglasses and a black panama hat was found only two hundred meters from the spot where Adsila Bucktooth was found. Sources say that documents on the man identified him only as 'Elathan', and that the man had died from numerous slicing wounds, consistent with those seen in black bear attacks..."

***

West Lake Road
Skaneateles, NY
Standard Earth Date October 4 3489

"This is very good wine."

"Shut up and kiss me again." *The dream! All this had to happen, to get here.*

"Yes, Sir! Madame President!"

"Not any more. I think my resigning the day you left stymied all of them. And that phony "we surrender" tape didn't fool anyone once that Bug "Queen" ship came out. Jock, our plan worked beautifully!"

"I don't like to lose. I am sad about Jeri, though. He didn't deserve that. At least they found his granddaughter, lost in the woods, cold, frightened, and confused, but safe. Poor kid."

"Things will be messy for a while, but we won't have a society that sees itself as immoral, or that sees immorality as the accepted norm. And, just maybe we've sown the seeds of something better for those yet to come. Do you think Mary has found her peace?"

"She's opened up an orphanage in Syracuse, in a refurbished ancient building that was an orphanage centuries ago. She's found her peace, Jock. She's found her purpose. Now, Oh Mighty Starclan Chief, come here and tend to your wife…"

***

United Space Force Academy
MacAlister Chapel
Cape Canaveral, Florida
Standard Earth Date June 18 3524

The new graduates parted as they watched the old man walk slowly up to the entrance to the chapel. Many found the old, wrinkled face familiar, but could not place it with the younger version adorning the Academy walls. Those who did simply smiled and moved aside out of respect. Rumor had it that each year, for a hundred years, he came to leave the flowers. Such exaggerated stories facilitated the promises

234

made between desperate lovers about to embark along divergent paths.

Each slow step seemed to pain the old man, yet his face carried a contented smile. He carried a small collection of blossoms, along with a small card. These he placed near the entrance. He glanced up at the words engraved above the portal just before he entered the place of worship. After a few minutes inside, he left with a tear on his cheek. Although he had come each year for some time, he never returned after this visit.

The flowers eventually faded, the card as well. It was simple, and said only, "Sharon, my love. Forever." One image was upon the card, an armored fist thrusting a dirk up through a circle with the word "FORTITER" inscribed upon the circle.

The fall after the old man came for the last time, an older woman came, accompanied by several men in black suits. She oversaw the placement of a stone pedestal onto the same spot where the old man had placed the flowers. The Clan Crest from the faded card was reproduced on the stone, with one word below it.

"STARCLAN".

Each year, each new graduate begins the first day of service on the first midnight after graduation by touching the word "FORTITER" and leaving a single flower on the pedestal. The top four in the next year's graduating class are brought along, so the story and tradition live on.

Almost three centuries later, a young commander would oversee the construction of a new Academy. Placed outside the chapel was a stone pedestal. The top of the pedestal was engraved with an armored fist thrusting a dirk up through the center of a circle, the circle was inscribed with "FORTITER." Below the fist was inscribed "STARCLAN."

Every graduating class from this academy continued the tradition of each graduate leaving a single flower on the pedestal on the first midnight after graduation.

Epilogue

House Of Providence
Syracuse
Standard Earth Date June 22 3761

"Do you understand what happened?" Jock MacAlister sat next to the young boy, the stars twinkling brightly all about them.

"I think so. The Bugs, were they bad, I mean, they did bad things, but were they evil?"

"They were tools, used by Evil."

"You were a tool, too weren't you? A tool used by Good?"

"Ah, you're learning, my boy. You are the next great tool, lad. Always do what you think is good and right, and your life will be the most powerful tool for Good."

"Where is the Evil really? Why is it hiding?"

"That is your task, young one. To find it. To confront it. To defeat it, by bringing goodness with you. By bringing the Evil into the light. It will not be easy, you must be persistent. You are the tool for that."

The boy thought he heard a deep, baritone voice, with a Scottish accent, calling off in the distance, but he could see only the stars. Jock looked off to his left in response. "Coming, Father," a young boy's voice answered from Jock's lips. Jock turned back to the boy and smiled, "I must go now," his grown-up voice told the boy.

"Thank you, great-great-great-great-great-grandpa Jock." The young boy counted the 'greats' on his fingers as he recited them. "I'll remember everything you told me, and I'll remember to tell her for you. I promise! Will I get to see you again?" The boy called after him as Jock and the stars faded into the morning's light.

"One day, yes! Yes you will!" came the reply from a great distance...

Mary was sitting by his bed as he woke up, his hair wet and face red from this warm summer night's dreams. He smiled at her when he noticed her kind face welcoming him. He lifted his shoulders up, leaning on his elbows as he spoke.

"Mother Mary, what do dreams mean? Can they really tell you things? True-to-life things?"

"They may mean many things, young Angus MacAlister. What did your dream tell you?"

"It told me I must live my life as a tool for good. And, it told me, well, great-great-great-great-great-grandpa Jock told me, to tell you that he loves you, Mother Mary, and he will see you very soon." Angus tilted his head a little, "Mother Mary, he's your father, isn't he?"

"Oh, Angus!" The old woman hugged her great-great-great-great nephew and wept. *Lord, you always answer my prayers! He is the one. Now I may rest.* She smiled as she went to sleep for the last time later that afternoon. It was a very contented and peaceful smile.

About James W. McAllister

I founded Fortiter Publishing LLC in November 2013 as a vehicle to let all these great Science Fiction and Fantasy stories out of my head.

"FORTITER" is inscribed on the MacAlister Clan Crest. The word means "to go forward, boldly." I am grateful for the Clan Chief's permission to use the Crest and Tartan in my company's logo, and to use "FORTITER" in my company's name.

My name is James Warren McAllister. I am a Registered Respiratory Therapist living near Syracuse in Central New York State. Currently I am employed in Healthcare Accreditation. I have extensive experience in both the hospital and the home care aspects of Respiratory Care, including management in both settings.

I have been interested in science fiction since reading the Lensmen Series of books by E. E. "Doc" Smith in Junior High School. TV shows like Star Trek and Battlestar Galactica, and movies such as Robinson Crusoe on Mars and Star Wars further peaked my interest in the genre.

My first novel, THE BEST LAID PLANS, has been selected as a Runner-Up in the 2013 MARSocial Author of the Year Competition.

See my Amazon Author's page here:
http://amazon.com/author/jwmcallister

If you enjoyed this story, please leave a review.

Now enjoy a sneak peek at the next Starclan book:

THE BEST LAID PLANS

Birth Of The Starclan

Starclan Book II

Prologue

Large Survey Vessel USF Sagan,
Star System 44G92216
Standard Earth Date July 21 3803

"Captain, I have an anomaly!" Senior Sensor Officer Ellie Joslyn exclaimed as obnoxious alarms fulfilled their purpose by agitating everyone on the bridge.

The Large Survey Vessel USF Sagan was following standard approach procedure for entering unexplored star systems, running in Stealth Mode Alpha. The four kilometer long exploration vessel emitted no energy, and moved with silent invisibility through the outer reaches of the star system designated 44G92216. The ship was traveling under momentum built up well outside the system. Now fourteen Astronomical Units, or AUs, out from the bright yellow star, the dull charcoal colored Sagan coasted at 0.3 effective light-speed.

The primary exploration vessel class of the USF, the Sagan was a Magellan class vessel based upon the Excalibur Heavy Cruiser design. While the streamlined dumbbell shaped, starship shared all the stealth and defensive capabilities of her military cousin, the Sagan was modestly armed with only four twin heavy rail gun turrets and two GravTorp Tubes as offensive firepower, along with two hangers for the one Wildcat fighter squadron and several transport and utility vessels used for exploration. Military presence was limited to one company of Marines. The extra space and power was used for an increased scientific crew along with an extensive sensor and communications array.

"Let's have it, Miss Joslyn!" Captain Howard Sloan prodded,

successfully hiding his nervous apprehension from his crew. No USF exploration vessel had ever contacted any evidence of an alien life form, let alone an actual live alien.

"Only visual, sir. And that is, well, weird!" The young blonde Sensor Officer could not keep the excitement and nervous tension she felt out of her voice. This could only mean one thing, she thought; Contact!

"On screen."

"Aye-aye, sir"

The huge viscreen display at the front of the bridge had been displaying a real-scale view of the star system before them. Now it quickly zoomed in to the third planet from the star. The advanced gravity optics bent the available light to give a miraculous view of incredible detail.

"Opinion, Miss Joslyn?"

"It's twelve AUs away sir. It's moving towards us, and fast. And, it's big. REAL big." Joslyn excitedly reported.

"Crew; this is the Captain: Execute Contact Protocol Alpha" Sloan announced throughout the ship. "How big is it, Johnson?" Immediately wishing he had phrased that differently when he heard Joslyn's combination giggle/whisper, "Told you that size matters!" directed at Sensor Chief Barry Johnson, seated at the adjacent station. Johnson rolled his eyes and nodded towards the Captain. A slight grin had crept onto the Captain's face as he relaxed just a little.

"Estimated diameter is......180 Kilometers, sir." Joslyn's awed voice nearly a whisper at the thought of those intimidating dimensions.

"ETA?" Before Joslyn could answer, the Captain Sloan added, "Can we get a better picture on it?"

"That is a true rendering, sir; it really does shimmer like that! ETA, is, um, now, sir. It's *here!*" she gasped.

The object stopped 200 Km from the Sagan, perfectly matching her speed and vector. A light grey sphere, it shimmered as if seen through very hot air rising off of sun-baked asphalt.

"Part of the ship has come into focus, sir. Like something underwater breaking the surface!"

"Energy emissions; it's scanning us, sir!" Sensor Officer Passives Johnson exclaimed.

"Capta...." Joslyn's shout began and died as a very bright, red light flashed from the surface of the object.

The standard procedure for exploring an uncharted system was to drop a Stealth Comm Recon Drone outside the system. And Captain

Sloan always followed procedure; the Mk 12 SCRD he had dropped dutifully recorded the huge ship and its 1,200-member crew evaporate into an expanding cloud of glowing plasma.

After six weeks of quiet sensors, the probe left for home.

Other James W. McAllister Books

STARCLAN Book I
THE TURRET
Starclan Foundation

STARCLAN Book II
THE BEST LAID PLANS
Birth of the Starclan

STARCLAN Book III
A MATTER OF HONOR
Starclan Chrysalis 2015

RODS
A John Martin Story

THE PAGE
The Year of the Dragons

THE UNIVERSE, While You Wait
28 short stories to read while you're waiting